OPAL

ALSO BY SANDY NATHAN:

FICTION

The Bloodsong Series:

Numenon: A Tale of Mysticism & Money
(Bloodsong 1)
Mogollon: A Tale of Mysticism & Mayhem
(Bloodsong 2)
Leroy Watches Jr. & the Badass Bull
(A Bloodsong Novella)
In Love by Christmas
(Bloodsong 3)
MINDSPEAK/HEARTSPEAK:
A Saga of Quantum Physics, Alternative Universes & Love
(Bloodsong 4)
Opal: A Poodle's Journey Home
(Bloodsong 5)
Willy Fish & the Mighty Fine Mule
(A Bloodsong Novella — coming in 2020)

Earth's End Series:

The Angel & the Brown-Eyed Boy
(Earth's End 1)
Lady Grace & the War for a New World
(Earth's End 2)
The Headman & the Assassin
(Earth's End 3)
The Earth's End Trilogy
(Earth's End 1 to 3 in a single eBook)

NONFICTION & CHILDREN'S LITERATURE

Stepping Off the Edge: A Roadmap for the Soul
Tecolote: The Little Horse That Could

OPAL

A Poodle's Journey Home

SANDY NATHAN

Illustrated by *William Renn*

BLOODSONG SERIES 5

SANTA YNEZ, CA

Book Cover and Interior Design of Print & eBook editions: Damonza.com
Cover photo: Many thanks to Mon Amie Standard Poodles for the cover image of their beautiful Standard Poodle, Sterling Time to Shine.

Publisher's Cataloging-in-Publication Data
provided by Five Rainbows Cataloging Services

Names: Nathan, Sandy, author. | Renn, William, illustrator.
Title: Opal: a poodle's journey home / Sandy Nathan ; illustrated by William Renn.
Description: Santa Ynez, CA : Vilasa Press, 2020. | Series: Bloodsong, bk. 5.
Identifiers: LCCN 2019909972 (print) | ISBN 978-1-937927-10-3 (paperback) | ISBN 978-1- 937927-09-7 (ebook)
Subjects: LCSH: Widows—Fiction. | Dogs—Fiction. | Poodles—Fiction. | Wildfires—Fiction. | Loss (Psychology)—Fiction. | Paradise (Calif.)—Fiction. | California—Fiction. | BISAC: FICTION / Action & Adventure. | FICTION / Animals. | FICTION / Disaster. | FICTION / Women.
Classification: LCC PS3614.A865 O63 2020 (print) | LCC PS3614.A865 (ebook) | DDC 813/.6—dc23.

To my beloved Standard Poodle, Margo. We rescued Margo from a very bad place with the help of very good people. Everyone loves to rescue an animal in need. What we must remember is whatever happened to them may leave lasting scars. Margo has been the most difficult and rewarding of a lifetime of rescues. She still has good days and bad. She's the real-life model for Opal.

But who could resist that smile? It makes up for the bad days.

*I know that dogs are pack animals, but it is difficult
to imagine a pack of Standard Poodles… and if
there was such a thing as a pack of Standard Poodles,
where would they rove to? Bloomingdale's?*

—Yvonne Clifford,
American actress

Oh, Yvonne, sweetheart, you are so *misinformed. Yes, Standard Poodles
are elegant fashion icons, but they're much more. Originally hunting dogs,
they'll still jump in freezing water to bring back a duck or two. They're
emotionally tuned to people, making great service and therapy dogs.*

*And—they are super smart: they work as police dogs and circus dogs
and excel in agility. Standard Poodles have served in the military as war
dogs since the seventeenth century. They even did all right in the Iditarod,
a grueling 1,100-mile sled race through the frozen North. Poodles are very
protective of their owners—forget the Doberman, get a S'poo to watch
your place!*

Poodles would never mob Bloomingdales. They'd head for Le Bon
Marché *in Paris, the classiest store on the planet. But don't worry,
Yvonne. You're about to meet Opal. You'll never think that poodles are
puff dogs again…*

—Sandy Nathan,
Award-Winning Author and Standard Poodle owner
(or maybe she owns me)

CONTENTS

LIST OF ILLUSTRATIONS

A Note from the Author

THIS BOOK *IS* part of the Bloodsong Series. If you're familiar with my previous work, you'll know that the Bloodsong Series first appeared in 2008 with the publication of *Numenon,* a book about the richest man in the world, a Silicon Valley billionaire, meeting a great Native American holy man at a gigantic spiritual retreat. It took place in 1997 in the New Mexico desert. What does that have to do with a tale about a confused and dangerous poodle and a devastating California fire in 2018?

Hard to find a connection, isn't it? It's there, as you will see as the story unfolds. All my books have been born in my deep subconscious and appear in my brain as dreams and visions. They pop out whole, as instantaneous, gigantic *AHAHs! Opal* was like that.

If you are familiar with my work and the intervals at which I publish books, you will know that I am subject to vicious, soul-sapping bouts of writer's block. For instance, *Mogollon: A Tale of Mysticism & Mayhem,* book 2 of the Bloodsong Series, was published in 2014, six years after book 1. That's a long time for readers to wait. The wait isn't over: the retreat is only half done at the end of *Mogollon.* All the characters are still where they were, thousands strong, frozen mid-action in the New Mexico sun. I *have* written the end of the retreat, but my telling of the story included what happened to every single person. I love all the characters and detail, but my editor thought that readers don't like telephone book-sized books these days.

I agree with her, but how to cut it?

I couldn't and didn't and was creatively dry for a long time. Until the Camp Fire raged, and California was on fire, and I rescued a troubled Standard Poodle who changed my life. (Her name is Margo, not Opal.) And then I started fixing up old furniture to look like fixed-up, pimped-out, old furniture. I became aware of a thriving culture: women who redo junk and make it art.

Bingo! The old subconscious kicked out this book in a single bolt of intuition. I do love those! When *Opal* popped into my head, my reaction was something like, "The ol' mare still has it."

I hope you think so, too. I loved writing *Opal.*

If you'd like to know more about the people in Opal, you can always read your way through the Bloodsong Series. The series is numbered roughly in the order the action occurs. All the books are on Amazon. There's a little-known volume called *Vanessa Schierman, PhD: WITCH* that introduces Vanessa. She's also a major character in *In Love by Christmas.* But *shhh!* No one knows in the early parts of the Bloodsong Series that she will end up Will's *wife. Don't tell.*

Ciao, friends. Time to feed the poodle and get on with life.

My blessings and best wishes. May your journey home be rewarding and fulfilling.

Sandy Nathan

ACKNOWLEDGEMENTS

BEFORE WE ENTER Opal's world, I'd like to acknowledge a few people who helped me tell Opal's story.

The wonders of the internet allowed my dear friend from high school, Barbara Peppard Sutak, and I to reconnect after more than fifty years. Barb wanted to read my new manuscript. Turns out that she was raised in Chico and knew the area of the fire well. She provided Chico trivia as well as describing what it was like to survive major fires. Her mother lived through the Tubbs Fire of 2015 and the Camp Fire of 2018. She didn't lose her home, but can describe the horror of a massive fire. Barb is a great provider of feedback and super catcher-of-mistakes. Thanks, ma'am!

The beautiful photo of a poodle on the cover comes courtesy of Mindy Mays of Mon Amie Standard Poodles. For the cover, I wanted an image that could convey Opal's beauty and complexity. Many stock photos of poodles exist, but when I saw a photo of Mindy's Sterling Time to Shine, I flipped. That dog *was* Opal. The kindness, beauty, and intelligence in his eyes conveyed Opal's shining soul. Mindy was kind enough to let me use Sterling's photo and to give me feedback about Standard Poodles and their world. Sterling is poised to begin his show career and is expected to be Grand Champion Sterling very soon.

Thanks also to the Animal Compassion Team of California and Laura Williams, Animal Compassion Team, Foster/Adopter/Volunteer, for bringing a Standard Poodle into my life. The Animal Compassion Team does amazing work saving animals. Our Margo is a Standard Poodle who needed rescue—and ACT and Laura rescued her. Margo came to Barry and me with some *issues*—she'd had a hard time—but is now blossoming as an elegant ranch dog. Poodles are *not* wimps. I'm a crazy poodle lady now.

I must acknowledge the DIY furniture redo/updo community. One day, I looked at my thirty-year-old dining room set and said, "I hate you." That was the beginning of a passion—or obsession—for finding wonderful old pieces of furniture and transforming them into gaudy monstrosities that embarrass my kids. No! Redoing them with paint and jewels to fit my senior style, which can be termed "elderly storybook" or "losing my inhibitions and taste."

I discovered a huge community transforming the world of interior design one cast-off headboard at a time. My chainsaw-wielding heroine, Cait Cummins, grew from my hobby and the group of mostly women transforming the old and outmoded into the unbelievable. I must mention a few people whose blogs I follow and read voraciously.

Thank you, Tracey Bellion, for your inspiration and our consultation. It resulted in my new/old dining room. Kudos to Christy James and her Confessions of a Serial Do-It-Yourselfer. This woman knows what to do at a thrift store. Sarah, of Thrifty Décor Chick, actually uses power tools and exceptional ingenuity and taste to transform her world. Many more: Do Dodson for gracious good taste with Do Dodson Designs. Nancy of Artsy Chicks Rule and Serena Appiah of Thrift Diving. Two more women unafraid of power tools. Plus hundreds more bloggers and everyone on YouTube for every kind of DIY tip. Thanks, ladies and guys!

Many thanks to the talented William Renn for illustrating this book. His fine depiction of the action and emotion in the text give it more dimension, letting the story leap even farther off the page. I look forward to working together in the future.

Kudus to the team at Damonza.com for the cover and interior

design. As always, they went over the top in interpreting my wishes. You nailed it again, guys! And thanks to Sue Soares for her eagle editorial eye.

As always, I thank my husband, Barry Nathan, for his support and "first reader" skill at catching errors and stuff that doesn't make sense in what I've written. And—I own all errors in this book and thank all contributors.

OPAL

1

INTO THE FIRE

THAD LEANED ON the handle of his extra-large scooper, contemplating the dogs and their top-of-the-line, concrete and chain-link kennel. Mounds of crap dotted the runs. Old poop. New poop. Thad sighed. He needed to clean up more often, but after a while, the excrement of a dozen big dogs got so gross. It never stopped.

"They're not worth feeding." Caitlin slunk up behind him. Thad winced at his wife's sour tone. It reached him at the same time as the acrid smoke from her cigarette. He flared back.

"I've told you not to smoke outdoors. This place is a firetrap. You ought to chew tobacco, if you have to have nicotine."

Caitlin bent over and ground out her stub. She shoved the butt into the gravel extra hard and scooped some pebbles over it with her foot. "See, fire safe." She paused and took a long breath. "I'm sorry I've been such a bitch, Thad. It's just… I can't take it anymore. We have to talk."

She wasn't angry. She sounded so dejected that he noticed her for once. Tears drifted down her cheeks. This grief was deeper and more painful than the dramatic sob-and-make-up routine their marriage had become.

"Please, can we go inside and talk?"

She grabbed him like a lifeline. He held her tightly, and she wept, her broken grief different from the violent storms that wracked their home the last year. He led her to the sofa and sat with her, holding her hand. His beautiful blond wife seemed shattered. She reminded him of a porcelain doll, cracked in a million places and barely holding together.

"It hasn't worked out, Thad. None of it. We had such a good plan to start with, but none of it worked." She looked at him, beseeching, begging, but not saying what she wanted—yet.

He thought about their move and the events behind it. They *had* had a good plan for their new life when they left San Francisco. They set the move up logically: He was doing tech stuff from home, an IT consultant. What was the difference between working from an apartment in San Francisco and a house in the country? None that Skype wouldn't handle. He could drive to the city and stay at his buddy Sam's place when he needed to. Same with Caitlin. She was a technical editor. She could do her work anywhere she could plug in a computer.

In an instant, his mind transported him back to those days when the need to move occupied their lives. Why should they want to move from the coolest city on the planet? They had a great apartment, which cost more than a Mars flight every month, but it was ultra-hip. Had a great view. It was in a cool neighborhood. They were cool. Hip, beautiful, young. Caitlin was downright movie-star gorgeous. They were foodies and wine aficionados with tons of stylish, well-educated friends banging on the door.

They were living the life, and they knew it. Except for the rent, and everything else that living in San Francisco entailed. They weren't saving, and they weren't growing their net worth. They didn't own a house and never would in the city, or anywhere in a half-day's drive of it. Their lack of advancement on the socio-economic scale gnawed at them.

Worse were the smog, traffic, and homeless drug addicts passed out in doorways. Peeing in doorways. The panhandlers and rising crime. When Caitlin got mugged, they knew they had to get out of the city.

She was bloody and shook up when he picked her up at the police station. She burst into tears and started to run to him. A cop stopped her on their side of a railing. "You have to finish the paperwork before you can leave, ma'am."

"Paperwork? Why should she have to do paperwork? She was mugged." Thad was outraged.

"I got arrested, too, Thad. That's what I couldn't tell you over the phone." Her pretty face screwed up, and tears flowed from under the bandage covering the side of her face. "This homeless person grabbed my purse and tried to run off with it.

"It was my Michael Kors. I wasn't about to let him have it. I ran after him, and he pushed me. I fell and hurt my knees and hand." She held up her bandaged hand. "I got so angry. I ran after him and jumped on his back. I grabbed my purse. He fell, but he rolled over and got up."

Thad stood, open mouthed.

"That's when he beat me up." Her mouth pursed, and her chest heaved. She had professional-looking bandages all over her hands and arms. Someone had seen to her injuries. "He would have killed me if these other homeless people hadn't gotten him off me."

"Cait, my God. But why are you here? Why aren't you at the hospital? Why isn't that guy here?"

"Well..."

"She assaulted a police officer, sir," someone behind the desk said.

"What?!"

"Don't worry about it," a voice bellowed from behind him. Their friend Jeffrey Hoagland, super attorney, walked in the door. His dad was a judge. "I got it dismissed. But you must take an anger management course, Cait. That was the best I could do."

"Oh, thank you, Jeff." Caitlin ran around the counter and hugged him.

"Hey, lady, you gotta sign this before you can..." the cop piped up again.

Jeff raised a paper. "She's free."

"Thad, I think I need to go to the hospital." She doubled over, holding her ribs.

"Okay, babe. I'll take you."

Three broken ribs and a big ER bill later, they drove home. Thad didn't say anything about what happened until they were in the car. "What happened, Cait? How could you get arrested?"

"Someone in the crowd called the cops. I was so mad. I didn't know I could be so mad. I jumped the homeless guy, grabbed my purse, and hit him with it. He knocked me down and kicked me. These other people pulled him off, and I jumped him again. I never thought, I just did it.

"Someone pulled my arm, and I turned and slugged him. I thought he was another homeless person trying to get my bag. But it was a cop. They don't like it when you hit them." Caitlin balanced her purse on her thighs, examining it. "It's scuffed up, but they didn't get it."

"Caitlin, there's something not right here. You get mugged, and the guy breaks three of your ribs, but you are arrested? What happened to the purse snatcher?"

"They never saw him. He ran off when the cops came. All they saw was me hitting him."

Thad was speechless. "We need to get out of here. Completely out of the area."

"Yes, but how? What can we afford? Where should we go? What can we do for work?"

It wasn't until he saw the picture of the dog that it jelled. After she was mugged, they didn't go out much. The streets seemed empty and menacing. Getting to friends' places or restaurants seemed like too much work. He and Cait felt lonely, sitting around their well-appointed flat during their time off. They worked insane hours, but even they needed outlets.

"We should get a dog. We live near the park. We'd get more exercise walking it. We're not going to have kids for another five years. A dog would be like a kid. Look at this…" He held up his laptop and showed her a picture of the most adorable dog he'd ever seen, a fluffy gold mop with a grin from ear to ear.

"It is cute. What is it?"

He studied the image. "It's a Goldendoodle, it says. A cross between a Golden Retriever and a Standard Poodle."

"It's big. A big dog could protect us." She flipped through some pictures on a breeder's website. "They're nice and big. I don't want a little dog— they bark too much. Yap! Yap! Yap!" They laughed at her high-pitched imitation. "And they bite, too. My Grammie's Yorkie bit me all the time." She peered into the screen, clicking on a tab that said, "Puppies."

"They've just had a litter. They're taking reservations for pups. Look at this one! We could get it!" Caitlin was so cute when she was excited.

"Look at this," he said, pointing to a paragraph that started with "We reserve the right to refuse to sell to particular buyers." And ended with, "Pet quality, $3,500. These puppies must be neutered. Breeding quality pups by private contract. Contact us for prices and breeding restrictions. An $800 nonrefundable deposit holds your puppy." The paragraph ended with, "We take Mastercard, Visa, and American Express."

"Holy shit! Thirty-five hundred a puppy, minimum. How many do they show in those pictures?"

"Nine new puppies. They just had litter of seven sell out. They've got another litter due next month."

"That is… $56K this year."

"No. It's more than that. They had two other litters before that one that sold out. And the site says they have three scheduled later in the year, after the one that's coming up."

"Okay. Two early litters at, let's be conservative, seven puppies each. That's fourteen pups at $3,500 each. That's $49,000. Plus, the sixteen they just sold and the new puppies. That's $56,000. And four more litters coming, we'll say at seven pups each." He did the math in his head. "$98,000 in the pipeline later this year. That's a total of $203,000 for the year."

They stared at each other, eyes wide. "And they can do that again next year, and the next." He shook his head in disbelief. "We should breed Goldendoodles. We could keep our jobs and make $200 grand playing with puppies."

"Why keep our jobs? Two hundred thousand is enough to live on." Caitlin frowned. "We couldn't do it here. We'd have to move somewhere with enough land."

"That dream farm you've talked about?" He grinned and waved a hand around their apartment. "This place is decorated in urban farmhouse. We could do rural farmhouse. You could live your dream."

Caitlin ran a search for Goldendoodles and their breeders, studying the facilities shown online. "There are some really cute places, Thad. Not so far from here, up in the Gold Country."

"Check the online real estate listings. We can afford something up to $500K. Let's see what they've got. And what do you have to do to get a business like that going—that's in terms of local government regulations and what kind of facilities we'd need."

Answering those questions and moving took two years.

Three years after the move, they sat next to each other in their brilliantly renewed Victorian in worse shape than they'd been as a couple. Caitlin would stop crying for a few moments and then plunge back into her anguish.

"We studied it so thoroughly, Thad. What kind of dogs to get and where. How to breed them. Real estate. You did that incredible website for the pups. We made up our kennel name and the logo… 'Charisma Kennels. Heavenly Doodles.' All for nothing. This *is* my dream farm. I hate it. I'd rather be dead than live here!"

"Oh, please, Thad, can't we go back to the city? And get rid of the dogs? And this place?"

That was the basic conversation, but there was more, much more.

"Remember when Irene *ate* her puppies? We weren't there when they were born, and she ate them. We walked in to see the last one's feet sticking out of her mouth. Blood…" Cait grimaced. "And when Opal attacked the Boss and almost killed him? That was $2,500 just in the first set of vet bills. And that kid, Blue, ripping us off? We thought we were so lucky to get a nice local boy to watch things when we went for a romantic weekend? He took everything we had. We never got anything back. He stole my mother's *silver…* " She wailed.

"I hate the country. It's all heat—and cold—and bugs. Snakes. Bats. Bats! They swarmed around my head, Thad. I opened the cellar door and…"

Thad clutched her. She hadn't brought up the worst that had happened to them since leaving the city. His demotion to a drone's job. *"I'm sorry, Thad, you're a great worker, but we can't get ahold of you,"* his boss said. *"I've got to have someone reliable."* He *was* reliable, it's just the internet service out there wasn't. They installed a microwave dish receiver, cutting into their dwindling savings. It worked, but it was too late for his career.

Caitlin lost her job entirely. Her boss had been sympathetic. *"Downsizing, Caitlin. I'm so sorry. It's industry-wide,"* he told her. Except her friends living in the city didn't get dumped. *"At least your expenses are lower out there."*

Lower, but not non-existent. Cait and Thad couldn't believe what their money would buy in the country. In San Francisco, they could buy nothing. In the Sierra Foothills, they bought a Victorian *mini* mansion on nine acres. It was the estate house of a larger ranch that had been subdivided. The gingerbread-trimmed masterpiece with its porches and turrets had the style Cait wanted for their kennel. "We won't even have to advertise with a place like this," she said. Of course, everything about it needed fixing. Their farm was near Magalia, a tiny town a little bit north and east of a metropolis named Paradise in the Sierra foothills. Paradise was the proverbial dream small town where every city-dweller longs to move. Life couldn't be better. Thad bought their first dogs. She set about fixing up the house. They were Jack and Jill with a puppy-based life.

It was Paradise to them, for the first year. But then, reality struck. The dogs didn't have puppies as easily as they expected, and when a litter came along, there were only three or four pups. Sometimes they'd die, one or two of the four. People didn't buy them for what they expected.

"I've got $400, take it or leave it." Most times, they took it. They learned that you had to have more than a fancy kennel and flashy website and good dogs. You had to have a reputation as a producer of top puppies. You had to be *known.* That took marketing and *money.* They had to go to Doodle events, where they were treated as total outsiders by the other breeders.

Their calculations didn't take that into account. Or Thad's buying more dogs thing. It was like a disease. "I have to have this bloodline. No one has it.… We got *Opal* for nothing. She's a famous dog. Look at her show record." He was more to blame than Caitlin for them going through their savings. They both knew it. Charisma Kennels had twelve dogs, all purebred poodles except for the two purebred Golden Retrievers. The stud dogs. They were planning on *four* dogs maximum to start.

But that was then, now was *now.* They sat on the couch for a long time, talking and holding each other. Really talking for the first time since they had moved.

"Thad, I called a dog rescue today. They can pick up the dogs anytime we want, no questions asked. They'll find them good homes… We can move back to the city. I talked to my old boss. And I talked to Sam, too. He said the guy they hired to take your place isn't working out. You have a good chance of getting your job back; but they want you to live in San Francisco. Oh, can we go? Please…" It was a wail, and he followed it with a wail of his own. Thad hadn't known how desperate he felt.

"Yeah. Let's go. Let's get rid of the dogs and go. We can sell this place after we move out." He was so relieved, tears burst out. He was crying as hard as she had been. "I hate it here. I hate the country. There's no good restaurants..." *And I don't like dogs much*, but he didn't voice that.

Somehow, things moved from weepy to romantic. They kissed and groped a while, which was interrupted by his stomach growling. Then hers.

"Hey, let's go out to dinner in town."

"Paradise?"

"No, a real dinner out. Let's go to Chico. To the Sierra Nevada Brewery. Right now! You don't have to get done up."

The Sierra Nevada Brewery was their favorite place, both for the food and the ales *and* the wines. You could get snookered on the ale sampler alone. They liked it because they could show off their knowledge of beers, wines, and cuisine. "Let's order some Viognier!"

"Thad, can we afford it?"

"We'll be able to afford a *lot of wine* when we sell that dump."

Dinner was a dream transported from San Francisco. The wine flowed, and so did they, ending up at the motel down the street.

"Oh, baby. We haven't done anything like this for so long..." Caitlin giggled, swaying on her feet.

"We haven't done this ever." He slipped off her blouse.

When they got into bed, it was Thanksgiving and Christmas and their wedding night. Things were going to be okay again.

He didn't think about the dogs—he had installed automatic waterers and feeders. They could leave for a week, and they'd be okay. That scum-bag kid who ripped them off taught Thad a lot about local people. Or kids anyway. Don't trust them: take care of your own ass.

The night wore on in a glorious coming together of soul and flesh and love. He adored Caitlin, always had, always would. This year had been a nightmare from another planet. They'd get back to San Francisco and real life. Rebuild their savings...

They awoke before dawn. Cait rolled over on her side and looked at him. "You know what? I don't want to go back to San Francisco so much now. I want to do what we did last night more and worry less. Can't we rethink our plan? Cut down on the dogs. Try to monetize my YouTube channel? You always said I should do that. If we weren't so stressed about money all the time, I'd kinda like Magalia."

"Really? I thought you hated it. I just agreed to leave because I thought you were so miserable."

"Not anymore." She smiled and stroked his chest. "I bet you could make me positively ecstatic."

He could and did.

They awoke late the next morning. The magic was still on them. Thad rolled over, embracing Caitlin with the adoration and ardor that had been missing for so long. "Let's do it, Cait," he whispered.

She giggled. "We're doing it."

He kissed her. "Let's do it, sugar. Let's do everything…" And they did.

Thad awoke first. The light coming in the window was dimmed and kind of orange. Was it afternoon? Had they slept the whole day? Caitlin slumbered on, looking like a pale angel against the sheets. He smiled at her, then got up, restless. Something was wrong. He pushed back the drapery and looked out. A haze filled the lot, and the sky to the east was lit up with an orange glow.

They'd been so engrossed in their personal conflagration the night before, they hadn't paid attention to what was going on around them. He slipped into his jeans and out the door. People stood around the parking lot, looking in the direction of Paradise. And Irish Town, the tiny hamlet beyond Magalia, where they lived. They spoke in hushed tones.

He went over to a knot of men rubbing their chins and looking at the wild-colored sky. "They say it's a big one," an old coot confided, turning the dial on his radio. "They're callin' it the Camp Fire. Some campfire!"

"Eatin' up the forest. Hundreds of houses already gone. Started yesterday north of Paradise and took off like someone poured gasoline on it."

"Zero percent contained. Heading this way."

Thad's eyes bulged. The dogs! They were in the path of the fire.

He climbed into their 4-WD van, biggest van Ford made. Their Volvo would have been a more likely car to take on a date, but it didn't do too well on rough roads and *no* roads. So, he and Caitlin took the van on their getaway.

The van was another financial boondoggle attributable to their being dog breeders. He bought the van in Texas when he was on a dog-buying frenzy all over the country. With a zero-down loan, it seemed cheap. Certainly cheaper than shipping six big dogs from one end of the country to the other when he made his first buying expedition. Turned out they needed it at home, too. They had to transport the dogs to the vet and to doggy get-togethers. You had to socialize dogs and train them, as well as petting them and posing them for photos.

He had one more thing to do with the van, then he'd sell it. He'd get the dogs and be back to Chico before Caitlin awoke. Easy peasy.

* * *

At Charisma Kennels, "Home of Magic Doodles," the dogs paced in their runs. The sky was orange. Their lungs smarted at the bite of smoke. They needed to get out of their prisons. But how? They'd already tried chewing through the wire mesh. They'd tried digging out. Opal had thrown herself at the chainmail door until she was bruised and breathless.

There was no digging out of the cement-floored kennel, which was built as tight and impressive as anyone could make an enclosure for dogs. No money spared for the canine colossus. No way out by tooth or claw. The first dog howled, and then another. The wails rose and fell, sobs of desperation. Pleas for help.

The next house was a half mile away. No one heard them.

The neighbors were busy. The volunteer fire department and sheriff's deputies had gone door to door. The entire basin was under a mandatory evacuation order. The fire had burned Paradise and was heading straight at them. Everyone was packing what mattered most. They had two hours before the cops would throw them out. No one thought about Cait and Thad's dogs.

2

OPAL

OPAL LAY IN her run's shelter, long nose resting on her front legs, eyes moving from side to side. She looked regal, even filthy and sporting a haircut so bad, any dog groomer would be fired for producing it. She got up, unable to be still. Pacing along the chain-link wall of her kennel, she stared at the sky. It was wrong. Everything was wrong. The air stank of smoke. Greasy, it clogged her nose and made her eyes run. White flakes drifted in the air, landing like thin snow.

Opal felt worse than usual. Her food fell out of the wall where it always did. She sniffed it and resumed pacing. Water was there. She daintily slurped a bit, barely pausing in her circuits of the enclosure. Something bad was coming. She couldn't get out. She whined.

The other dogs answered her, looking in her direction. She was the boss, even though she never romped with them the few times the man let them out together. She had sniffed noses with some and let them sniff her, but that was it. Opal wasn't a friendly dog. They knew that. Most had been here when the Boss tried to force himself on her.

As he tried to get friendly, a killing rage came over her. She grabbed him by the throat. She grabbed and bit, driving her teeth deeper, feeling her jaws lock and the blood rage take over. A human grabbed her hind legs and picked them up off the ground, crossing them behind her. Someone else grabbed her chain collar and tightened it. She continued to bite the ugly, hairy dog, not letting up. The collar ground tighter around her neck.

"When she passes out, her jaws will release. Pull him away. Don't let go of her feet—if she comes out of it, she'll lunge at him again. And watch your hands." Human voices, but she didn't hear them. Everything turned black.

When she awoke, she was in her kennel with a coppery taste in her mouth. She came to growling.

"You're sure a girl who knows how to say no!" The female human was at the kennel door, making that strange barking noise at her. "The Boss isn't such a boss right now. Thad just called from the vet. You almost killed him." Her barking said one thing, but *she* said something else. She didn't mind what Opal had done. "You're going to cost us a pretty penny, you nasty bitch." The voice stilled. "I'm sorry. I hate that word. No, you just know what you want. It was too early for you, wasn't it? He was going to rape you."

Opal got up slowly and limped to her waterer. She drank gently, feeling the copper taste fade. She had lived so many places. Most were like this, hard ground she couldn't dig into. Walls she could see through, but not get out of, no matter how long she chewed.

"You are a real beauty, girl, even with Thad grooming you. We forgot to budget grooming for twelve dogs. We forgot a lot of things." The human female was sad, Opal knew. Her sadness would have made Opal sad when she had been with some of her people from earlier times. She had loved the old man. She loved his pup, the young man. But this human's sadness didn't affect her as much.

She lay on the bed they gave her, the only soft thing in the cement den, watching the female human carefully. When she came to the door and opened it, Opal stood, a growl turning over in her throat.

"It's okay, girl. We're in the same boat, stuck here." The woman extended her hand to Opal. The growl deepened, and her hackles rose. She took a step toward the person, poised to leap.

"Jesus! You are such a bitch! I thought we could be friends, but you are *impossible!*"

That was the last time the female human approached Opal. The man fed her and shaved off her matted hair. She stood like a good show dog while he sawed at her. She knew what would happen if she showed any temper to the groomer.

"You know, Opal," the man said, finishing shaving her. "When you're like this, I can see you winning all those awards. I can see you living with a family. What happened to you?" She was civil long enough after grooming for him to put her through the paces she'd learned for the show ring. She'd done them so many times, head up, tail up, every step perfect, a moving symphony even with her dazzling silver coat shaved off.

He ran her up and down the driveway until he got tired.

"You're my favorite, Opal, even if you're a pain in the ass and may get us sued someday, biting somebody. Or me." She bolted to the rear of her enclosure when he let her go.

"No, 'See you later, Pop?' No, 'It was fun?'" The human stopped his barking and left, heaving a great sigh. "Que sera, sera."

Opal watched him go, suddenly wanting him to come back. She raised her muzzle and made the shadow of a howl. Curled in a ball with her nose tucked into her body, she spent the night dreaming of people who'd left her. These people would disappear, too. The minute she showed them she loved them, they would go.

3

DRIVING

"SHIT!" THAD RUMMAGED through the junk on the passenger seat with his right hand as well as he could while driving. He'd forgotten his cell. Also his wallet. He didn't go back to their room when he had decided to get the dogs because he didn't want to wake Caitlin. He also didn't want to let her try to dissuade him. He was on a stupid mission. He knew that.

"Damn." Now he couldn't call her and tell her where he was—he'd been in such a hurry, he hadn't left a note.

But he did have the van's shortwave radio. It was the twin of the one in their house in Magalia. They got the pair because cell reception was so sketchy in the little valley where they lived. He could talk to Caitlin anywhere with the shortwave. Turned out he could talk to people on the other side of the world, too. He did that when he was learning how to use the shortwave set, sometimes crashing private conversations.

Now, he was handy with it. He punched some numbers, gave his call name and ID then, and said into the mic on his dash, using his call name and that of his pal, Cliff. "Cliff Hanger, its Puppy Thad. Where are you?"

"I'm at home, packing up, Puppy. Where are you?" Cliff was Cliff Madsen, one of his neighbors. They all had funny IDs for the shortwave.

"I'm driving up Skyway Road, heading home from Chico. Cait and I had a getaway there last night."

"Why are you going *home*? Don't you know there's a huge fire up by Paradise? You're heading right into it." The reception crackled. "This is not a place to be, buddy."

"I can't leave my dogs to burn. I can get up there and back before the fire gets to the farm."

Cliff's voice boomed out of the receiver, leaving shortwave manners behind. "Thad, this is a frigging fire volcano. The fire guys gave us two hours to clear out before the cops haul us out."

"It's only forty minutes to the house from Chico. Hey!" Thad was getting peeved. "I gotta get there. I need you to call Caitlin on her cell phone and tell her what I'm doing. I forgot to bring my cell. Tell her I'm fine and will be back for lunch."

"Thad…"

"Seriously."

"Okay, buddy, but stay off the main roads. They're shutting them down. Outgoing traffic only."

That was a problem: the fastest route to their house was Skyway Road, which he was on. It was also the only direct route and the only road, main or not. *What* smaller roads should he take? There weren't any.

Sweat broke out on Thad's brow. What was he doing? Nevertheless, he sounded confident when he replied to Cliff, "Don't worry. I'll watch out for roadblocks. Call Caitlin."

"Do you want any help, Thad? I can haul dogs. Meet you at your place. I'm a mile away."

"No. Take care of your family. You know what a chicken I am. I wouldn't be doing this if I wasn't sure I'd be okay. If there's any trouble, I'll turn around."

"We'll watch your back, buddy. The Commandos take care of their own."

Thad laughed. The Commandos were his bowling team. He never thought he'd be on anything so dim as a bowling team, but there wasn't much to do up there. He rationalized it at first, saying he was networking and marketing dogs. Turned out, he liked it. And the guys were great. They would always watch his back, even if they weren't super-educated professionals.

"Okay. Keep your channel open. I'll tell you where I am and yell if I need you. Call Cait for me. Gotta drive, man."

"I'm gonna get the Commandos to track you. We can come for you if you need help. An' we can also spot roadblocks and find you back roads and shortcuts. You got your GPS tracker that we made you get on?"

"Yeah." Though it was never mentioned in so many words, Thad thought that his buddies' surveillance capabilities and equipment had to do with the bedrock of the county's economy: growing weed. They made him "suit up" with their spy gear. He was glad they had all that stuff now. They could see where he was on their computer screens if they were tuned to his station.

A new voice cut into the conversation. "Hey, Puppy Thad, it's Whirlin' Ernie. I'd take the chopper or the Cessna up to spot you, but the fire's messed up the air. I got you on my screen. We'll watch out for you."

"Thanks, Ernie." Thad felt his eyes sting and then tear up. None of his fancy San Francisco friends would offer to do that. "Thanks, you guys. Get in touch with Cait for me. Hey, you guys are the best. I came across as an asshole when I got here, but I learned. You're the best…"

"Go on and drive, buddy. You'll have us boo-hooing. You're coming back, no problem, with all the dogs."

"And puppies," said a familiar voice. "I got my eye on that big one, Thad. He's mine. Bring him home."

"Is that you, Red-eye Sam?"

"Me an' all the rest of us. Tell 'em who's here, guys." The chorus rang out, his entire bowling team was spotting for him, while packing up their own families to flee a fiery disaster.

Thad Drives to Save the Dogs

Then they were silent. Thad drove on through the smoke. No sign of fire here, but the smoke was more intense than he'd experienced. He was alone. All alone, surrounded by smoke and magnificent forest that looked fog shrouded, except for the orange glow. His solitude was as overwhelming as the smoke.

He had been moved by his friends. Tears plummeted down Thad's face. He couldn't take a hand off the steering wheel to wipe them. He had *real* friends here, even if they weren't lawyers and doctors. He was bouncing along a cattle road, a rut really. The Commandos had spotted a roadblock, a big one. Everyone was being turned back, except for the fire trucks that barreled through.

Cliff Hanger's voice piped up out of the speaker, "Thad, there's a roadblock ahead, but you can get past it by turning left in about a hundred feet. Barbwire gate. That's the Hansen place, cattle ranch. Leave the gate open so the cows can get out in case they didn't get all of them out already. Drive into the ranch past that line of trees, then head northeast again. There's a dirt road. You can get back on Skyway at the entrance to the ranch. You'll see the house and barns. No cops around there, or roadblocks for quite a while."

Thad drove as directed. To his right, he could see the pile up of cars, cop cars with the lights going, barriers with lights. And a stream of fire and emergency vehicles headed up Skyway. No civilian vehicles. The civilians were making their way carefully in the other direction, toward Chico.

"We gotta go dark for a while, while we get out of here, but at least one of us will be listening for you all the time. We gotta evacuate right now."

"Did you call Caitlin?"

"About fifty times. She's not picking up." Thad's heart grabbed. "Don't worry, buddy, she's probably hungover and has her phone off."

Thad laughed despite himself.

"I've been to that brewery myself, boy. Them ales are *ales.*"

Yeah, that was all it was. She was a little hung. He must be, too, to be doing what he was.

He fell into a reverie, driving. The guys were silent, fleeing their homes for safety somewhere. The bouncing of the van and closed windows made him sleepy. His mind didn't rove; it felt like it was pulled by a powerful magnet to a specific time and place.

He found himself remembering Texas, when he got Opal. He'd searched the net for Standard Poodles. They were in short supply, the ones he wanted: great genetics, health-tested parents, hips and eyes and everything else clear.

He didn't know much about dogs, but he knew a lot about research. Didn't take long to find out about unscrupulous dog breeders and the genetic deficiencies of pure-bred dogs. No one could say he and Caitlin were unscrupulous!

When he got to his destination, it looked like a frigging castle. Hundreds of acres with a stone mansion in the middle, with sprawling stone buildings spreading from the center. In the distance was another stone complex. He could make out horses in fields. That was the horse end of the operation. He had the address to the kennel, but he got lost and ended up at the main... château.

He'd heard this was the most prestigious kennel in the country. It certainly looked like it. The owner was a billionaire. Made his money in something... The outside of the building was so impressive, Thad's mind shut down.

He rang the doorbell, and an English guy in a tuxedo answered. "I have an appointment to see several dogs. Is the owner here?"

"No, sir, he lives in Manhattan. Mr. Kenyan takes care of kennel business. You will find him in the first bungalow to the left, near the kennels."

Uh. "Thank you." God, did he feel like a rube! Couldn't remember the owner's name because he was starstruck by a butler in a penguin suit. And of course, the billionaire owner wouldn't live in a palace in Texas. He'd live in a castle in Manhattan.

Thad found the "cottage." It would do nicely as an estate house in Silicon Valley. He knocked on the door. A voice rang from around the corner, from what must have been the kennel.

It was like a horse barn, configured with stalls for the mama dogs and babies, wash racks, a bunch of things he didn't know about. Grooming stations, maybe. At the end were wide swinging doors like hospital doors. He could see a corridor extending back though glass windows in the doors. Someone was walking toward him.

"Ah, Mr. Cummins. I'm glad to meet you. Lyle Kenyan." The kennel manager, dressed in khakis and a perfectly ironed shirt, wiped his hands on a towel before extending his right hand. "I was just checking one of our bitches. She whelped last night. Nine beauties." He jerked his head for Thad to follow. They went into the kennel.

"This is the most exciting part of raising dogs. That and winning at shows."

Thad looked over Kenyon's shoulder into a stall. A magnificent black poodle lay on her side, nursing a pile of puppies.

"A multi-best dog in show. More royal blood than Queen Elizabeth. And a good mother."

"She's beautiful."

"A lady is always a lady, in the throes of labor or in a ball gown."

His reminiscence was broken by a voice from his shortwave. "Hey, Puppy Thad, how goes it?"

Then more voices came over the shortwave. He was jerked back to his van and reality, away from the glossy life he'd glimpsed in Texas.

"It's Shirley You Jest. You okay, Puppy Thad?" Shirley was the one female member of the bowling league. She could out-bowl and out-drink all of them. Also had a swear-word vocabulary to rival international champions. Her radio name was a pun.

Thad could hear a lot more static. "I'm okay, Shirley You Jest. Who else is listening?"

"The brothers opened the frequencies, Thad. Everyone in Northern California is listening. Just want to keep you company while you save the puppies. You're not alone, Thad."

Others spoke up, but he couldn't take it. "Hey, I gotta drive and do this thing. Can't talk. Just maybe keep an eye out—and say a prayer."

"Will do, Puppy Thad. Over and out."

Whatever was grabbing at his mind pulled him back inside. It was a strange sensation, like being in a bunch of places at once. He was driving through smoke so dense, he could practically chew it, but his head was back in Texas at that classy kennel. He was driving through the smoke, and he was at their farm with Opal's black eyes gleaming before him. It was like she was hovering a foot before his face. Her intent black eyes were what had gotten him into this crazy dog game. He could hear Opal saying, *Save me, Thad. Don't let me die.* But she didn't have to say anything, the message came from her eyes. She had mesmerized him from his first glimpse of her.

At the Texas dog palace where he got Opal, he and Lyle Kenyan had sat in the kennel office—or state room or something. The room was enormous and paneled with dark oak like an English lord's retreat. Photos of poodles lined the walls. All of them were with handlers and large trophies. The entire ceiling was covered with ribbons hanging from wires. Every square inch bristled with shiny satin tags and garlands, all blue.

Kenyan followed Thad's eyes upward. "After a while, you don't know what to do with them. That's as good as anything."

They got down to it. Thad had come there to look at three dogs. Opal was the one he wanted most. He'd seen a video of her winning Best of Group at the Westminster Kennel Club Dog Show in New York City. It was a few years back; no way he could afford a recent Grand Champion.

She was the most beautiful animal he'd seen. She was silver, never to be confused with gray. Her face was a silvery white, while the hair above her eyes went from white to silvery as it moved back along her head. Silver light seemed to wash over her from front to back. Her front bracelets, the puffs of hair on her front legs that some found ludicrous and others beautiful, were white. In back, her bracelets were white, with silver behind the ankle. Her long, flowing hair shimmered from white to silvery beauty.

On the videos of dog shows Thad had watched, her coat gleamed like opals under the lights. She pranced in a way that no other dog could come near, seeming to float. Opal had been two in the videos, at her prime as a show dog. At six years old, her show career was over, but she should have years of health and puppy-making ahead of her.

She was advertised as healthy and fertile. She was to be sold without the right to show, as a companion. For $500.

Thad should have seen that sum and run. The other two bitches—he hated that term, but it was what they were called—were $5,000 and $6,000. He thought he could bargain their price down… maybe.

He couldn't. Kenyon acted insulted that Thad would even try to get him to drop his price.

"Well, why is Opal only $500?"

"Opal has a complicated history. She is not a dog for everyone. Would you like to see her?"

They went outside. In a few minutes, a uniformed attendant led the queen of all dogs into their presence. Thad almost dropped to his knees in adoration when he saw her. A video from a dog show couldn't capture her magnificence. She had the same flowing hair, parted by bands of almost hairless clipped areas. A show cut, Thad knew. She held herself with the regal air of something too good for this earth.

Kenyan looked at him with an amused smile. "She is quite impressive. She's Shutzhund trained, too."

"What's that?"

"Shutzhund trained dogs compete in a sport involving trials in obedience, tracking, and attack."

"Attack? That dog?"

"She's best at that, actually. Don't say 'Faa! Faa!' around her. That means 'attack.'" He smiled.

"An attack-trained poodle?"

"Poodles are seen as fluffy jokes. They are in fact tough, hearty, and very athletic. And highly intelligent and trainable. They are protective of their families. In Europe, they are used as police dogs. They've been used as war dogs since the seventeenth century.

"At this point in her life, Opal is best as a breeding dog. The pups in the three litters she's had for us have been almost as good as their dam. Not quite, but very, very good. Let's go back inside."

Thad followed. It wasn't until he tried to unload Opal from her crate back in California that he realized Kenyan had made no attempt to touch her, nor had he offered to let Thad pet the dog or lead her around.

"Here is her unvarnished story," Kenyan launched, and Thad listened. Opal was six. She'd had at least five owners, a couple of shady transfers besides. She'd been bred by an old poodle aficionado who loved the breed and loved her. He didn't have the money to campaign her the way she deserved, but the old man didn't want to sell her. Until he got cancer.

"One of the wealthiest aficionados in our breed made him an offer he couldn't resist, and he sold her—with the caveat that his grandson should be her handler and travel with her. We know she's had at least one home where people loved her. From then on, in terms of dog psychology and handling, it was all downhill. She went from show kennel to show kennel. Some must have been abusive for her to turn out as she is.

"She is not a normal poodle: poodles are jolly and happy. The nature of the poodle is kindness and bravery and sweetness. I don't believe a better breed of dog exists, or a more perfect one. That's why I have dedicated my life to them, and that is the reason my employer maintains this kennel.

"But, many people who own places like this," he waved his hand around the office, "show dogs to win. That's what they care about. The dog or horse or cow is a thing to bring them glory. They'll do whatever they must to produce that winning exhibit.

"That's not good for Opal. She's high strung, and she's not afraid to defend herself. If you're rough with her, she'll be rough back… Maybe twice as rough." Thad gulped at the last words.

"I don't know where the old man's grandson disappeared to, but he did early on. She's lived in a hostile, loveless world most of her life. Dogs are the brilliant animals you see in the show ring, because of their conformation and breeding, but mostly because of their souls. Opal's soul is wounded.

"When we acquired her, I thought we had the expertise to heal her.

Make her more of a normal dog. She gave us three brilliant litters. We haven't healed her psychological wounds at all. The people here are good. Top dog men and women. Very competent, and kind. No one has been able to get past her wall.

"If she's bullied, Mr. Cummins, she will attack the bully with everything she's got. She's a strong dog, despite her elegance." *Thad barely breathed.* "She's been shown to death and almost bred to death. I don't know how many puppies she's had. She's been used, Mr. Cummins, like a whore to satisfy people's greed for her perfection. They thought one more litter could bring an offspring to equal her.

"She had a hard time with her last litter. Our vet has pronounced her healthy and fertile, but you may want to have your own studies done." *How much will that cost?? Thad thought. Kenyan wasn't done:* "I'm not sure she can carry another litter—or should if she can." *He paused, pursing his lips as though considering how to go on.*

"Legally and morally, I am compelled to tell you one last thing. The most damning strike against Opal is that she's bitten two people. Those are the people who filed complaints. I don't know how many others she's bitten. I don't think it was her fault; I think she was yanked around by idiots, but that isn't how the law sees it. One more 'mistake' and the sheriff could claim her as a vicious dog. She would be euthanized. If you're still interested, we can make shipping arrangements, but we do require that you sign a liability release stating you understand what I've told you."

That rocked Thad back. He looked out the window, and the handler walked by with Opal. She seemed even more beautiful. The light shone on her coat, and it ruffled in the wind.

"You seem quite taken by her. How about if I give her to you, with breeding rights?"

"I'll take her."

He came home from that first buying trip with the van, six dogs, and Opal. He wasn't quite sure she qualified as a dog. When he got her home and let her out of her crate, she flew out, mouth wide open and snapping. She jumped out of the van and ran off into woods on their property.

"Oh. Well done, Thad," Caitlin said. "Are they all like that?"

And Charisma Kennels, the real kennel with real dogs began.

His reverie ended abruptly, dumping him in a hell of embers and blowing ash. He'd reached his destination. Instead of being cheered by seeing the farm, he felt more dejected. But he was alive, breathing for the moment, and the dogs were safe in their kennel. Smoke curled around the *Charisma Kennel* sign that Caitlin had designed and made, making it look planted in fog. It wasn't fog. It was smoke, capable of killing, even without the fire that made it.

No visible fire yet, just the roar of the flaming beast in the not-so-great distance. The house and everything they owned would burn, that was obvious. Everything smoked, sort of, releasing its essence before getting cremated.

He caught and loaded eleven of the adult dogs and the two litters they had at the time.

"Opal! Here, Opal!" He'd tried to load her into the van first, but she slipped past him and ran off. She could move and dodge faster than anything on this earth. He chased after her for a while, then realized he didn't have time for this game. "You'd better come here, or I'm going to leave you." She stood at the edge of the forest, gleaming silver and white in the gloom. He couldn't leave her.

"Okay. You win. You want *treats? Chicken treats? Chick-uuun?"* She licked her lips but didn't come any closer. He went in the house and got the bowl of broiled chicken nuggets Cait kept there for bribery.

"See, Opal. Treats! You love these." But she'd never taken one from his hand. She could have been a major league outfielder for her ability to catch them when thrown, but Opal had never grown trustful of him or Cait.

He threw her a few, but she didn't come closer. "Crap! Why do you have to be such a jerk? You've been here for three years. Why don't you trust us?"

The shortwave's crackle broke into his anger and helplessness.

"Puppy Thad? You okay? It's Cliff Hanger. I'm in a motel near Sacramento. We're okay for the time being. You okay?"

"I'm at our farm." He was exhausted, but the dogs were in the van. The smoke was unbelievable. He looked up while talking, his last glimpse of Charisma Kennels, the gingerbread dream that had lured Caitlin and him into the woods. Like the evil witch did Hansel and Gretel. "I've got all the dogs loaded, except…"

"Opal."

"Yeah. She ran off. I can't catch her. She won't come." Smoke forced Thad to stop talking while he hacked.

"Buddy, let her go. Don't die for her. You couldn't help her all these years. Get out of there!"

Thad hacked from the smoke and got in the van. "You stinking bitch," he whispered, staring at the place Opal had disappeared into the ferns. "Why won't you let me save you?" He set the bowl of chicken pieces on the ground by the van and climbed in. She could eat them when he was gone.

As he drove out of the driveway of their dream farm, the place they'd lavished with all their affection and cash, that Cait had made into something a magazine would feature—and had. He forgot how many times they'd been in country homes magazines and dog journals. And on videos. Cait had made herself into an internet personality with her home renovation projects and the dogs.

He rattled down the dirt road toward the highway. Before, he couldn't see the flames, just feel the heat and oppressive smoke. Now everything around him blazed. Nobody else was fleeing, they'd already gone.

The sound of it: a monster roaring. Gods beating drums. The nuclear arsenal going off all at once. Through all of it, voices from his radio drowned out the inferno, "You there, Puppy Thad?"

"Here," was all he could say. He passed burned-out hulls of cars and trucks. The first wave of the fire had already been through here. For some reason, the roadway seemed to open for him. He seemed blessed.

"We're all here, Puppy, waiting for you. All of us…" A chorus of call names, many he'd never heard. "The whole state is rooting for you." "Bring it home, Puppy." "Hey, you get that big male pup for me? I'm gonna hold you to it."

Their voices cheered him on when he could barely see through eyes reddened and almost sealed shut by smoke. Trees went up like torches all around, but he wasn't touched.

He knew; the truth hit him like a flash. He had to say it now. Something inside him pulled the words out. "Puppy here. Tell Caitlin I love her. I never meant for this to happen. I just couldn't let them burn up. I had to save them. Cait, I lost Opal. She wouldn't come. And now I've lost you. I can't make it, baby. I'd fight past a million devils to be with you. I'd face anything. But I can't beat this fire. I love you as much as a man can love a woman. I always will. Goodbye, my darling."

He pulled around a perfectly clear bend and found the road blocked by a gigantic fallen tree. Every inch of its three hundred feet flamed. He stopped hard and looked around, trying to find a way to get around the tree. He spun the van in reverse, gravel flying.

The fire moaned and howled so that he didn't startle at the CRACK! It was a pine tree bursting into flames next to him. The shallow-rooted pine, as big as the one that had fallen across the road, flamed. It was like a newly lit torch, or a body just touched by a lethal virus. It blazed and toppled.

Thad and the dogs never felt the fire. A sharp, flaming branch pierced the van's roof, and then Thad's skull. He died instantly. The tree fell the length of the van, crushing its occupants before incinerating them. None of them suffered long.

4.

ASHES

CAITLIN'S EYES OPENED slowly. She registered the smell of smoke but was too sleepy to make much of it. She stretched. "Thad?" He wasn't there. Of course, he wasn't. He got up early. It was late. Very late. Dim, orange-tinted light came through the draperies over the motel window. It must be four p.m.! Thad must be bored out of his mind, hanging around tourist shops and waiting for her.

How could she sleep so long? Cait knew that perfectly well; she'd taken a sleeping pill after their early morning lovefest. She smiled a bit. She and Thad could be so wonderful. But their interlude of love-making barely silenced the worry that had consumed her for months. She was jangled afterward, wanting to sleep more and knowing she wouldn't on her own.

Cait knew she needed to see a therapist and that she and Thad needed couples' counseling, but they couldn't afford either. All her doctor could do was give her something for anxiety and insomnia. The pills would get her through until they got back to the city, then she'd settle down. She took the pill that morning, feeling guilty as it went down. But it had given her hours of untroubled sleep.

Now to find Thad and take the next step. Whatever that was.

Noise from the parking lot jogged her mind. People shouting. Some crying. They were talking about a fire. It must have gotten much bigger for that many people to be clustered out there. Thad! She threw on her clothes and stepped out of the motel.

The parking lot was jammed with RVs of all sorts, trailers, campers, and people. Mostly people. Their faces were drawn, streaked with ash. Eyes bulged. They were utterly silent, in shock, or jabbering like magpies.

Across the highway, a gas station had been taken over by emergency vehicles, fire personnel, and cops. Red fire trucks mingled with highway patrol black and whites and the new sheriff's yellow cars. They were "Putting a friendly face on law enforcement," with pastel cop cars. News people with microphones accompanied by cameramen wandered around, taping anyone who would talk.

She walked over to a group of people. "What's going on?" They looked at her like she was crazy.

"The fire," some grizzled codgers said.

"Fire?" Cait looked back blankly. "There was a fire last night. I thought they'd have it out."

"Where have you been? It's burned up Paradise and everything around it."

"No." Time became slow. "It couldn't have. That's impossible. It certainly wouldn't reach Magalia or Irish Town…"

"Honey," a chubby, but very comforting, gray-haired woman sidled up to her. "They're gone." She touched Cait's arm, and she didn't pull away the way she would normally. Cait wasn't very touchy-feely, but now she was numb.

"No. That's impossible."

"Do you have friends up there? Do you live there?"

"Yes." Her voice was a squeak. "My husband and I live there. We have Charisma Kennels."

The crowd went silent. Most of them had heard of the kennels, and most had shortwave radios. The police certainly did, as did the press. They'd listened to a heart-wrenching series of broadcasts between Puppy Thad and his friends. He had been silent since broadcasting that tragic goodbye to his wife.

Who must be the woman standing before them.

"Honey, come over here with me and sit down. I need to tell you something."

The woman led her to an RV and sat her in a camp chair. "Do you know where your husband is?"

Cait shook her head. "No. We did a getaway here last night. I slept in. I thought he'd be hanging around town, looking in thrift shops. But I don't see our van..." She looked around the crowded parking lot. The group ringing the camper where she sat grew larger. A pretty, dark-haired woman with a microphone pushed forward, followed by a guy with a camera.

"Where is he?" Cait choked out. "He's here, isn't he?" Her eyes begged the older woman, *Tell me he's okay. Tell me he's fine.*

The woman's face was compassionate and serious. Her expression didn't dampen the impact of what she had to say an iota.

"What's your name, sweetheart?"

"Caitlin Cummins. Cait."

"I thought so. Thad left for your kennel early this morning. He didn't want the dogs to burn up. He forgot his cell phone, so he called his buddies on the shortwave to get a hold of you. Cliff Hanger and the rest of them."

"His bowling team."

"Yes. They were with him on the radio all the way, Cait. He wasn't alone."

Cait got it. "I don't know what you're talking about!" She jumped to her feet. "No. Thad!? Thad?! Where are you?" She looked around in a circle hopelessly. "NO! He is NOT dead! He is NOT!"

Rather than accept the comforting arms offered to her, Cait bolted across the street to the cop station. They had set up a command post, with shortwaves, computers, lots of personnel. Civilians ringed it, looking for news of loved ones. Little thing that she was, Cait pushed to the front of the line.

"Officer! People are spreading lies over there. Magalia and Irish Town are all right. Tell me they're still there." Fire simmered in her eyes. She felt the way she had when the homeless guy tried to rip off her purse. She could fight anything.

The cop looked her up and down. Tiny woman, as pretty as a woman could be. "I'm sorry, ma'am. Magalia and Irish Town burned. There's nothing left of them. Paradise is gone."

Her mouth opened. She fell to the ground, knowing nothing, feeling nothing.

"Medic. We need a medic here."

When she awoke, Cait lay in her bed in the motel room. An IV was hooked up to her arm with a monitor taped to her body with a bleeping machine next to her. Her chest ached inside. She looked around. Thad's wallet and cell phone were on the nightstand. Her cell phone lay with them, the message light blinking fiercely. She reached for it, and someone took it away.

"I don't think you'd better listen to those right now," a paramedic said. "We're monitoring your heart. Sometimes symptoms like you've got are from shock, but sometimes they're the real thing. We want you to stabilize before you hear more. Do you have any friends or family nearby?" She shook her head.

"We'll get someone to sit with you…"

"Did the dogs burn?"

He nodded. "Yes, ma'am. They all perished in the fire."

"And the puppies?"

He nodded. "All of them, except one dog named Opal. She might be alive. He couldn't get her in the van; she ran away."

"She's such a *bitch*… *She* would be the one to live." Cait sobbed and dropped off a cliff. She felt like she'd fall forever. Her chest hurt; she couldn't stand it. Someone put something into her IV, and she slept.

When Caitlin awoke, it was dark outside. The smell of smoke was more intense and even the darkness seemed orange tinged.

"We're going to have to move you to Sacramento or the Bay Area," someone said from the other side of the room. "Too many refugees here. They need the room. This is a field hospital now. You're one of the lucky ones…"

Cait heard that and was stunned. Then she laughed. She was lucky! That was so funny. She'd lost her husband, her dogs, including the puppies, her home, every penny they'd invested in the place, all her clothes. Everything. And they had no savings.

Thad might have paid up the life insurance, or not. He thought it was unnecessary. "I'm young, Cait. There's not a thing wrong with me." He'd fought having insurance from the moment they bought the lousy term policy. Had he paid on it?

Well, maybe the fire insurance company would cough up something for the farm. And maybe Opal was alive. Of course, she'd never touched Opal and had every indication the dog hated her.

But she was alive. That was one good thing.

"Can I watch the TV?" But there was no one in the room to give permission. Okay. Do what you want. She grabbed the remote and channel surfed. Not much to surf: all the local stations and even the national ones were about the fire.

"Here, in one of the greatest tragedies of the Camp Fire, is the story of a young couple, Thad and Caitlin Cummins, who came to Chico for a romantic getaway on the night the fire started. Thad drove back to their farm the next morning, leaving early. They have a kennel, the well-known Charisma Kennel. Thad wanted to save his dogs."

His voice came out of the speaker, while his photo covered the screen. "Tell Cait I'll be back for lunch. I can't let the dogs burn."

Cait's eyes bulged. She sat up, furious. Were they bugging his shortwave?

"Thad forgot his cell phone and called his bowling club by short-wave. They opened the channels so all of us could hear. This is what happened to Thad Cummins, a dog lover who paid the ultimate price for his passion."

They played audio clips from Thad's conversation with Cliff and all his friends. Tears streamed from her eyes. She wanted to *kill* that stinking reporter. She was the hard-looking woman she saw near that nice lady who sat her down when she first found out. The broadcaster was an attractive Asian woman who looked like she was dressed for a safari-themed fashion show, not to catalogue the destruction of people's lives.

Cait seethed and sobbed. When they played Thad saying goodbye to her, she froze. Didn't feel. Didn't cry. He loved her. The last thing her husband said was he loved her. She couldn't take it. She was about to dissolve, when the plastic-faced announcer filled the screen.

She wore the smug expression of someone who had bagged the story of a career, something that captured the essence of the disaster unfolding around her. And moved her to the front ranks of news hacks for good.

"Sadly, I was there when Thad Cummins' wife heard the news of her husband's death. Here is Caitlin Cummins."

The footage rolled. Cait saw her own frozen face, the life and color leeched from it, shockwaves playing around her. That nice lady with the RV sat next to her, holding her arms out.

Cait shot out of her seat, saying, "No. No. That's not true."

The filthy newscaster followed her to the cops' station with her cameraman and got Cait hearing what happened from the officer and fainting. Even got them hauling her away with an IV in her arm.

The syrupy fake voice of the announcer went on, "At this moment, Caitlin Cummins is resting and being monitored for a potential heart attack. We'll keep you in the loop on the woman who may end up being the face of the Camp Fire."

Caitlin's image filled the entire screen, an expression of anguish beyond anguish, of pain that no mortal should have to bear.

"So long for this segment of KXIT News! Allison Chao reporting."

5.

OPAL

OPAL WATCHED THE van pull out and whined. She stood out of sight, just beyond the tree line, picking her feet up and putting them down rapidly. She whined, stamping and whirling. Her eyes were fixed on the spot the van had been. She acted as though she was on a tight chain that wouldn't let her move. But there was no chain.

Minutes went by until she could overcome whatever had held her. She ran to the road and stood by the bowl of chicken treats. She didn't eat them and didn't look at them. She stood staring up the road where Thad had gone. *Come back! I want to be with you. I love you.*

I want to be your dog… but I don't know how.

I don't know how. She loved Thad and Cait, her man and woman. She thought of them and dreamed of them. But she didn't know how to be a family dog.

Something red landed on her back and bit her, biting harder and harder. Smoke arose from her coat. Opal threw herself down and rolled until the biting stopped. She got up. Many orange biting things danced around her. She ran, bolting down the drive and then the road.

Terrified, she ran, dodging and darting to avoid flaming trees, shrubs, houses, cars. And mostly the biting flies in the sky. Explosions happened, turning the air orange. She didn't know they were propane tanks blowing up. She knew that this was hell. But she didn't even know that. She didn't have concepts to make such a description.

It was grinding, wrenching, roaring chaos. It was fire and ashes blown by a hellish wind. This was the end of the world.

Opal couldn't conceptualize even those things. All she could do was run. She ran from the thing trying to devour her. Once, she had been able to run a long way. Her trainers took her for runs over green grassy meadows and turf tracks. Through the woods. Always supervised, all choices made for her. No free rein.

This was all free rein. She would die if she made a bad choice. She couldn't run far; she'd stood in Thad and Cait's kennel for years instead of being conditioned by her handlers. Her breath came in huge gulps, as she tried to push herself faster and farther. Stay ahead of it. Outrun the white flakes swirling in the air, the hot ground. Scorching air that burned her throat and lungs.

She kept ahead of the beast for hours, stopping when she could to rest, and trying to figure out where she was. She knew where her home was, exactly where Charisma Kennels was. Or had been, having been burned to the ground by that time. She didn't know that, but she knew the direction of her old home.

Where was she now? She lay under a big tree in a part of the forest that was green and leafy. The only evidence of the fire was the smoke that permeated everything. That and the fact no birds sang, no animals rustled in the brush. Nothing, man nor dog, shouted out. She was the only living animal there.

Her stomach growled. It was past dinner time and getting dark. Her man didn't bring her food. She thought of the chicken treats. The woman brought those, usually. But they were not here. Nothing was here. Her head drooped. She curled up and slept.

Opal leapt up as a CRACK! like the loudest and most terrifying thing in the world had pierced the quiet. It was close. A tree turned bright red/orange/yellow and black smoke billowed off it. Stinging red dots filled the air. The burning tree fell with a boom that shook the earth and made more burning branches fall. Just over there, she could see many burning trees. A house on the other side of the road was a home one moment and covered with crawling redness the next. It moaned and fell.

The monster had caught up with her. Opal ran again. This time there seemed no way out: everything was covered with tongues of fire. Her eyes darted side to side. No escape. Another piercing CRACK! and the tree to her right burst into flames. She ran, breaching a small rise. Something hit her and knocked her forward.

Opal toppled over the embankment and down the other side. At first she slid, but then she lost her footing and plummeted out of control. She landed with a splash in water, a lot of water. A flaming tree fell and entangled in another tree, still fresh and green. Both toppled in her direction. The dog fought to swim in the mucky water as the trees bounced down the bank on top of her. They settled into the irrigation pond.

The branches pushed Opal under the water, leaving her struggling to get air. Pine needles surrounded her, giving her barely enough room to get her nose out. Everything went black.

She opened her eyes. Much time must have passed, because the roaring flames were gone. Only sparks of orange and smoking ash surrounded her. She was in the water, lodged into the fresh tree with her face stuck in its green needles. Opal pulled her head back gingerly. She moved out from under the tree and looked up. The green tree had shielded her from the burning one. That tree smoldered, popping when sap hit the still-alive coals.

She was sore everywhere, but not hurt badly. Opal pulled herself out of the water, first taking a long drink. It tasted terrible, nothing like the purified water of the kennel, but it quenched her thirst.

Where were her people? Where was breakfast? This place was

different than it had been the night before. Everything was black, or black and smoking, or still burning. The ground made her feet sting. She wasn't safe there.

6

CAITLIN'S NEW LIFE

"YOU'RE OKAY TO go. Dr. Morse says you're fine," a nurse said, pulling the sticky tags from the heart monitor off Caitlin's chest.

"Where do I go?" Caitlin had the clothes she'd worn when she and Thad went out to dinner and her purse. She had registered that Thad, her farm, and everything else she had were gone.

She'd never accept it; at best, it would be like the Loma Prieta quake of 1989, the one that knocked down the Bay Bridge and set San Francisco on fire. You might have lived through earthquake, but you trembled when the wind shook the house for the rest of your life. She could get out of bed and put one foot in front of the other. Cait couldn't think.

"The Red Cross is putting people up in the high school auditorium. Also at the Y. They have a list of people offering rooms in their homes. The state is supposed to be providing emergency relief... you'll have to ask around. We need this motel room, miss."

Mrs., it's Mrs., Cait thought. *I'm Thad's wife.*

Not anymore, a darker voice said from deep within.

Cait walked into the breezeway outside her room, unsteady on her feet. She didn't want to stay in the high school gym, or some hall jammed with beds and people she didn't know. She wanted to go home. Her eyes looked toward Skyline Road and the town of Paradise without any direction from her. Hopeless.

Some of the circus of the day before had abated. Just the news crews and emergency vehicles filled the parking lot and gas station beyond. The cops had gotten the disaster tourists contained. Where could she go? What could she do?

Cait gasped when that lacquer-faced reporter from the night before approached her, cameraman in tow.

"Good morning, Mrs. Cummins. I'm Allison Chao of KXIT News. How are you feeling?" The concerned expression on the perfectly made-up face *could* have passed for real.

"I feel like a person who's lost her husband and everything she has. Now, if you'd excuse me." She tried to dodge past the commentator.

"But where will you go? What are your plans?"

"I don't know, and I don't have any. Get out of my way." Caitlin Cummins was a tiny bomb that exploded when pushed. She headed across the parking lot toward the gas station and the law enforcement officers. A law against harassing destitute new widows had to exist.

Someone tapped her shoulder. She wheeled, about to slug Allison Chao of KXIT. Or bite her head off.

"Whoa! Take it easy, Cait. It's Cliff Madsen, Thad's old bowling buddy, Cliff Hanger."

"Oh, Cliff. I'm so glad to see you." Tears fell at the sight of a friendly face. She fell into him, a mini faint like when she found out about Thad. He grabbed her and steadied her.

"Where are you going? Do you have a place to stay?"

"No. I don't know what to do. I have nowhere to go."

"Yes, you do. We Paradise Commandos take care of our own." He smiled kindly. "I want you to stay with us."

"I thought you were in a motel in Sacramento."

"Not anymore. My brother has a vacation house in the Delta. Uses it for fishing and jet skiing. It's right on the water. He said we could use it for the duration. You're welcome to join us."

"Oh. Is there room?" Cliff had a wife and five kids.

"Oh, yeah. It's a party house. Has five bedrooms and a big loft. The kids can stay in the loft."

"Okay." A problem solved so easily. She felt faint again. This time he had to grab her to keep her from falling. He held her tight, this big, strong man with his red beard and muscles.

"It's okay, Cait. All of us will get through this together." He kissed the top of her head. "Let's go."

As they headed to Cliff's truck, Allison Chao spoke to her cameraman, "Did you get that?" He nodded. Another sort of story was emerging: Caitlin Cummins kissing and hugging, then going off with a man when her husband's remains hadn't yet been found. She'd sit on that.

People like nice stories about pretty widows coping, not trash acting out on her husband's grave.

But if Ms. Caitlin showed herself to be a slut or *anything*, she'd have the material she needed.

7.

WILD DOG

OPAL WAS VERY hungry. Her food had always been delivered on time, twice a day. It consisted of the finest kibble, mixed with whatever her trainer of the moment thought was the best source of protein. Ground chicken, ground beef. Even ground buffalo. And supplements to keep her coat glossy and eyes bright. She wasn't given raw meat or bloody bones, ever.

She had never provided for herself, never stalked and caught anything, even a lizard.

Opal moved all day, heading away from the fire. For a long time, everything she passed was burned. It was a black, charred world. At first, many trees had burned and fallen. As she ranged farther, the land changed to hilly with grass and fewer trees. The grass was burned along with the trees. Long stretches of burnt grass separated the trees.

And finally, the grass wasn't burned. She could smell the smoke from behind her, but she was clear of the fire. For now—Opal remembered how a new fire had risen out of nowhere and almost killed her earlier. She kept walking. Stickers and burrs caught in her coat; she had to pull away from some plants, leaving hair behind.

Still no birds or animals… Until she heard dogs quarreling with high-pitched yips. She crept closer, using all her senses. A large animal lay on the ground, with the dogs on the other side, snarling and snapping at each other. They tore at its belly. The animal didn't move.

She had seen animals like the dead one through the fence. They had shaggy reddish hair and ate grass. This animal had charred places with red flesh showing through. The fire must have killed the animal. Opal had seen a dead puppy, one of her own. That was what she knew of death. She knew the steer had been changed very fundamentally, as that puppy had.

The smell rising from the animal made her lick her lips. Her stomach growled. She dropped close to the grass, her smoke-stained coat blending with the dry, yellow pasture. She crept forward, watchful. Were these strange dogs dangerous? Her nose wrinkled. They smelled terrible. No decent dog would smell that way.

The way of pack was ingrained in Opal and not something she had to learn. She knew all about "top dog" and "bottom dog" and every position in between. She was the top dog, always. She had been turned out to "play" at several kennels and found the *play* involved sniffing other dogs and sometimes walking stiff-legged around them. Growling. And getting into all-out brawls. Which she always won.

The AKC didn't set maximum heights and weights for Standard Poodles. If it had, Opal would at the top of both. Her size drew every eye in the show arena, giving her more presence than other dogs. She was super-athletic and fast. Her aggressive attitude and ferocity marked her as a killer.

"She's a natural fighter," one of the humans barked to another, cleaning up the loser of a fight. "A natural fighter and a bully."

"She could be a pit dog," one of the others responded.

"Not with those ears dangling, but cut them, and she'd take down most pit bulls. They're not as fast as she is, and she's got a lock-jaw bite, too."

"She's a beautiful, elegant killer," said still another. "They should put her down." He held up his arm, showing the stitches they'd taken to repair Opal's bite. "She shouldn't be around people."

A couple more fights, and she wasn't allowed in the yard—any yard. Exercise was on the leash only.

She crept up to the stinking dogs on the other side of the dead animal, eyes sharp, sniffing. They weren't dogs! They were the animals that howled around the kennel at night, driving her and the other dogs crazy. They were the enemy of dogs.

Snarling, she leapt at the coyotes, surprising them as they bolted down the dead steer. They looked up. By the time they could react, she had the closest by the throat. She tore his gullet and shook him, tossed him aside, and went for another.

They grouped to fight her, but they were confused. What was this animal? She was so fast and big. She smelled like a dog, but she was so much faster and meaner than the dogs they'd encountered. Opal ripped into another before they retreated, yipping and shrieking. One snapped at her ear as he ran, tearing it. She sank her fangs into its throat, but not until it raked her face and neck with its sharp canine teeth. Blood ran down her shoulder. She shook her head and turned to the eviscerated steer.

The dead steer lay on its side, ripped from breastbone to pelvis by the coyotes. Its guts spilled out. The coyotes had been feasting on intestines and rich organ meat, the first part of a prey wild dogs and carnivores ate. Opal buried her snout and devoured everything she could. She gobbled things she'd never tasted but knew they were what she was supposed to have been eating all her life. This was proper food for a dog.

Opal was so gorged she could barely walk when she turned away. A hunk of intestine trailed from her mouth. She held it tightly for later. Now she needed to sleep in a place safe from whatever other unknown creatures lived in the forest.

The coyotes silently returned to finish their meal. They raised their heads from time to time, keeping track of Opal's progress through the pasture. She was something to be feared.

Opal vs. the Coyotes

8

THE DELTA

CAITLIN FELT HER spirits rising as they drove to Cliff's brother's house. It was in the Delta, which was the intersection of California's two great rivers, the Sacramento and San Joaquin. The Sacramento River converged on the Delta from the north, its water flowing from Chico and beyond. The San Joaquin entered it from the south, from the Central Valley.

Together, they formed a vast water world filled with wide tracts of open water and narrow sloughs snaking through shallow islands and watergrass. Eventually, all of it flowed into the Pacific through the San Francisco Bay.

She had never been to the Delta. Caitlin and Thad always used I-80 through Sacramento to get to their farm and back, skirting this area. The Delta was as flat and wide as Magalia had been treed and mountainous. From the road, she could sometimes see a shimmer indicating a canal, but that was it for topography. Reeds, water, and sky. Couldn't be more different than Paradise and Magalia. Her shoulders relaxed.

They crossed a bridge onto Bethel Island. A river flowed beneath them. Docks with boats tied to them lined both sides of the river. The riverside bustled with restaurants and bars. They passed through town and drove down Gateway Road, turned on Piper, then right on Willow Road. The house was right on the water, on what looked like a narrow canal fronting on Frank's Tract, which Cliff had told her about. It was a huge expanse of wide-open water.

When they stopped, Cait gawped at the house. It looked like a derelict from the 1960s, its redwood siding faded pale gray from sun and rain. The wood trim around the windows hung raggedly. Gutters swung in the afternoon wind. The street was lined with houses of the same vintage. They were built on top of a rise—a levy to protect them if the river rose, Cait figured.

She bolted down the embankment to the river. A sharply inclined path led to the house's dock and boat slip. Caitlin could see the vastness of Frank's Tract through the reeds on the other side of the waterway.

Cait stared at the sparkling movement in front of her. Thad's face came to her, as it did whenever she wasn't concentrating on something. His image faded as the lapping of the waves and soft wind gripped her. Gradually, her ribs relaxed, and her breathing eased.

The river brought her to herself. Its current was slow, but she could feel it tugging against the pier. Its never-ending pressure reminded her that the water would be there when humans were gone. The canal lapped softly, its surface marked with areas of glossy stillness and whorls that indicated underwater creatures fed. The river's eternal power was disguised with softness. That's what released her tears. She ran to the house and almost bumped into Jennie, Cliff's wife, who was organizing her brood.

"Cait, honey, go ahead and cry," Jennie, said, holding out her arms. Caitlin collapsed into them, all her San Francisco reserve and sophistication flown.

When the power behind her sobs had dissipated, Cait sat hunched, wiping her eyes. "I don't know what to do, Jen. Thad did all the practical stuff, and I made videos about puppies and rehabbing old furniture. I don't know how to do *anything*. And I don't have anything to do it with. My computer is burned, and Thad's. All our financial records. I don't have a dime."

Her cell phone rang. "I'd better get that." She picked it up and clicked it off moments later. "Somebody wanting to sell me a medical-grade brace for my leg." Shaking her head, Cait said, "How could they get my phone number? Why do they think I need a brace? I need a miracle. I need Thad…" That set her off again.

"Go ahead, hon. It's okay. You've got lots of tears to shed." Jennie patted her back. Eventually changing the subject, "Do you want to pick a bedroom, or take what's left over?" Cliff and the children had held off from entering when they saw Cait crying. Now they milled around the entrance hall, wanting to get settled.

"I'd like to pick my room, please." Cait cracked a tiny smile and directed her eyes around the room. "Boy, look at this place. Do they ever need me? This mess is in extreme need of PuppyCait."

"Who?"

"PuppyCait. That's my moniker on my home decorating and dog training tapes."

The grungy living room of Cliff's brother's house was straight out of the 1960s; the interior was redwood, *all* redwood. The walls were faded planks with huge beams supporting the great room's high ceilings. A warren of bedrooms spread down a dark hall. The floors were matted orange and avocado hi-lo carpeting. Dust floated idly. The place had been lived in hard and never renovated.

"Oh, they had parties here. Cliff's brother and the whole clan," Jennie said. "I suspect their teenagers were here more than their parents knew. This is *old* Delta. This house was built before they put up Russo's Harbor, down the road, and that was in the early sixties. Now, there's tracts of expensive homes just around the corner, and the place is a zoo on the weekends. It's like trying to waterski on a freeway."

"I'll pick a room, Jennie. Or you can tell me where you want me to go. I don't need anything fancy."

"Oh, fancy isn't part of this place. I'd stay away from our room.

Cliff snores like a freight train. And the kids play video games to all hours. If I remember, there was a little room upstairs. You might like that."

Cait's cell rang again. She jumped to get it. "Thanks, Samantha. I'm not up in Magalia now. I'm at Jennie and Cliff's brother's place. That's sweet of everyone, but they should give the clothes to people up there." She got off the phone.

"That was a neighbor with free clothes. People are sending them from all over," Cait said to Jenny, sounding peeved. "I'm waiting for my insurance lady to call me. I've called her *six* times. Normally, she gets right back. Now that I need her, nothing."

"She's probably up to her eyeballs. The whole town burnt up. I'm sure she'll get to you soon. You did have good insurance, didn't you?"

"I think so. Thad took care of that. He was very thorough. But I just want to hear from our insurance broker that I'll be okay. They'll cover everything."

9

OPAL'S
FURTHER ADVENTURES

THE THING WAS crunchy and had skin that prickled her mouth. She had seen such things before at the places where she lived, flat things with legs and long tails, darting about on the rocks. She was seldom allowed out, so she hadn't chased one. The other dogs loved to chase them, but she'd never seen another dog catch one. She was faster than they were. After all the trouble, it tasted terrible.

It was her first kill! She'd finished her piece of intestine from the day before when she awoke and by late afternoon, she was hungry. Opal realized she would have to hunt—finding coyotes feasting on dead meat wouldn't feed her very often. And she didn't intend to live on what she had just caught. Lizards didn't have enough meat.

She had to catch something bigger, and she had to find a good place to sleep. Opal liked to sleep in a kennel, and not one with wire-mesh sides and top. She wanted something solid above and around her, something that no enemy could break into. At home, she had a long run with chain link sides and top and a concrete floor. In the back was a concrete room with a solid kennel in it. *That's* what she liked. That felt safe.

The previous night had been a nightmare of yowling coyotes and other animals she didn't recognize. She didn't have a kennel or anywhere to hide. Rock outcroppings stuck up all over the pasture. She found one that had an overhang and an indentation between rocks that sheltered her. It wasn't a cave, and it wasn't safe, but it was the best she could do.

So many things about the world were a mystery to her. In the night, coyotes had yowled close and all night long. A terrible smelling black and white thing the size of Cait's cat walked past her shelter. Opal had always wanted to chase that cat and tear it apart. Even though it was the same size as the cat, the stench of the black and white thing was enough warning. She let it pass.

Coyotes, skunks, foxes, bobcats, all ambled by her hole. She didn't know what the humans would call them in their strange barking, but she knew them distinctly by their nighttime smells and stealthy movements. They were carnivores and a danger. If other dogs had been there, she would have jumped out and run at the predators, but she was alone.

Worse than being alone was the nagging feeling that *more* creatures existed in the wilderness, large animals that ate meat and would eat *her*, if they caught her. She didn't know what they might be, just that they existed, and she'd better avoid them.

The faces of her owners, Thad and Cait, swam before her eyes. She hadn't been nice to them when she lived with them, but Opal thought of them all the time now. Opal knew who they were and knew their names. Thad and Cait. She knew many human words. Heel. Sit. Down. Come. Stay. The commands that every civilized dog knew. She obeyed them when she felt like it.

She knew many other human words: the names of all her owners, at least when they owned her. She remembered Thad and Cait most. She liked them, but she just didn't want them to know it. Sooner or later, they would breed her to that ugly, hairy yellow dog they had. She'd have puppies, and then they'd take them away! She hated that. She wanted to live with her puppies forever. And she wanted a mate that *she* picked, not one foisted on her during her *time,* when she couldn't resist.

Oh, she knew a great deal about humans and the human world. And language. She knew the names of all the other dogs in the kennel. Also of the people who visited often. Cliff and Jennie. And their pups, four males and a female. They were called "children." She knew "outside," "go potty," "Hungry? Are you hungry, Opal?" "Chicken? Do you want some chicken?" She knew "car" and "let's go." A terrible word: "The *vet* is here." Many other words seemed to have flown from her mind. "Good dog." She seldom heard that. She knew many words and could tell what humans were thinking and feeling by tiny changes in their posture and expression. And smell. Their smell changed slightly when they were afraid, or angry, or dozens of other feelings.

Humans knew nothing of what she felt and what her physical movements meant. They didn't care about her or know anything about how she felt.

Until she bit them. *Then* they cared. They jumped away, screaming at her. "That dog is the nastiest bitch I've ever seen." Sometimes they bled. That made a warm feeling arise inside her, just for a moment.

Things were always worse after she bit someone, but she didn't care. They could put the *collar* on her and shock her. They could hurt her and make her stay alone. All of that made her more angry, but not afraid.

As the day waned, Opal grew desperate. She felt sick. The crackly thing she ate upset her stomach. Her ear and face and neck hurt where the coyote had bitten her. At first, red blood flowed from it, but now pasty green stuff dropped onto her shoulder. She couldn't reach the wounds with her tongue to clean them. She threw up the lizard, but her stomach still felt poisoned.

Her ear and face hurt all over, not just at the bites. The side of her head throbbed in time with the beating of her heart. Opal knew she needed help, from a human. They could do many clever things with their paws that she couldn't do. They could stitch up wounds that she made when she bit other dogs, for instance.

Where were Thad and Caitlin? She wouldn't go to anyone else but them. She trusted them, not that she'd let them know. Maybe she even loved them. That was *dangerous*. When she loved someone, she usually found herself living somewhere else with new people she didn't like at all. If her most recent owners didn't know she loved them, she might be able to live there any longer. That was how life was.

Opal trotted along a narrow path, looking left and right. No humans at all. Lots of birds. And… she leapt to the left.

It was over quickly. Opal knew the death bite, the hard-crushing grip to the base of the skull. She knew that instinctively, as she would find she knew many things. The rabbit died instantly. The dog ripped it open and feasted in the hard justice of the wild. She ate what couldn't eat her, just as something larger would eat her if it could.

She carried the rabbit's carcass as far as she could, saving it for later. Saving it to save her life with its rich flesh. Opal was so tired. She staggered. She turned her head and lick the yellow stuff. She could reach it now; it was bigger. Her shoulder was stained by it. The side of her head throbbed.

Smoke still permeated the air, but far away to the south and west. Its ghost contaminated the fresh mountain atmosphere. The fire still raged; she headed directly away from it, in unpopulated grasslands that had turned to forest during her journey.

As night fell, she came across an ancient oak, the trunk of which split at the base. It made a very satisfactory lair. She couldn't pull her entire body into it, but most of it. Her teeth would face an intruder handily.

In the morning, Opal felt worse. She had been totally unconscious in the night, missing the visits of forest creatures she should have feared. A bear. A mountain lion. They didn't attack. She whined and cried in her sleep, peddling her legs, running from the terrors of the dream world, when real terrors walked by. They let her sleep. The stench of her rotting ear and face kept them off.

She felt sicker in the next morning, and worse the next. She kept traveling deeper into the forest, away from the fire. Away from danger. Away from anyone who could help her. Opal wove with each step, barely staying on her feet. Her ear stank. Yellow and green guck coated her side, and she had no will to lick herself clean. Her body hurt. She felt hot. She was sick, she knew that. She'd never been sick. She needed to find a human to care for her. Where?

Thirst was the worst. She would catch the slow bunnies, if she felt a bit better. If she could raise her head. But water? Where was that?

It came to her, not that day, but the next or the one after that, she would die. She would fall in a stinking heap, and other creatures would eat her body. A noise barely penetrated the fog of her mind. What? Water. A brook. She stumbled forward and careened down a mossy bank. A creek meandered along. She drank a little, a sip, but enough to revive her so she knew she had to find help very soon.

Smoke came from the other side of the stream. Little smoke, tame smoke, not the giant of the fire that had destroyed the world. She headed toward it, dragging her way. Pain was all she was. Pain and nausea and stinking guck.

When she got to the top of the bank, she saw a human living there. There was a tent—she knew what it was because Cait set up one of those at home on the lawn for Cliff and Jennie's pups to play in. They were "children." A blanket for sleeping was in front of this tent. A smoldering fire sent up a stream of smoke. She dragged herself across the trail and collapsed on the sleeping bag. Everything went black.

Opal Finds the Camp Site

10

PUPPYCAIT

WHEN THE CALL from the insurance company came, it wasn't from the agent they'd used for years. "Mrs. Cummins? This is Weldon Thaller of First Western National Insurance. I'm handling your claim."

"Oh, thank heavens you called. I've called our agent so many times. We've worked with Shirley forever."

"I didn't get the calls, and she didn't either. We've closed our Chico office and brought everything back to San Francisco."

That seemed weird to Cait. If all the claims from the fire were near Paradise, shouldn't the insurance adjusters and agents be there, too?

"Oh?" Her hackles went up. Were they going to try to screw her?

"First off, I'm sorry to hear of your loss." He seemed to be consulting a paper. "Mr. Cummins has been our client for many years."

"His dad used you, too. Thad thought you were a good company."

"We are. I have a few questions to ask you about your property. I understand from the documentation that you ran a breeding kennel from the premises we insured."

"Well, yes. Our name is on everything we filled out: Charisma Kennels. Our agent Shirley knew; everyone knew."

"I didn't know, and the company didn't know you were operating a business from the property."

"You saw our kennel name on the first page of the application. We told Shirley. Everyone knew we ran a kennel. Look at YouTube! I've got tons of videos of puppies for sale and us working with them."

"No one here in the headquarters knew about it."

"Is there a problem? Everyone around us had a business going at home. Appliance repair. Painting. Tractor work. Plumbing. What's the problem?"

"The problem is that we have no record of you applying for business coverage. We can't cover your business. That would be everything that wouldn't be included in a straight homeowner's policy."

"The kennel." Cait's mouth was dry. It had cost over $100,000. It was concrete and galvanized steel, but she had seen similar structures charred and bent on the news.

"And the fences, garage, and the room where you gave your PuppyCait seminars for the dogs and home decoration podcasts."

"But I didn't make much money from the furniture part of PuppyCait or the seminars."

"Did you declare your sales on your income tax? How about fees for workshops?"

"I didn't sell that many pieces of furniture, and I've only had two workshops. It wasn't enough to live on…" What was happening? Her world was tilting again, out of control. "It was just a hobby."

He chuckled. The sound had a bite. "You have 83,000 followers on YouTube. More than 50,000 on Twitter and 20,000 on Facebook. That's some hobby."

"I made almost nothing on it. I didn't do it for money. I didn't know about all that online stuff. We didn't have good internet service at the house. I couldn't check my rankings."

"We have to study your case. The fact that you have over a hundred videos about the dogs and your furniture rehabilitation business plus the massive internet following speaks to you operating two significant businesses from a residential address. This is not permitted."

"It was permitted! Thad got a business permit for it."

"Where is it?"

"I don't know. Burned up with everything else. The county records…"

"The business license is actually a minor part of the problem." She could hear rustling, as though he was looking through papers. "We understand that you made major renovations to your home and property. But the county has no record of building permits."

Cait choked down a gasp. "I don't think anything we did needed permits. I did most of the work myself. I weigh 110 pounds. What could I do that required permits?"

"Lots of things, Mrs. Cummins. Electrical work. Plumbing. Many types of structural work with proper tools."

Cait was stunned. Thad didn't want to get permits, and she had followed his lead. "They will just increase our property taxes. They take forever to get and cost a fortune. Go ahead and do what you want. You don't need permits for redecorating."

That was before they discovered the dry rot and sagging beams. They got to know their neighbor Cliff Madsen, when he offered to help. Cliff and his men had done work that certainly required a permit. But if she told on him, he could lose his license as a building contractor. He and his family would be without a livelihood. She couldn't say a word.

"Well, Mrs. Cummins, I will keep you informed of our progress on your case."

"But I am insured? I will get something? I'm a widow, I don't…"

"We will consider all aspects of the situation and get back to you. Our attorneys may wish to depose you. Do you have representation?"

"No." She could feel the grit leeching out of her. Then she remembered Thad's old friend Jeffrey Hoagland who'd helped her when she got arrested for hitting that cop. "Yes, yes I do."

"You can have your attorney contact me. We won't get the IRS or other jurisdictions involved until this is straightened out."

She was shaking when she dialed the number of Hoagland, Moore, Cassavetes, Peters, et. al. in San Francisco. Things had changed for Jeffrey. He was the head of his firm. That's what being listed first in a list of partners meant, didn't it? Cait had gone over her spiel a dozen times, but her hands shook, and her lips trembled when she talked to the receptionist.

"I'd like to speak to Jeffrey Hoagland, please."

"Is he expecting your call?"

"No. I'm an old friend, but it's about… I need a lawyer."

"I'm sure one of our junior…"

"No, I need *Jeffrey.* Just tell him my name. Caitlin Cummins. He knows me." She bit her lips while waiting. When they lived in San Francisco, she and Thad went out to dinner with Jeffrey and his wife… what was her name? Deidre? Something like that. They went out three of four times a year. They weren't close friends, but they were strong acquaintances. Thad and Jeff went to high school together.

"Hey, there, Cait! It's been a long time. I heard about the fire up there. You and Thad didn't get caught in all that, did you?" Jeffrey sounded younger and more full of life than he had when she saw him last.

"We got very caught up in it, Jeffrey. Thad was killed trying to rescue our dogs. They're all dead, and the house and kennels are gone. I've got nothing."

Jeffrey was silent. "Jesus, Cait. That's horrible. I'm so sorry."

"I think my insurance company is trying to get out of paying me for everything. They say having a business wasn't part of the insurance and that we did lots of renovation without permits. That nullifies our coverage." She didn't cry, just got very still. Brittle, again, the way she had when ashes permeated everything. "They said their attorneys wanted to depose me. And that I should have representation.

"I don't have any money, Jeff, but I thought since you helped me when I hit that cop, maybe… Maybe I can pay you when I get something for the farm."

"Cait, I will do everything in my power to help you, *pro bono.* You've suffered enough. I'm so sorry about Thad. He was a good guy. And now this…" He cleared his throat a few times. She sensed he was fighting for control.

"Unfortunately, I'm preparing for a big trial, so I won't be able to help you myself. But the firm has over two hundred attorneys on staff. I need to think about it for a day or so—I'm sure I can find a couple of lawyers who are perfect for you. Don't worry, Cait, I won't let you down."

He was serious, calming, and reassuring. Why didn't she feel reassured? Was he passing her off on some flunky? "Um. I do have one thing. I started doing videos for the dog business—for customers, but also for people interested in dogs, or having trouble with dogs. And the cottage we bought was a mess. We cleaned it up, and I learned how to do all sorts of decorative things for the house. Rehab furniture. Even replace walls. I did videos for that, too. And one of the paint companies sponsored me.

"It didn't amount to a lot of money, but the insurance man said I'm wildly successful online. He's using the number of people following me as proof we were doing a big business. I didn't know about my following, but it's huge. That's my resume, Jeffrey. I'm PuppyCait. Check me out on any of the social media—YouTube, Instagram, Facebook, Twitter."

"I will, Cait. Don't worry." She gave him the address where she was staying. He said, "I'll be in touch."

When they got off the phone, Jeffrey looked around his magnificent office. On the corner of the building, wall-to-wall, ceiling-to-floor windows formed two sides of the room. Being on the sixtieth floor gave him one of the best views in the city.

He felt bad for Cait. On the other hand, he always had thought that Thad was the kind of dufus who'd relocate to a fire trap pursuing a stupid dream. Breeding dogs? That's what you did when you'd made your fortune. It was a hobby, not a livelihood.

He spoke to his computer, "Look up PuppyCait."

Jeffrey rocked back as the screen disgorged page after page of listings for PuppyCait. He clicked "Images" and saw what old friend Cait looked like now. He whistled.

"Time hasn't hurt that little dolly one bit." His eyes narrowed. Poor little widow. He'd help her all right.

11

OPAL MAKES A FRIEND

WHEN OPAL AWOKE, she was inside the tent, lying on a matt. It was daytime. She couldn't think very well, and everything looked fuzzy. And didn't sound right. She tried to lift her head and couldn't.

"Oh, you're awake!" a cheery voice said. "I thought you'd make it, but you were in pretty rough shape when I found you." She tried to get up but could barely raise her head. "No, stay down. *Down,* do you know that? *Stay!*" Opal stayed. "Ahah. We have a trained dog. A poodle. I took the liberty of trimming you a bit with my electric shaver. Only a registered poodle would have that needle nose! And all that curly hair. Matted now. My razor couldn't do much with that. But I can see your pretty face."

He moved to where she could see him better. In the trickery of fever and drugs and fear, her eyes did a strange thing. The old man who had been with her when she was born lived forever in Opal's mind. He was tall, thin, white haired, kind, and he knew everything about dogs. He had been her first owner, and she considered him her real father. Opal loved him more than any dog or man she'd met since.

Her memory of that man came to her and wrapped itself around the man in front of her. Who was tall, white haired, very thin, and knew everything about dogs. It was him! It was him! The man who raised her, who she loved above all others came back! He came back! He was here! She was certain it was him, come back to save her.

Opal's tail thumped on the pad, and she whined, lifting her head and licking at his fingers. He moved his hand to her mouth and let her lick.

His eyes swam with moisture. "You aren't the only one who needs a little kindness, are you? Lick away, girl, and I'll tell you what I did to you. First, let me take your vital signs." He got a stethoscope out of a bag and listened to her heart and all along her belly. He was a veterinarian. Opal knew all about them. *Never bite the vet!* That was a mighty rule. She disobeyed it once and was severely punished.

The man put the stethoscope back in the bag. The satchel had gold letters on the side: Roger E. Welbourne, MD. "You were near death when you came here two days ago. Mauled by coyotes, I would say. Some predator. I hope you gave as well as you got, girl. You ran from the fire, too, didn't you? You had burned patches along your back. Hard for fire to get started in dense wool like yours. You got those cinders out, probably by rolling. And then mixed it up with the wild boys. Dirty wild boys.

"I had to take off most of your ear, sweetheart. The infection was out of control. Gangrene had already set in. I cleaned up your facial lacerations and your neck. That coyote almost killed you: half an inch and it would have severed your jugular. But you're a lucky one!" She moved her head. Something dangled from her neck. "You've got drains for the seepage. And IV antibiotics. And painkillers.

"You'll be here with me for a week or two, sweetheart. But that's all right. That's about how long my errand will take. I brought supplies." He went silent. His head fell forward, and his eyes closed. Opal nudged him with her nose. He didn't wake up, so she went to sleep.

"I've got something I think you'll like," the old man said, coming into the tent. "Here, I let it cool. If you're anything like Addie's dogs, you'd gobble it down straight off the grill and burn yourself." He held out a pan with delectable-smelling meat. "My morning catch, or half of it. Mountain trout. Enough for both of us. I boned it for you, too. You'd gobble those little bones down and make yourself sicker."

Opal was a picky eater who smelled the fish thoroughly before taking a dainty bite. Then she gobbled.

"Hah! A poodle is a dog under all the fuss!" the old man chortled. "Let's see how you're doing this morning." He checked her bandages and changed her drains. "You are one healthy dog. Amazing! Amazing.

"You know, Addie—she was my wife. Adelaide, but no one called her that—loved dogs. She had boxers. Very athletic. Nice dogs. She used to show them. They're like popcorn. Soon, we had a kennel full and raised a couple of litters a year. I moved my practice to be out in the country where we could have more land. I'm an MD, but I did more veterinary work than anyone knew. Someone could have turned me in, but all the neighbors knew I was the only 'vet' available night and day." He chuckled.

"Aren't you lucky? You ran into the only MD with extensive canine veterinary experience available on this mountain during a catastrophic wildfire." He chuckled more. "I'm glad you're here. These might have been lonely days and nights on my 'last vacation.'" He coughed, and Opal looked at him, concerned.

"I'm going to do more of that as the days go by. You'd better get used to it. But we'll have a time, you and I. Would you like it if I made sure you had a home after this? I can fix that."

Opal crawled closer and licked his hand again. She didn't like the tone of what he was saying. She couldn't understand his words, but the feeling made her scared and sad.

"Okay. I'll walk slowly with my canes, and you can follow beside me. No jostling, or I'll fall over and not be able to get up."

Opal stared at him. He was *very* thin. He should eat more. He was very weak and seemed barely able to walk, even with the sticks he held.

"We'll do walks like these as long as I can. When I can't, you can run off by yourself and catch rabbits or squirrels. You'll stay in at night with me, so you'll be safe. That's after I remove your drains."

They went for their slow, short walk.

"Oh, my dear poodle friend!" He stopped every few feet. "Look at those trees! Magnificent cedars! First growth! And look at the ferns. Aren't they lovely?" She measured her pace to his and looked at him every few feet. He made her nervous, but the happiest she could remember.

They went along like that for quite a few days, Opal had no idea how many.

"We're not going out together, today, sweetheart. I need to rest. But I have a game we can play. I'm going to guess your name.

"Have you heard this joke? One old codger says to another: 'I can't remember a thing. I can't remember my dog's name.' The other guy says, 'That's easy. I sat out in the backyard with my dog and shouted all the dog names I could remember. When the dog came to me, I knew I got his name." The old man laughed, and then coughed long and hard.

"I'm okay, girl. Don't worry. Now, let's try that." He barked out all sorts of words for a long time. Opal cocked her head from one side to the other. "Princess. No. You're not Princess. Sally. Fluffy. June. July. You're not any of those. How about April?" Opal got up and went to him. Was he trying to say Opal?

"Your name is April! Good girl, April!"

He seemed so delighted to almost get her name that she jumped up and danced in a circle.

"Well, April, I have to do some homework now. Do you feel up to chasing squirrels? Or rabbits? I wouldn't mind a rabbit for dinner. Go! Run!" He motioned for her to go. She looked into the forest and then back at him. "Go! But come back!"

She sprinted off, reveling in the joy of running free. She went quite a way before remembering the old man. She charged back and happened to catch a fat bunny just before camp. She brought it to him and laid it at his feet. He was barking into a little box and smiled at her. He did something to the box, and then said, "Oh, good. I'll correct what I dictated and then dress the rabbit. We'll eat tonight, April!" She wiggled all over.

He touched the box, and it barked back to him. Opal listened hard, tilting her head from side to side. His voice was coming from the box!

"Well, Craig and Alice, I know you're worried sick about me. I know you have called every law enforcement agency that will listen to you. I need to make you clear about this: I am the one who is dying, not you. This is *my* death, not yours. I am the one who should say how it happens. I tried to tell you this, and you wouldn't listen, so I did what I had to." His voice got stronger.

"I *will not die* in some damn, sanitized hospice or hospital. *I will not.* Your insistence that I live my last weeks slurping Pablum and being treated like an infant is *your* idea of my perfect death. What you're insisting on is for *you, not me.* If I'm trussed up like a turkey in sterile sheets, it's so that you can say, 'We did our best for Dad. Always, and especially at the end.' You're lying.

"You *didn't* do your best for me. Your mother and I devoted ourselves to seeing that you had the best of everything, even when we could barely afford it. You got private schools, and university. When your mother died, I allowed you to convince me to sell my practice and the kennel and move into the city, near you.

"I hate the city. All I wanted was a few more years of the pastures and forest. Camping trips like your mother and I used to take. That's it. What I got was a stinking condo with a Gestapo condo association. All so you could 'conserve my resources.'

"They're *my* resources. If I want to give them to a dog rescue, I can. And maybe I have, huh? You won't know until my will is read. *My* will.

"I'm going to stay out here and croak. I have enough morphine to give me a pain-free exit, at exactly when I want it. Your cops and sheriff won't be able to find me. They've got enough on their hands with this fire. Hundreds of missing people. Thousands of houses lost.

"They won't have time to find an old man who wanted a quiet, natural death. Death is *natural.*"

He stopped listening to the box, tears in his eyes. "Oh, God, April. I wish I didn't have to do it this way. I wish they could understand. I wish they'd stop trying to be the best kids anyone never had and looking so damn correct. Why don't they see me? The real me?"

Opal whined and poked him with her nose.

"You're a good listener, aren't you? Well, maybe I won't leave that message. Maybe I'll erase it. Sure felt good to say it, though."

Every day, he moved less and less. One day, he didn't get out of his bed. Opal poked him many times, but he didn't get up. She licked his fingers. Ran out in the forest and brought him a bunny.

"Addie!" he called. "Addie, is that you? I can see you."

That made Opal frantic. Who was he talking to? She barked and barked again.

"Oh, April, are you mad at me? I would never leave you, darling, but I don't have any choice. Can we play a game, girl? Go to my bag. Bring it here." He motioned. She hauled it over to his bed. "Good girl. Such a good girl." He looked down by the cot. A collection of rabbits and squirrels, some quite ripe. "You've been feeding me... I'm beyond that, darling." He coughed, but weakly.

"It's cancer, April. Can't beat it. Neither could Addie... I loved her so. We had such a life. Could you bring my cell phone?" He pointed at the little box at the end of his bed. She did, and he spoke into it.

"My dying wish is that you find my dog, April. She's been the dearest, best friend I could have had. She stayed with me at the end. Bringing me rabbits..." He managed a chuckle, as sick as he was. He coughed. "She needs to be loved and cared for. No lousy walk twice a day in some city park. Craig and Alice, I'm sorry if I seemed stern earlier. If only you could listen to me as well as this dog does." He turned off the device and closed his eyes.

She nudged him with her nose, but he was sleeping. Opal ran out and caught a squirrel for him. They weren't as tasty as bunnies, but she didn't have to go far to catch it.

Dropping the squirrel by his bed, Opal approached. She poked him. He didn't move. Poked again. She realized what had happened. She poked him hard, and jumped up on his bed, licking his face.

He had left.

Oh, no! This couldn't happen. This was impossible. He had gone. He wasn't there.

Opal howled. She howled louder and harder than any dog ever had. She screamed. Jumped off and on his bed. Cried.

She had to get help. Humans would help him. They could do many things she couldn't. Where were humans? Opal barked, running from one side of the clearing to another, barking in the corners. Barking in the middle.

Help! Help! You have to help him!

Back at the parking lot for the national forest, three rangers sat in a 4WD SUV boosted high off the ground and equipped for any sort of disaster. The vehicle was covered with mud and ash and beat to hell, as were its occupants.

"Why are we here?"

"We're here because that woman cussed our boss out ten ways from Sunday if we didn't try to find her dad."

"She thought he was in Costa Rica, she said at first."

"Yeah, but she found out that was bullshit. His friend down there had mailed the letter that said he was there with him. They pulled a fast one on her. The old man was making a run for it."

"Because he wanted to die in peace. The way she talked to our boss, I can understand him wanting to run from her."

"Look, there's people who are really lost and in danger out here. Let's find this old geezer and get back to work."

They walked to the trailhead. Paths going in a half-dozen directions departed there. Signs marking the major camping spots pointed every which way.

"Do you hear that?"

"That dog?"

"Yeah, that's one upset dog."

They walked toward the sound. "Here, boy! Here, girl! Come! Come here!"

The dog barreled out of the underbrush, panting like it might explode. It was a very dirty white poodle with most of one ear missing. When it could gather breath, it barked hysterically. It ran to them, then back into the trees. Then back to them.

"Okay, boy. We got it." They pulled some first aide equipment from the SUV and followed the dog.

They never would have found the camp; it was nowhere near an organized campsite and far off trail. The dog kept running back and forth, more hysterical as they got closer. Its frenzy indicated the proximity to disaster. For that's what the rescuers felt. They were heading toward a tragedy.

"Oh, phew." The stench greeted them in front of the tent. "Smells like he's been dead a while."

But that wasn't it: a small zoo of dead rabbits, squirrels, a possum, and even a garter snake was arrayed around the body. *They* smelled, not Dr. Welbourne. He was fresh as a daisy, with a contented smile on his lips.

"The dog's been bringing him gifts."

"Our cat did that.'

When they approached the body, things changed. The dog jumped between them and the still figure, teeth bared.

"You have to let us help him, buddy. We won't hurt him," one of the Rangers said.

The dog snarled and growled furiously, jumping forward as though it might attack.

"*PLATZ! PLATZ, BLIEB!*" One of the rangers moved forward forcefully, speaking in German. The dog dropped and stayed down as though she'd been stuck. She lay there, every hair trembling, but in control.

"She's Schutzhund trained," he said. "That's a type of German training and a canine sport. The dogs are trained for obedience, tracking, and attack. Very demanding."

"Why would anyone train a poodle to do that? A *poodle?*"

"Poodles aren't sissy dogs. They're super smart and trainable. When they're big like this one, they can be war dogs or police dogs. Or service dogs. This one was probably trained because…" The guy shrugged. "Maybe to get more control over it. Maybe the owner had won so much in the show ring, he wanted to extend the range of the dog's influence. And winning…

"Who knows. He's lying there. He doesn't like it, but he didn't attack." To the dog, he said, "I'm going to examine your friend. You need to stay there and let me do it." He said some more in German.

"How do you know it's a show dog?"

"K-9 core in the Army. And I like dogs."

"Should we call the coroner before we move him?"

"I don't see any signs of violence, except for all those rodents. They came to a violent end." They laughed, a short, not very humorous burst. "Everyone's busy now. We could probably get a coroner out in a week or so."

They packed up Dr. Welbourne and his camp, taking numerous pictures to show the police and other authorities. They picked up his cell phone but didn't listen to the message. "We'll let the boss do that. Maybe he left a note."

Opal ran out to the trees to relieve herself.

"Oh, we have to take back all those 'he's.' She's a girl."

Opal watched with increasing anxiety. They put her man into a big sack and zipped it. They put him in their car. They took all his things but left the presents she had given him. She whined and ran from one man to another. When they got in the car, they beckoned to her.

"Come, girl. We'll take care of you."

The dog guy used his best German commands, but Opal wouldn't obey.

"Okay, I've had it." One of the guys took off his belt and made it into a loop. He held it out, planning on looping it around her neck like a leash.

When Opal saw the swinging belt, she froze and moved toward the trail head. There, she danced from foot to foot, whining.

"Boy, she knows what a belt is for. Poor thing. What a life she's had."

"Come on, girl. We'll take you somewhere safe."

Opal sat back and howled. She howled again, and again. The voice of agony. Ceaseless pain.

He was gone. They were taking what was left of him away. She would never see him again. Her best person had left her. She was alone.

Opal bolted into the woods.

12

CAITLIN WORKS OUT

"I'VE LOOKED OVER our professional staff and have two possibilities to represent you." Caitlin could hardly contain her excitement. Super-lawyer Jeffrey Hoagland had called her back! She hadn't heard from him for a couple of weeks and assumed he was blowing her off. Not at all, from what he was saying.

"These are the available attorneys I think would do the best job for you. Jason Bridger is known in the firm as our 'widows and orphans' man. He's very bright, very competent, and has a knack for appealing to juries and judges emotionally. He creates a feeling for sympathy for his clients, even in opposing counsel, sometimes! I hesitate to describe you as one of the poor, helpless widows or orphans, but you are to some extent. You need someone who can exploit that, if need be. And Jason's a great lawyer. His 'win' record is amazing.

"Celeste Ramon is as good an attorney, but more like a shark. She'll win in whatever pond you put her, and she'll do it without mercy. She's also a woman, and I thought that might appeal to you. She's very compassionate to women in tough spots. If you were accused of murder, I'd recommend her over Jason. But it depends upon what they throw at us.

"Have you heard anything more from your insurance company?"

"No. I guess they're still 'studying my case.'" She sighed.

"We'll have to get going and surprise them. I'm going to have Jason and Celeste call you today. You can chat and make up your mind as to which you'd like to represent you. Then get whoever you decide to work with copies of everything you've got. And cc me everything between you."

"All I've got is the insurance company's notices and what that guy said on the phone."

"That's right, you escaped with the clothes on your back. Well, Jason or Celeste will be able to get the documents from the insurance company. Now—how are *you* doing?"

"I'm doing better here than sitting in a parking lot in Chico with smoke in my eyes." They laughed. "It's good to be here with Ellen and Cliff. They were always good neighbors, but I didn't know *how* good until now. I've got all the clothes I can wear, thanks to the Women's Guilds of the churches around here. They heard what happened to us and sent us their old clothes. I'm *amazingly* stylish..." The trembling in her voice was real; the local people cared about her. Jeffrey Hoagland cared about her...

"Jeffrey, I'll pay you when I get money from the insurance."

"Don't worry about it, Cait. My pleasure..."

"No, I want to pay you."

"Okay. Would you like to give me a retainer?"

"I don't have any money."

"This won't require money. Make some more of those PuppyCait videos. I'm totally hooked."

"What?!"

"Yeah. I watched one. They're like salted peanuts. You can't just eat one. I've watched all of them."

"Four years' worth?"

"Every one. The ones about dogs, and the ones about furniture. I told my daughter she could get a puppy after watching them. I figure

I've got the know how to handle a pup after watching years of you getting chewed on."

"Really?" She had no idea her videos would appeal to him.

"Yeah. You're hysterically funny and have a great stage presence—and sense of timing. With better sets and a camera man, you could have a cable show, or even real TV. We can talk about that downstream.

"And all those ideas for fixing up broken down furniture. I loved the one where you took two chairs and made them into a bench. And where you took the old phone booth and… de… de … what?"

"Decoupaged it."

"Yes, into a replica of the Sistine Chapel."

He started laughing, and so did she. "That was one of my better works."

"Do more of those. And check your YouTube and social accounts. I think you'll be surprised."

"Can I look at one of your laptops?" she asked Cliff's brood of kids. All of them had laptops, even the littlest. Their house hadn't been burned to the ground as Caitlin's had. The Madsen home had merely been damaged, not burnt entirely. It could be restored. Cliff had been up there, measuring and figuring out how to restore their place. He was having no problems with his insurance company, even though he ran his contracting business from his house.

But she wouldn't get upset over that. She would keep her mind on what Jeffrey had said; checking out her social media. Cait had mastered social media well enough to post anything she wanted, do killer videos on her cell phone, and upload them. People had told her she should "monetize her content," but she thought of it as a hobby. Now she needed to see what had happened in the weeks she'd been prostrate with grief.

In the minutes the Madsens had been given to evacuate their home in Paradise, their kids had packed all their most important possessions: listening devices, computers, game consoles, cell phones, and athletic shoes. They forgot such important things as toothbrushes, clothes, and orthodontic retainers.

"First things first," Cait thought, logging into her Facebook account. Her jaw dropped. Hundreds, no, thousands, of people had visited her page and wished her well. They'd posted pictures of her taken from her blog articles and videos. Pictures of her and Thad and the dogs smiling and joyful. They made her eyes tear up.

When somebody dropped a bombshell, like announcing that Thad had died, the comments bore paroxysms of grief. People were just guessing, because she hadn't posted anything, but they were guessing accurately. Or watching the news.

"All the Charisma Kennels dogs died!" Her followers went into hysteria. Convulsions. They posted GIFs and images showing dog angels. She couldn't imagine it. Instagram and Twitter were worse, or *more. Thousands and thousands* had commented, asking her questions, wondering how she was.

"Are you going to do any more PuppyCait videos? My dog club loves them."

"I just bought the most hideous table. I want to do something like what you did with your jewel-box suite. I hope you come back soon. …" A pause. "And I'm so sorry about your husband and the dogs."

Shit. She lost everything and this broad wanted free advice on how to decorate furniture? Fast? Cait wanted to fire back, "Thanks a bunch, Sweet Patootie, I'll remember this when *your* husband dies."

But she didn't. She knew that would tank what she had going. She had *gone viral* because of the worst thing ever to happen to her. She intended to capitalize on it.

"Do you kids have video cameras?" She'd done all the vids she'd put up on YouTube with her cell phone. She and Thad talked about getting her a better camera but got burned out before they could decide which one to buy.

They hadn't only video cameras, but better tech stuff and skills than had ever been applied to "PuppyCait—Love your Puppy and

Live with It!" and "Puppy's Got a Brand-New Home—with Puppy-Cait." Not good titles, but what she'd gone with for years.

Turned out the kids knew all sorts of editing techniques and could add music and special effects. They were far beyond her in their skills. PuppyCait was going to upgrade. Cait had some ideas. With the kids' help, she could post a new video the next day.

Cait stood in front of the old barn in her hand-me-down finest and ragged jeans. She added a few bits of lace and such, ending up with a funky thrift shop/bohemian look. Her look. A very feminine look.

"I just looked at my social media. It's the first time I've been online since…" She teared up and let it show. The kids were filming from several angles. "I just saw all the notes and well-wishes. Thank you so much for thinking of me—and Thad." She let the tears flow. "The police told me they found our van with Thad and the dogs in it.

"There's one bit of news that wasn't released. Opal, the big mama of our pack, wasn't in the van and may have escaped death." A glimmer of hope appeared in Cait's blue eyes. "I'm not holding my breath, but she may be alive. I'd offer a reward for her, but I don't have anything to give.

"Except PuppyCait."

She whirled and dashed into the old barn behind her. More of the kids were in the barn, ready to film.

She walked to a heavy wooden workbench arrayed with a few power tools. Grabbing a gigantic chainsaw, she held it up to the cameras, grinning wildly. Cait fired it up. The thing bucked like a bronco. She ran toward the barn wall. A large rectangle had been chalked on the side. Cait lit into it like she was cutting chocolate cream pie. In short order—which the kids sped up on the video—she had carved a gaping hole in the side of the barn.

"There! That's how PuppyCait does it," she crowed, turning off her saw and putting it back.

Cait Remodels the Barn—with a Chainsaw

"What have you done?" They hadn't scripted this part. Cliff charged into the barn. "This is my brother's barn. What am I supposed to tell him?"

"Tell him he's been PuppyCait'd!" Caitlin grabbed him by the hand and led him to the hole in the wall. "Look at that: the best view on the property, hidden in an old tool barn. It's going to be the new master suite! I'm going to PuppyCait this whole place, to thank your brother for giving me a place to stay."

"You're gonna '*PuppyCait*' it?"

"Yes! Your brother's family is the first to be Puppy'd. You've seen what I did around our little cottage back at Charisma Kennels."

"Yeah, it was really cool. But Cait, my brother doesn't have all sorts of money to finance a remodel."

"I did everything on the cheap. Scavenged everything. Like look at this." The kids threw the barn doors wide. A caravan of trucks rolled up the driveway.

"You the lady that wanted the old church window?"

"The molding and millwork left over from the mall redo?"

"The PVC pipe?"

"Dinged-up sheetrock?"

"Yes, I'm Cait Cummins, the PuppyCait! I'm going to redo this house, so you won't believe it. Thank you SO MUCH!" She ran around the lot, hugging and kissing the drivers. "You can put it in the barn. I'll work around it. If you have friends who have leftover building materials, tell them to call me and bring it here! Nothing too weird to work in somewhere."

The guys stacked things in the barn.

Cliff said, "But, Caitlin, what are you going to do for labor? There's no budget for that."

"Ah, Cliff, we have a built-in labor supply. You have five kids. They're all older than my grandpa when he went to work. If I can do what I do, I can sure teach it to your kids. While I'm homeschooling them!"

"Homeschooling them?"

"Yeah. I have an MA in English from Stanford, and a teaching credential. I can homeschool your kids while giving them a trade. You're going to have your house up in Paradise fixed in a few months. No sense in them having to adapt to a new school. I'll teach them here. Can't beat that!"

"You sure can't." Cliff grabbed her and gave her a big kiss on the cheek. He held it a little longer than felt comfortable to Cait. He whispered when he let her go, "The kids were filming. Thought I'd give them a show." He winked and ambled away.

I hope no one else sees that, she thought, wiping her cheek.

"So, that's the latest episode of PuppyCait. I'm going to be busy, redoing Cliff's brother's house. But it will provide lots of wonderful Puppy Tunes!" She stood still as the kids filmed the closing material for the show. "I said I didn't have anything as a reward to offer if you can help us find Opal, but I do. I can PuppyCait a room in your house for free! And I'd be glad to. This is what she looks like—"

Two photos filled the screen. One was Opal in a full-on show trim, with pom-poms all over, looking like a hairy bon-bon. The second was Opal after Thad trimmed her.

"Thad was a great guy and loved the dogs, but he was the worst dog groomer in the world. She'll look like the second picture, except probably worse."

"So long everyone and remember 'Pet a puppy.'"

13

BREAKIN' BAD, OR
JUST BREAKIN'

OPAL SHOT OUT of the camp. The rangers called after her and tried to get her to come, but she would never go to them. Her human had left her. That man took out his belt. She knew what that meant: he was going to beat her. Opal tore into the heart of the forest, running into its shrouded darkness and as far from people as possible.

She was colder than she had ever been, even with her coat a grown-out mass of ungroomed matts. The Camp Fire had started on the eighth of November, which was normally well into the fall-approaching-winter stage in the Sierra Foothills and darned cold. Winter didn't come at the normal time that year: the inversion layer held the fire's smoke and heat in and kept the season from changing.

Several weeks later, when her human left her, the weather caught up. It was almost December. Opal ran northeast, into the wilderness near Buck's Lake, some of the roughest terrain in California. A ferocious wind arose, and the temperature plummeted. Trunks of trees raked each other, groaning like meat-starved demons. Branches popped as leafy giants fell. Opal skittered from one near death to another. Her heart pounded from exertion and terror.

The wind came, and then the rain. It dropped like the buckets of slop Cait had thrown to their hog. Opal had seen rain, but nothing like this. She was quite dry, her matted coat keeping moisture from her skin, but the gusts tossed her off her feet. She had trouble clawing her way forward. Thunder boomed loud enough to have her cowering at each crash. The booms were ceaseless.

After the rain, the snow. Opal had seen snow. She started life in a New York kennel. She knew snow, but not the snow of the wild Sierras. It blew sideways, it whirled, it flattened her to the ground. Her feet with their tough pads couldn't take the icy cold of the banking snow. She could barely flounder through it, and still it came.

She was going to die. She'd escaped before, but this freezing nightmare was as bad as the fire had been. She had to find a place out of the raging blizzard. She needed water, and food. She hadn't eaten much when her person was dying; she kept watch by his side and didn't move. She was starved and nutritionally deprived.

The forest was cleft with gullies and canyons. She darted up one, the only way she could go with the wind, and found an opening in its side. A cave. She'd never seen a cave, but it seemed like her kennel, deep and dark and safe. Pulling herself inside, Opal collapsed.

When she awoke, she had a bad feeling about the place. It stank. The ground stank, and now she stank of it. A movement caused her to look up. The ceiling was covered with something alive! A blanket of softly furred black forms undulated at her movement, watching her with bright black eyes. They made high-pitched noises and then launched off the cave ceiling. She scrambled to her feet as they flew at her head and shoulders, beating her with leathery wings. A swarm enveloped her.

Opal flew out of the cave, a cadre of bats following her. The storm had passed. The sky was bright white, reflecting an invisible sun. The blizzard blanketed everything in new snow. Opal plunged her way through it, yelping as the flying creatures struck her. They flapped in her eyes. Bit her. The bites didn't hurt, thanks to her matted hair. When she had fought her way through the snow much farther than she knew she could, they flew back to their cave.

She wanted to throw herself down and cry. What were those things? This world held dangers she couldn't conceive. The image of Thad's face and Caitlyn's floated before her eyes. *Please Cait and Thad, come for me. I'll be good. I'll let you touch me, Cait. I'll never growl at you. Help me! Please,* something *help me!*

Opal crawled the last few yards on her belly. She didn't know how she made it up the stairs to the wide porch. The lights had called her to the house, a friendly house like Cait and Thad's had been, with lights in the windows and a thin stream of smoke escaping from the chimney. Snow draped the place and covered everything for miles around. Only the track Opal had made indicated the world wasn't covered with snow.

Help me. Help me, Opal whispered in silent dog talk.

The door opened and a gruff voice spoke, "What the hell are you?" Hands pawed her. "A beat-up mutt. Dirty as a…

"I better get you in or I'll have a dead dog on my steps when they come back. Won't say much for my house sittin'."

The guy hauled her into the living room and laid her in front of the wood stove. "What you doin' out here, piggy? You forget your groomin' appointment?" He laughed, an unpleasant sound. She couldn't fight it. "What? You got one ear? Wha'd you do, lose a fight?

"I don't got any dog food, but that cheapskate doctor that owns this place has a freezer full of elk. That ought to hold you. I'll go defrost some." He got up, and Opal heard him moving around and the whirring noise of a machine.

"There you go. Eat up." He put a plate of half-frozen, half-microwave-fried meat in front of her. "Eat up. You look like you could use a square meal."

She ate, gingerly at first, and then ravenously. She looked up at him.

"You want more? Okay. Today only. I can't let that doctor think I ate all his game."

She watched him very carefully, keeping as much distance between them as possible. He didn't act like any human she had known. He liked to stay in one of the rooms, keeping the door shut. He also kept the doors and windows to the house shut and watched her whenever he was out of his room. He was thin and had sores all over his face. His teeth were rotten. She had never seen that, either. Sometimes he was happy and danced around the big room where she spent most of her time. Then he'd be angry and yell at her. He chased her with a broom once. She turned on him snarling, ready to attack.

"Oh no, sorry, girl. Just feeling a little cranky. You know how that is."

He forgot to feed her, sometimes for days, but when he did, he fed her large amounts. She did okay. He didn't hit her. Sometimes he talked to people she couldn't see and ran to the windows, peering out the closed draperies, screaming at nothing.

"Damn feds. None of their business what I do in my own house." He abruptly started laughing. "Ain't my house, of course. Belongs to stuck-up SOB doctor thinks he's better than me."

He talked on the telephone, one on the wall and one in his pocket. His voice sounded oily and fawning, like a pup standing up to its mother.

"Aw, Doctor Milt, that's a shame that you and the family won't be able to come up this year. Yeah, well, being in Barbados for Christmas is better than here in the cold. Don' you worry, your place'll be ready for you in May. Okay, well, you know that ol' Chet has you covered as long as you want."

He laughed hysterically when he got off the phone, acting like he was talking to someone Opal couldn't see. She looked around. "Dumb asshole. That gives me plenty of time to finish. The boys will pick up my stuff, and I'll be out of here and in fat city."

He scratched himself all the time. That, she understood. No one had given her flea medicine, and she scratched too. "What you looking at, bitch? You can't *look* at me…"

Opal ran down the stairs, into the basement. This was the most horrible part of her being trapped there. He didn't let her go outside to relieve herself. She went as far as she could in the house to find a spot. That was the cellar. It was littered now with months of her waste. It smelled. The man never cleaned it, just like he never cleaned up the bowl he put her meat in. Or the house. It all smelled.

She stayed down there while he raged and raved above. She heard dishes and furniture shattering, everything in the house being smashed and broken. Then he screamed. She heard a noise she knew—gunshots. One of her owners liked to hunt and shot guns at his estate. What were the gunshots for? Would the man be dead like the deer and other animals?

When the upstairs had been silent a long time, she crept up the stairs. He wasn't dead. He lay on the floor. He was twitching in slow, convulsive movements. The stuffed elk head over the fireplace was shot to pieces.

Opal looked around, running from door to door, window to window. All were locked. Worse, snow covered everything. Even if she could get out, she'd die in the snow. She had no choice but to stay there if she wanted to survive. She had been through bad times, but this was the worst of all.

"Well, dipshit, I'd better get to work. I'm supposed to make my delivery in a couple of days. That means double batching. But I can do it. I can do anything if I need to." He turned on the TV, contradicting his impulse to work hard.

"Lookit that! You like the Animal World?" The huge screen showed a German Schutzhund competition. German Shepherd and

Rottweiler dogs, and a smattering of other types, were shown tracking scent drags in some shots. The action switched to another area where others demonstrated obedience.

In another area of the competition grounds, handlers gave commands, and the dogs attacked highly padded participants. The dogs looked like they'd like to kill their quarry but called off at a word from the trainer. "This is what I like, lookit that! Those are just killing machines!

"That's what I'm gonna get. If the damn liberals take away our guns, I'm gonna get me a dozen of them. Do you know how to do that, girlie? How about you: *Auf?* That's right *Auf!*"

He had commanded her to get up. She did, her training was so ingrained, she had to obey.

"*Hier! Hier!*" Here, come here. She did. Then in fast order, "*Sits! Ahh-tuunk!*" Sit! Watch out! Finally, his eyes gleaming crazily, "*Faa! Faa!*" In German, *Fas*—attack. He pointed at the torn-up sofa. She shot after it and tore an arm completely off the wrecked couch.

"You *are* worth something! You're a Schutzhund! You're like an atomic dog! Do I have a job for you!"

He turned and walked away, as though the interlude hadn't happened. She shook the sofa arm another time, dropped it, and disappeared down the stairs.

He remembered to feed her that night, then stood muttering by the sink.

"I've gotta do it. It's gonna have to be shake and bake. I don't got any choice."

She didn't know what that meant, but he was shaking and wiggling around again, more than usual. She grabbed her meat and went down to the stinking basement.

He screamed, "They were supposed to bring me everything for a real pro cook. So I wouldn't blow up this place. But they didn't. Stinking sons of bitches! They left me here high and dry with a contract to fill!" Then he raved—loud, angry barking. She didn't know the words, but what he felt with his wild barking was clear.

Other humans had hurt her more than this one had, but none had frightened her so much. She growled most of the time she was with him, low in her throat.

"You the atomic bitch? You gonna bite me? Try it, bitch." He kept a gun in his belt now and would pull it out and point it at her. Sometimes he would whirl and shoot it at something in the house.

Opal's chest was so tight; she almost wished he'd shoot her. Then it would be over. She didn't know how long she'd been there.

The snow was mostly gone now, just covering the ground in patches. If she could get out of the house, she'd run. He could shoot her running away, and she wouldn't care. Anything to escape.

He had bottles that had held the bubbly dark liquid he liked to drink. He'd given her some. She didn't like the bubbles. But this was an empty bottle. He had lots of them on the sink and was putting little stones, little round things in them. All around the bottles were things that humans used. She recognized some from what Caitlin had used making things. Pliers, scissors, jars. Lots of things. He poured other things into the bottle.

He was quiet, mixing, and then he shook the bottle. And another, and another.

She ran downstairs and hid. An aura of danger and a horrible smell followed her.

"Hah! Look at that! I'm the best cooker in the business! They didn't bring me my stuff, but I'll get the job done! Shake 'n' bake city!" He was laughing and cackling, waving a pistol around. The door burst open..

"SHERIFF'S OFFICE! D.E.A.! FREEZE! HANDS OVER YOUR HEAD!" The front door exploded inward, and men poured into the room. They wore the same clothes, and all had guns.

Opal felt the rush of overheated air leave the living room and crept up the stairs. The front door was wide open. She could escape. Trying to make herself as small as possible, she crept toward the door.

"What's that? A dog?" one of the newcomers said.

"Yeah. That's *my* dog. She's the toughest bitch in the west. See her ear's gone? She did that fighting. Come spring, I'm taking her to Nevada and put her in the pit!"

"You're not going anywhere, Chet. We've been watching this place all winter. We picked up your partners on the way out here, with all the ingredients of a major cook."

Her captor looked around the room frantically.

"Drop it, Chet. It's over." The leader of the men moved forward, pointing his gun at Opal's captor.

"*FAA! FAA!*" he shouted at Opal. Attack! Attack! He swung his head from her toward the cop. "*FAA! FAA!*"

Opal stood in the open, frozen. The man who kept her prisoner had told her to attack the other man. Both men stood, pointing guns at each other.

With no hesitation, Opal pivoted toward her jailer and grabbed his arm. They could hear the crack of bones breaking. The gun discharged into the air, and the law enforcement officer lunged forward, grabbing the dealer and putting him in cuffs.

Opal dropped to the ground in a perfect "down." The cops circled her.

One recognized her. "One ear? Shutzhund trained? Boss, I know who this dog is. That cute little gal on YouTube just posted a reward today. You gotta see this." He pulled out his cell and showed the guys Caitlin talking about Opal on YouTube.

"I think Opal is still alive. If you can help me, I would appreciate it so much." She was so sweet and pretty, she could have had a viral YouTube channel just standing in front of the camera. "I'd PuppyCait your house!"

"What was that?"

"She's some kind of decorator. Lost her husband and dogs in the Camp Fire. One of the dogs may be alive."

"A white poodle with one ear."

They looked down, but Opal was gone.

"Was she a poodle?"

"Yeah, one that had been living wild for months."

"Whoa. She's like a ghost."

"A real ghost. I'll tell you one thing; she sure knows the good guys from the bad. She jumped ol' Chet here without a second thought."

Chet was carrying on about his arm.

"We'll get you a doctor, you lousy…"

"What we need to do is report finding that dog. And find out what being PuppyCait'd means."

The Meth Lab Raid

14

CAITLIN CONQUERS A
LOT, BUT NOT ALL

"CAIT, THERE'S SOMEONE here for you," Cliff Madsen called into the living room. Cait was on a twenty-foot ladder, putting a sealer on the redwood ceiling planks so their stain didn't seep through the paint she'd apply next. Sheets had been draped over all the furniture. The room looked like a lived-in construction zone.

"Oh, Cliff, I can't get down now. Can they come back?" She had paint smudged on her face and hands, a big work shirt covering her clothes.

"No, I don't think so…"

"Ma'am, I'm Officer Duncan. I've got some news…" A heavyset man in a khaki uniform stepped into the room.

Cait's face turned white. She took a step down the ladder, faltered, and missed the next rung. Cliff clambered up the steps and grabbed her, guiding her down.

She clung to him for a moment. "I'm not too good at getting news from law enforcement officers…" She swayed like she might faint.

Jenny Madsen walked into the room as her husband released their houseguest from his grip. Her mouth tightened, but when she saw the cop, it relaxed. "What's happening?"

The officer looked at Cait.

"You can say whatever it is in front of Cliff and Jennie," Cait said. "They're family. Who died?"

"No one died, man. We have positive ID on your dog, Grand Champion Contessa Opal's Elegant Masquerade. She was alive when spotted."

"Opal? You found Opal?" Cliff had to grab her again. She raised a shaky hand, "I keep doing this…"

"Members of the U.S. Forest Service encountered Opal. She's been positively ID'd, ma'am."

"Where is she? Do you have her?"

"No, ma'am. She wouldn't go with the rangers and ran off into the forest."

"Oh, no!"

"Ma'am, she's up for a Canine Hero Medal with the Forest Service. They want you to come up to accept the award.

"Opal?"

"Yes, ma'am. She found the rangers and led them to the man she'd been guarding for weeks. He left a recording about the dog on his cell phone. I have a copy for you."

"Oh, where is he? Can I meet him?"

"No, ma'am. He perished before the team could reach him, but Opal went out, found them, and brought them back to his camp. They never would have found him, but for the dog. He was dying of cancer and went out in the woods so he could die the way he wanted to. The dog kept him company and cared for him, as best she could." The officer cracked a smile. "Mostly, she brought rabbits and squirrels she'd caught, but also his water bottles and such. I've got pictures of that in his tent."

"Opal?"

"Yes, she led them to him, but when they got close to her, she got skittish and ran away."

"That sounds like Opal. But how did they ID her?"

"From her ear, ma'am. He had to amputate it: Coyotes mauled her. That was in his notes. They tore her ear up. It was infected and rotting when she came to him. He put it in a baggie in his ice chest. We had the vet school at UC Davis do a DNA test on it. American Kennel Club's DNA records confirmed the dog was Grand Champion Contessa Opal's Elegant Masquerade. We got your name from the registration and traced you here."

"Oh." Cait had to sit down. "I keep fainting. I never used to faint. How did you find me?"

The officer smiled. "Everyone knows PuppyCait. You've been broadcasting about Opal all over the 'net for weeks. Everybody knows you."

Cait had been producing new videos for her YouTube station every day. The remodel of Cliff's brother's vacation place was coming swimmingly. Donations poured in—both the old broken-down furniture type, and the money type, and the volunteer labor type. The place looked like a very hip, cool river hide-away. She had it about half done, thanks to Cliff, his kids, and handy neighbors.

Since she didn't have dogs or puppies anymore, the puppy part of her persona flagged until one of the folks living down the slough brought her a problem dog. "He chews up everything and pees all over."

That took one session for Cait to handle. "He's a puppy, he needs to chew. Give him big bones that won't splinter and make sure he's got them 24/7." Bingo. "The peeing? He doesn't know where *his* space is. Keep him in a crate inside the house and take him straight outside every hour. Go to the same spot every time. Reward him when he pees where you want him to—a piece of hot dog or treat. And you pee there, too," she told the owner. "Thad always did that. Great outdoor bonding with your dog." The neighbor burst out laughing.

"I'm serious. We're all just animals. You're his pack leader. And get him a doggy door. Do you know how to train him for that? Tape the plastic flaps up to the wall so he can go in and out freely. Have your wife on the outside with treats. You point him out from the inside. Should take about three tries like that. Then let the flap down, little by little, so he gets used to the plastic hitting his back..."

Another solution. The whole neighborhood came to watch and bring their problem animals.

"I'm not really a dog trainer," Cait said to her millions of fans. "I just fell into this. Thad and I thought raising dogs would be a nice break from our city jobs. And then we got the dogs. He researched health and bloodlines like mad, but dogs on paper are way different from real dogs with hair and teeth. I just sort of knew what to do..."

She came back to the moment at hand. Opal was a hero... "Oh, Officer, thank you so much."

"That's all I can tell you. She was alive last December. We don't know what's happened since. It took months to figure all that out."

"Oh. I'll PuppyCait your station! I promised!"

"We'd all like that, ma'am, but we weren't the ones who found her. That was the Forest Service. And none of us have brought her in."

"I don't care. I'll do the Forest Service office, too. You brought me hope. You made me happy." Tears streamed down her face. "I never thought I'd be happy again. I mean..." She looked beseechingly at Jennie and Cliff, "You have been the best friends and neighbors *in the universe*. I don't know what I would have done without you these last few months.

"But Opal. If she could live through that fire, I'll live. There's a future for me, too." She broke down sobbing. Tears ran down Jennie and Cliff's faces. And Officer Duncan's, too.

The Madsen kids considered it their masterpiece. They'd filmed the whole high-intensity, high-emotion interlude with several cameras. They edited it and posted it without Cait's permission. Or their parents'. Or the officer's.

"That was personal stuff, kids. It's not right to film it and post it without my permission. Don't do that again." Cait was as stern as she could be, which was very stern, as her bleeding guts hit the internet.

It went viral worldwide. Caitlin Cummins' channel, PuppyCait, trended on every social media outlet. YouTube, Twitter, Instagram, and many no one had heard of before.

'She's a phenomenon! She's gorgeous and so sweet. Poor thing!" People watched this stirring episode, and then watched all the rest. Four years' worth, that's how long she'd been doing her PuppyCait videos. Her stats shot off the charts.

Super-lawyer Jeffrey Hoagland called, "Cait, you have to come to San Francisco. I have you booked on three talk shows. The network wants you for a series. When can you come?"

"Tomorrow? If I can get my car to work." She'd 'adopted' a junker from one of the local lots. Sometimes it worked.

"I can send a car for you. Or, how about Jason Bridger? He says you two get along great. Your work with the insurance company is coming along. He can drive out and pick you up. The Delta isn't that far from the city."

"Okay. But where will I stay? I can't afford anything."

"Never worry, my dear. You're in Jeffrey Hoagland's hands. We have a great guest house at our place in Atherton. You haven't seen the new place, have you?"

"No. I don't have any clothes either, just the donations people gave me. They're fine for YouTube, but not for TV stations."

"Do not worry, my damsel-in-distress. You're in *my* hands now."

Something about the way he said *in my hands* gave her the creeps. What was she getting into?

15

OPAL'S TIME

O PAL RAN OUT of the house and into the woods after biting the evil man. More men stood around the front with guns, but they didn't bother her. She ran as far as she could. It wasn't far; she was in poor physical condition from being locked up.

How long had she been in that terrible house? The storms were long gone, and the snow was almost melted. Rain fell every day, but it wasn't harsh. Plants grew luxuriously, and the trees put out new leaves. She found some spots of new green grass, which she ate hungrily. She'd had nothing but elk to eat for months—her teeth seemed loose as she chewed the grass, and her gums ached.

' All the time, Cait's face swam before her eyes. Cait and Thad's faces and voices and the noises of the kennel. The barking of the other dogs when someone came. Howling at the coyotes circling every night. She could smell the smoke coming out of the chimney and smells of Cait and Thad's food. Human food, which wasn't so much different from hers. That was *home,* but she had never allowed herself to be home there. She was always a stranger.

Cait held the other dogs and played with them in the broad green grass in front of the house. She took them into the house, too. She sang and chased them, and the puppies too.

If you come back, Cait, I'll be nice. I won't growl at you. I'll play with you. I'll play with Thad and everyone there. The other humans like Cliff and Jennie. They were friends. They came and ate and drank with Cait and Thad, and their children did, too.

Opal had realized that, no matter how angry she was and how bad she thought Charisma Kennels was, things could be much, much worse. She set her course to home, to Charisma Kennels. Maybe it wasn't burned. Maybe it came back, if it had been burned. Thad and Cliff knew how to make things. They could make it just the way it was.

A lovely white home with fancy trim surrounded by flowers and lawns. Cait on the porch playing her guitar. Thad talking to someone, talking about buying a dog. Ducks lighting on the pond.

That memory made Opal's mouth water. In the old days, she didn't know what ducks really were. She let them splash and honk at the pond at the kennel. Now she knew what they were—dinner. A very tasty dinner and easy to catch. In the water or in the air, they were fast, but on the ground, they waddled slowly and awkwardly. That was when she grabbed them. She wanted a duck to eat.

She was in a forest with high pine trees, densely packed. She needed water. Opal listened but heard no sound of running water. She would find water along the way. Resolute, she turned and headed toward Magalia and Charisma Kennels. She had always known where they were. Her inner compass could guide her home from anywhere. Especially now, when she was sure it was *home*. Cait and Thad's faces glowed in her inner eye, her memories producing maps as clear as any a GPS could produce.

I'm coming. I'm coming home.

She didn't get far that day. Hunger and thirst demanded she pay attention to them. She found a creek, but it was a roaring, thundering rapids as the snow melted and was carried off to lower elevations.

Whining, Opal trotted along the bank. Here was water, but she couldn't get to it. She found a place where the bank wasn't a cliff and waded slowly down to the water. She soon found it would have been better to jump off one of the steep embankments and into the creek.

The embankment crumbled beneath her feet, sliding her into the torrent. She tumbled and fought to keep her head above water as the current took her downstream, bouncing like a cork. She careened off rocks and roots, ending up half-dazed in a shallow outlet. She lay there, winded and bruised. That would have been a painful accident even if she were in excellent condition. But she was not.

Opal lay in a stupor, finally lifting her head and shoulders. The creek widened into a shallow pond where she had washed up, while the rest of the water roared off with the stream.

When she finally gathered her wits, Opal realized she had water! She drank her fill, then picked herself up and carefully made her way over the lip of the low embankment. By now, she knew that *anything* could be around the corner. Best be careful before showing herself.

As it turned out, a wide meadow was over the rise. Flowers humming with bees dotted the space, and the later afternoon sun flooded every inch. It seemed safe. Putting her head down, Opal explored. Rabbits lived in places like that, and so did squirrels.

A quick scamper and a snap, Opal had dinner. She feasted on the rabbit's nutrient-rich intestines and organs, then carried the carcass into the woods to be consumed later.

The trees were tall and close. Not good if a fire erupted: they'd burn hot and fast. The number and size of the trees indicated that humans were nowhere around. They would cut down these big trees. Opal felt herself relax. This was a good place. She could mend here before she traveled. Home was a long way away, but a journey she could accomplish.

First, she had to undo the damage done to her. The smell of what the evil man had made clung to her, permeating her coat. It made her sick, too, and weak. She developed a routine… swim in pond several times a day. Catch a rabbit or two, or squirrels. Rest under the trees with pine needles for her bed.

Opal didn't know how long she stayed in the meadow, just that she felt better and wanted to move on. Her muscles were strong, and the stench of her captivity had dissipated. Hunting was good; her bones didn't poke her as she lay in her bed under the pines. Cait and Thad's faces swam before her constantly. She wanted them. She wanted to be home. She knew how much home meant now. She wouldn't waste it because of anger. She didn't remember where her rage came from.

She didn't notice it at first, she was so absorbed in the spring softness, the lush time of growing and blossoming. She felt slowed down and tranquil. Happy. Her muscles relaxed, though she felt strong once again. Her mind relaxed, too. Opal breathed easily, taking in the soft air as insects rose and fell above the meadow grass. Squirrels played, chasing each other up and down trees, rolling and clutching. Mating. Everything blossomed.

Not until her belly felt warm and the part of her body below her tail started to throb and swell did she realize what was happening. Her *time* was coming. All her life she'd dreaded it. She loved the puppies that appeared after her *time,* but she hated all the rest. Opal had been bred to many dogs. She had even been bred to invisible dogs!

Sometimes, the vet would come and examine her carefully, keeping his hands and face away from her teeth. She'd go to sleep. She'd wake up in her kennel, and many weeks later, she'd have pups. She didn't even have a chance to hate the dog they bred her to! Other times, they'd bring a dog to her. He would dance around, being stupid and proud of himself. He'd play with her and eventually mount her, usually several times.

She didn't like the dogs they picked for her.

"Great bloodline match," a human would comment.

"Yes, and he has a terrific temperament. Maybe it will do something to that witch."

Laughter. She knew they were laughing at her.

They never got it—she didn't like the stupid dogs they picked for her. Blue-blood, fussy pants, hair all in curlers or tied up. Smelling of perfume, not dog odor. She wanted a mate who could run with her, and tussle and roll. She wanted a mate that was a *mate*.

They never gave her that. When she went home to Cait and Thad, they would want her to breed with that disgusting, slobbering yellow dog they had. He was the worst yet—stupid and lacking in spirit. But she would do it. To have a home and master and mistress, she would do that disgusting thing, instead of terrorizing him so he wouldn't go near her, as she usually did.

That was how serious she was about going home.

It was getting dark. She would catch a rabbit and start out in the morning. Opal hid in the trees and watched the rabbits dance slowly in the moonlight. So beautiful. They danced and hopped with each other, spinning sweetly and silently. It had to do with their *time,* she thought. They were beautiful, but that didn't stop her from making one of them dinner.

He was silent, standing in the deeper shadows of the pines, watching her while she ate. Silent and dark with glowing amber eyes. His coat was almost black, and he stood with the assurance of a pack leader. He was bigger than she, quite a bit bigger, and strong. She could see his muscles under his heavy fur. He had a few scars on his face, but that didn't affect his beauty or magnificence.

Opal jumped up, a snarl rising in her throat. Could she fight this one? She'd never seen a dog like this. He took a step closer to her, stiff legged, as though he wanted to fight. She growled again, standing over her rabbit. He looked at her quizzically, as amazed and bewildered by her as she was him. He got closer and T-d off with her, moving his body so his breast was at ninety degrees to her side. If he tried to mount her from there, it was a sign of aggression.

Opal did something she couldn't imagine doing. Fast as only she was, Opal dropped her front end down, extending her front legs in a puppy-play movement. She jumped up and ran around the meadow, legs scissoring in and out, making sharp turns with her hind end way under the rest of her.

"Go, Letty! Be crazy!" Thad and Cait used to say to the other dogs when they let them out. They'd career around the lawn, like wild, nutty puppies, but all grown up. "Go, Letty! Go, Princess! Go, Sally!" they said to all their dogs as they gamboled freely. The humans would laugh while the dogs played.

Opal just watched and never participated. Until now. Now, she was a crazy wild thing, heart beating so fast. She zoomed by him, and he watched, bewildered. She wanted to make this stranger notice her. She wanted to engage him.

Finally, she stopped in front of him and barked, once. He jumped. As though he'd never heard a bark! He bounced up and down as she had, and then followed her on a romp. She was faster than he. She had to slow down, so that when he finally caught her, he was panting. He moved next to her and grasped the back of her neck carefully, using the leverage to pull himself on top of her.

They mated and mated again. Opal was wild with love and lust. This stranger was the mate she'd wanted all her life. He smelled of the forest's wildness, of kills fresh and old, of himself, a real dog, not sanitized by humans. They danced and romped, chasing each other as the days passed. They hunted together. Slept next to each other, or wrapped around each other, in her pine needle bed. And they mated, breeding often enough to create a thousand puppies.

One day, he brought down a deer. They feasted. She looked at him with glowing eyes. He could provide for her and their pups. She wouldn't be in danger if she was with him—he was so big and strong he could fight anything. They could live in the woods together, raising their pups. The pups could stay with them; no one would take them away. He felt the same about her, staying next to her night and day.

So deeply in love was Opal that she didn't notice her body changing. Her anatomy gradually shrank to its normal size. The wonderful-smelling discharge that had drawn him dried up. She was Opal of old, everyday Opal, still as in love. Nothing could dampen that love. He was her mate! At last, after so many dogs had disappointed her, she had found her soul's desire.

Opal didn't notice that her thoughts of Cait and Thad had diminished and then disappeared. She had thoughts for one creature: him. Her god and beloved, her life's mate. Home was wherever he was.

Then one night, a plaintiff howl came from deeper in the forest. A long, drawn-out howl, not a dog's howl. Another followed it, from a different location. Then another, still farther away. A dog just like her mate appeared from the forest. She was a lighter color, gray. She stalked toward them, showing no deference or fear at all. She approached Opal's mate and rubbed his neck with her face. Then she looked at Opal, unblinking, and sauntered back into the darkness. Her howl broke the silence. Opal stared. He had another mate. She thought he wanted *her* alone.

He looked at her, then prodded her with his nose, *Go into the forest. Come with us.* She didn't move. She didn't want to go into the forest. She wanted to live there, in their meadow, forever. She wanted a home, either a beautiful glen or a home, like the one Thad and Cait had. She wanted him, just him, and their pups.

The dog-like creatures in the forest howled, a chorus playing around them, calling them, or at least him, to join them.

He threw his head back and responded, his deep-throated cry destroying Opal's dreams. He poked her with his nose one more time, *Let's go.* When she didn't move, he walked away, looking back once before disappearing in the blackness of the night timberland.

Opal could barely breathe. He left her, just like everyone. She didn't want to live in the wild; she wanted a home. She thought he was like her, but he wasn't.

And he wasn't a dog.

Opal's Meadow

16

CAIT'S RISING STAR

"YOU'LL BE GREAT," Jason said, ushering her into the studio. "Are you sure? Do I look okay?" Cait was panicked. Jason had picked her up at Jennie and Cliff's place in the Delta with a casual, "Oh, by the way, you're on *Babbling Brooke* at four p.m."

"What?" she'd said. "I've never been on a TV show. I don't have any clothes. My hair… Who's *Babbling Brooke?*"

"The real name of the show is *Afternoons with Brooke*, but she babbles, so people call her that. You'll be lucky to get a word in. Brooke Burdette is a low-level TV hostess—one step above YouTube."

She had glowered. "I'd like to see you get the numbers I do on YouTube."

"No offense meant. She's a good starting point. We'll work up to the big guys later. And I have clothes, and everything handled. Not that your current Haute Goodwill isn't lovely."

He made her laugh. That's why she'd chosen Jason Bridger to be her attorney over Celeste Ramon. Celeste seemed nice enough on the phone, but she was straining so hard not to say anything that would trigger Cait about Thad dying, or the fire, or losing everything she had, or the insurance company's treachery, that Cait wondered if they'd be able to share a normal conversation.

Jason, on the other hand, was as affable as a high school BFF. And openly gay, which Cait considered a plus. He wouldn't hit on her, and he sounded like he knew his stuff legally and in terms of how to set up a case. What they were doing was getting her a platform and setting her up as everyone's wished-for best friend.

"Regardless of what happens with the lawsuit, I want you to be set up to make a living. Your online presence and skills should monetize nicely. That's what we're going for."

They stopped briefly at a boutique/salon in San Francisco, and Jason introduced her to his husband. "Willy can do wonders with *anything. Dust mops. Cleaning rags. Anything.*"

She left, coifed and dressed to appeal to down-to-earth, upscale housewives. A contradiction, but not really. Every woman wanted to swing a chainsaw like Cait, whether she knew it or not and regardless of her social position.

And then she was walking onto the set. The lights shone in her eyes. The cozy nook where she and Brooke Burdette would chat was like upholstered Styrofoam. She was *on.*

Was she *on.* Cait recognized a hint of euphoria in her mood. Uh-oh! She got herself in trouble when she felt that way.

Babbling Brooke was true to Jason's description. Cait thought she looked as though she'd spent her life wrapped in facial products, or Saran Wrap. And she *talked.*

"Oh my, what you've been through! I can't believe it. Let me say how sorry I am about your husband, and all those dogs… And your *home…*" Tears burst from Brooke's eyes. "The *fire…*"

The reference out of the blue made Cait mad. She understood why Opal wanted to bite so much. But suddenly, her eyes teared, and she and Brooke were in BFF-style talk-a-thon like they'd known each other forever. "I don't understand why I'm still alive," she said. "It's been my friends—Jennie and Cliff. All the people on Bethel Island. And construction therapy…"

Brooke bubbled like the wellspring of effervescence. "Yes! I've been watching your YouTube shows, the ones about the puppies, of course, but your home and furniture fix-up programs. They're *amazing*!!!! I *love* them. How did you get into things like chainsaws and power sanders?"

"I have to say, sometimes a chainsaw is a girl's best friend. Starting on Cliff's brother's house after everything happened *saved* me. But I got into construction and renovation because of our house up in Magalia—which is a little town right next to Paradise. That *was* next to Paradise.

"Thad and I were just an ordinary San Francisco couple—fantastic taste in wine and no money." The audience laughed. Brooke looked like she might fall off the couch. "We were never going to have any money, and we never would own anything, including a fruit stand…" More laughter… "anywhere near San Francisco.

"We got this crazy idea to breed Goldendoodles after figuring that we could make $200 grand a year on the puppies. That was my husband, the math major/information technology king, who figured that out!" She winked, and people laughed again. "It actually took us three years and every dime we had to figure it out that it wasn't possible, but we've never been *quitters!*" The way she said everything made it a joke. "Not while we're alive anyway." That one caught her. Thad died. It wasn't funny. Tears welled in her lovely blue eyes.

"Oh. I'm getting ahead of myself. Once we started looking at real estate, we couldn't believe what we could get for our money in the Sierra foothills. We couldn't buy *anything* in San Francisco, but in Magalia, we found the most beautiful fantasy house surrounded by massive trees. It was big; it had been the estate house before the original farm was sold off. The property came with nine acres. We could have hundreds of dogs there with the zoning. The house was a *real* Victorian over one hundred years old, complete with gingerbread trim and a wide porch.

"Of course, it was falling down. The windows were painted shut.

That's the windows that weren't broken. Plus, it had been vandalized dozens of times. And it had dry rot and termites. Needed a new roof, plumbing and electrical. But it came with pets: mice. Rats. *Bats.* We didn't notice these shortcomings until we closed *escrow.*"

The audience was in a strange state of grief, pity, and rollicking hysteria. They greeted Cait the way they would a famous comic who was an ace in home repair who just lost everything.

"The first night in our dream house was like living in a rodent speedway. Thad awoke when a rat ran across his forehead." She held up her hands and shook them, mouthing a scream. "Before, Thad had taken my comments about the condition of the house and poo-pooed them. Like I was a sissy. After that night, he'd hardly go into the house. 'I feel like I'm living in filth,' he said.

"We were. And no one could fix it but us. I learned right away that Thad had absolutely *no* construction skills. Well, I knew that from San Francisco. I forbade him from doing anything around the house after seeing what he did hanging pictures.

"My life as PuppyCait hadn't begun when I started out as Chainsaw Caitlin! I had to. Trees were falling. The house was disintegrating. I learned to love industrial strength glue and rat traps.

"At first, I didn't want to trap them. But we had to. I got a special humane trap. The rat, or mouse. Or squirrel, or even racoon, possum, moose—whatever—entered the trap because of the bait. Grain mostly, though they did like locks of Thad's hair... Rodents *loved* him." The audience roared. Cait's mirth was continuous. "Anyway, the *creature* would enter the trap and not be able to get out.

"You would then take the trap and release the animal somewhere else. The first time I did it, I released the rat into my next-door neighbor's backyard. That's a great way to meet the neighbors..." She mimicked someone erupting in anger. "He wasn't happy. So, the next trap, I drove out of the county and released the rat in a park. Rangers didn't like that, either...

"My trapping stopped when I found a rattlesnake coiled around the trap, rattling like crazy. I had created a rattlesnake feeding station!" She looked around, brightly. "The snake just got madder because it couldn't get to the critter in the trap. That was a fun day.

"Whatever you do, *don't poison pests.* Their dead bodies are just as poisonous as whatever you gave them. Lovely creatures like hawks eat the dead vermin and die. Hawks mate for life, you know." Tears again.

"Oh, dear. Look at me. I'm quite raw. Let me just say that life in an apartment in San Francisco hadn't prepared us for the country. I won't tell you about how we got rid of the *bats...*" People cracked up again. "It involved bad-smelling perfume and fishing net. Works every time. You can't kill *them,* either. They're protected by law. And they do swarm around your head if you surprise them..."

They took a commercial break. Jason had been frantically grinning and giving her the thumbs up from backstage. The audience rippled in their seats, fascinated and entertained.

Brooke smiled at her. Cait thought she saw the Saran Wrap on her face drooping a little. "You know, you've been through so much. Let's lighten up and talk about the dogs after the break. Then we have a special surprise for you."

Lighten up talking about creatures that had been burned to death in the fire that killed her husband? Cait ground her teeth.

"I turned into PuppyCait with our first litter. We didn't have a clue as to what we were doing. You can only learn so much on *YouTube,* you know." Every sentence was punctuated with laughter from the audience. "After we rushed our first mom to the vet for an emergency delivery, we should have gotten it. We wouldn't make $200K from puppies any year soon." She heaved a sigh.

"Turns out, I have a knack for puppies. That *was* from YouTube. And going to every dog training seminar I could find, West Coast to East. That ate into the dregs of our savings, but it was necessary. I got good training. And I just know what a puppy or a dog needs. I give it to them.

"For instance, I know Opal is alive. She's trying to make her way home. She's fighting for her life. She will make it, if she gets help. If she has any luck. And if the good Lord watches out for her. I can't help but feel she's already got that."

While Cait spoke, some dog show pictures of Opal flashed on a big screen. "Oh, that's Opal in her glory. She is a Grand Champion in the show ring." Images of Opal doing an obedience course. "She was also highly trained. Schutzhund trained. But she doesn't look like this at all now. If you're trying to ID her, don't look for that dog." Cait spoke to the guys behind the screen. "If you could find a picture of a Standard Poodle in the pound, that's what she looks like. Minus an ear."

Another screen lit up and a grungy, ungroomed poodle with matted hair and caked eyes appeared. "That's Opal now, except for the ear." Cait looked down, unable to speak. "If you find Opal, and your information results in her being returned alive, I'll 'PuppyCait' your whole house. And just ask Jennie and Cliff Madsen what I can do. Their family house in the Delta is awesome." Cait looked down and went silent, overcome. Her attorney's phone number and email contact played in a band across the screen.

Brooke took up the slack. "Opal is becoming a dog hero on her own. She received an award for leading a team of forest rangers to the body of a doctor who had saved her," Brooke spoke. "Cait, I have some more news about Opal. We thought we'd let Sgt. Broadhurst of the Plumas County Sheriff's Office give it to you."

"What? Do they have her? Is she okay?" Cait jumped out of her seat.

A screen lit up and showed a serious, middle-aged man in a uniform speaking from what looked to be a law enforcement office. "How do you do, Mrs. Cummins. I wish I could be there in person, but we're mid-case. I can't give you details about what happened, as it is an on-going investigation, but we in the department wanted you to know that Opal will be given her second award for bravery. She saved my life by restraining a perpetrator in a gun battle. I think the world of that dog, and we're committed to finding her. She clearly chose to save me, over a perpetrator who had been holding her captive."

Cait jumped up, put her hands to her face, and burst into tears. Then she fainted.

17

OPAL LEARNS ABOUT LIFE—WILD AND NOT SO WILD

OPAL STOOD TO her knees in the cold stream, practicing a new skill. Her sharp eyes marked the subtle movement of fish in a deep spot. She was fast enough to catch them, sometimes. She struck hard and missed. Opal gave it another try then walked to the bank. And looked around. The forest was a beautiful place.

The stream widened into a grotto tossed with rocks and gravel. Pine trees and cedars marched up the hills on each side. The summer had burst into the Sierras in full glory. Insects hovered above the water, rising and falling on their own rhythms. The birds trilled and the forest was quiet though it, too, burst with life. Everything that slumbered during the winter was awake and active, trying to fill its belly as best it could.

Opal had seen many new types of animals since she'd been alone. She kept a sharp eye; not all were friends. Many thought of her as dinner, just as she viewed her prey. Standing very still, she saw something that filled her heart. A large animal with rough brown fur waded in the flowing water upstream, swatting the water with huge paws. The paws had long claws on them. Opal had never seen such claws.

She watched carefully. The animal had two puppies playing on the bank behind her. Seeing them made Opal happy, and sad. Her mate would never see their puppies, if she had any. The large animal tried to feed her babes, but they were thin. Ribs showed through their harsh coats. The mother was even thinner. Watching carefully, Opal saw patches of bare skin on the mother's hide. Scars. Opal moved, and the animal swung her head toward her, acting like her eyes were closed. One eye was missing, and the other was mostly white. Could she see? This animal had survived the fire. She'd been burned.

Opal felt such sadness at that. She'd seen many dead animals and others scarred and maimed by the flames. Most didn't live as long as this mother bear. Opal turned and saw the outline of a large fish in the shallows. She snapped at it and got it.

Opal retreated up the bank to eat her dinner and saw the bear splashing around in the water, trying to catch a meal for her pups. Opal stopped eating. The pups waded into the water, seeing if they could fish, too. They were far too slow and noisy.

Slipping across the stream with the fish in her mouth, Opal approached the other animal. It snuffled but didn't come closer. The dog pushed the dead fish toward the large brown creature so that it floated toward her and bumped her leg. The half-blind mother grabbed the fish and turned to the shore with her little ones.

Opal didn't think about what she had done. She didn't think about generosity or kindness; she thought as a mother would. She couldn't let the little ones die. Too many had died. That was all.

She was on her way home, heading through the wilderness of Plumas County on the way to Magalia. Since she'd given her dinner away, finding another prey was her focus. The pine forest surrounded her. The bunnies would be coming out into the glades soon, as they did every evening. Opal hurried to find an opening in the woods.

She never saw it coming. A colossal force struck her and pinned her to the ground. It smelled rank, like one of Cait's barn cats, but rancid wild. She fought, struggling as hard as she could, but she was outweighed and overpowered. Her adversary had a rough beige coat and huge claws. The claws held her, piercing her flesh. It tried to grasp the back of her head and neck with its stinking teeth. She would die. This creature would kill her. She fought.

As suddenly as it had attacked her, the creature was yanked off her back and thrown through the air. It snarled and ran away. The bear rose far over them and roared. Opal felt the roar rather than heard it. Light faded from her eyes. Her life faded as rapidly. All was still and dark.

The bear's cave was rank, filled with smells of hairy animals living in tight quarters. Opal opened her eyes as the mother bear licked her wounds, softly cleansing the blood and keeping pus from forming with her antiseptic saliva and tongue.

Opal drifted in and out of consciousness. It seemed that humans were in the dark cave. Ancient, shadowy humans with rattles and drums sang to her. Their voices rose and fell. They beseeched some power to guard her, to make her well. The sound soothed her, and she slept.

The feel of the mother bear's tongue, the soft sound of singing, the feel of smooth brown bodies, human bodies, around her. Opal drifted in and out, perhaps alive, perhaps dead. Or both.

When she awoke, the cave was empty, the bear and cubs gone, and any spectral healers departed. She didn't know if they had existed. The bear was real. Opal could feel her tongue caressing her wounds, which were healed now.

The dog rolled up on her breastbone and looked around. She was alone. And she was ravenous. Opal made her way to the cave opening and peered out. The birds twittered in the trees; the forest and stream-bed were cheerily empty. Predators had flown. That, she could see.

But she had had no inkling of the mountain lion's presence. It materialized out of nowhere. Not true: it was stalking her from above, looking for oblivious prey.

Opal had learned something important: When traversing cougar country, the most important direction to look is up. She was one of the few creatures who had the opportunity to learn the lesson twice.

The Mother Bear Saves Opal

18

WELCOME TO ATHERTON, CAIT!

"HEY, GIRLFRIEND, YOU were great. Fainting at the end was the *piece de resistance*." Jason's face greeted her when she came to. She'd been moved off the set to a small office with a cot. "The doctor's coming back in a minute. Jennie and Cliff called to say you've been fainting a lot."

"A couple of times," she bridled, "I'm not someone who *faints*. And I'm not weak."

"I didn't say that. They were concerned. They thought we should check it out medically, and I agree. You have a doctor appointment tomorrow."

"What! I don't even know if I have medical insurance... I can't let Jeffrey do everything for me!"

"Let's talk about this on the way to Atherton. I want you to get settled in before it gets dark."

Jason was quiet, driving out of the city. They cut over to Interstate 280 before he started speaking again.

"You were saying you can't depend on Jeffrey for everything. Well you can. He's one of the richest men in the Bay Area."

"An attorney?"

"The principal partner in the biggest law firm in California. Not to mention what his IPO did to his net worth."

"IPO?"

"Initial Public Offering. It's the first time a privately owned stock is offered to the public. Original owners in a private firm can get access to a bigger pool of capital, diversity, prestige, etc. by selling stock to the public. If you price the offering right and have good underwriters, you can get filthy rich overnight. That's what Jeffrey did. Have you heard of Verbs?"

"No."

"Well, you will. Google's parent is Alphabet. Verbs is going to be the parent to almost as many companies as Alphabet; they're just not well-known yet. Jeffrey and his buddies have been headhunting and idea grabbing, patents included. It's in the works.

"All this has happened since we left the city three years ago?"

"Yep. In the last two years, mostly. Jeffrey has upgraded everything in his life since then."

Cait had the feeling Jason didn't like his boss very much. "I'll be okay living there, won't I?"

"Sure. Not that Jeff doesn't have ulterior motives." He grinned at her. "Not *that* kind about you. I think he wants you for his cable network. Something like *The Property Brothers,* with a pretty hostess with a chainsaw fixing America's housing stock. You're perfect. All the crafty ladies will love you, and so will their husbands."

"Really?"

"I guarantee that all the media power brokers in the city and L.A. have seen tapes of your show and are talking concepts for *your new* show. Talk to *me* before signing anything. I'm your attorney."

She was silent, considering this turn of events.

"On the other hand," Jason continued, "the guest house you'll be living in is fit for royalty. Jeff is never home. His wife spends most of her time flying around on a broomstick. Her daughter hides under the bed."

Dede? That didn't sound like Dede. She and Jeffrey didn't have a daughter.

"Oh, my God, Jason! You didn't say it was Buckingham Palace." They pulled into a driveway on a street threaded between ancient oaks. The drive opened into the vista of a home that Cait couldn't imagine. The place was so big, so heavily colonnaded, crenelated, ornamented, and plain impressive, she could barely breathe. The landscaping tripled the effect, flowing in burgeoning cascades of color, mounds of greenery, all framed by the oaks and flawless lawns.

"It isn't Buckingham Palace. Buckingham Palace is dated and drafty. Hoagland Palace is perfect in every way, and up to date. I'm going to drive you to the guest house." Which was behind the main house, across a lawn measured in football fields. It was a charming, English-style cottage of about four thousand square feet with a steep slate roof and more magnificent landscaping.

"With a house that big, who needs a guesthouse? Or a guesthouse like *this?*" Cait was mind-boggled by the turn her life had taken. "How did I end up here, Jason?"

"Well, hopefully, it won't be the witch's cottage in the woods. Things at *Chez Hoagland* can get a little intense."

"What do you mean?

"You'll see."

A brand-new BMW convertible was parked in front of the house. "That's for you to use while you're here."

Cait didn't know how to drive such a car. They had an old Volvo station wagon, the van, and a truck for hauling. Nothing so fancy and complicated as this.

"Get in. Go for a test drive." He climbed in with her and sat, waiting for her to turn the car on.

"What do you do? Where's the key?"

The Hoagland Residence in Atherton, California

"Oh, it's keyless. I've got the control in my pocket. Step on the brake and push that button. It will turn over."

It did, and she jerked around the driveway.

"I'd better get someone to drive you to your doctor appointment tomorrow."

"Or get me a 1980s car!"

"I'll work on it. Listen, I must get back to the city. Mrs. Hoagland is out tonight. The butler is going to bring dinner to your room. Uh, fantastic castle. I'll see you soon."

The butler brought her a five-star meal for one on a silver tray. Cait was so lonely, she wished for the barely constrained bedlam of Jennie and Cliff's place by the Delta. She hadn't seen a hint of Jeffrey's family. The next day, a maid drove her to her appointment. It was in a fancy office on Welch Road, the only possible address for a successful MD in Silicon Valley.

Having seen the Hoagland residence, Cait wasn't surprised by the posh doctor's office. The doctor surprised her. She was a mid-forties, hearty, Native American woman with more than the requisite number of awards and degrees on her wall.

Seeing her surprise, the doctor said, "I'm Evelyn Morningstar. I inherited this place from Elizabeth Bright Eagle." Cait's brow furrowed. "Ancient history. But let's look at *your* history while your lab work is being processed." Cait realized that a perk of enormous wealth was the ability to get things done *fast*. Her test results would be available *during* her appointment.

"Your history seems quite normal. Except for the anemia, all your tests are where they should be, given your age and condition. You need to take iron. And you're underweight for a woman who is over six months pregnant. That's what's causing the fainting, I think."

"*What!?*"

"I'm sorry, I thought you knew. Can't you feel the baby move? It doesn't show much yet, but you should be able to feel it."

"Uh. Maybe. I get this kind of movement like a fish inside me, but I thought it was indigestion. It was a baby?"

"When was the last time you had your period? You must have noticed you haven't had it."

"My period is always irregular. That's why Thad and I put off having kids. We didn't want to have to face my infertility."

"You're not infertile. You're going to be a mom in three months, if you chose to continue the pregnancy…"

"No! I'm having this baby. Oh wow! I can hardly believe it." She felt like Thad was reaching out to her from beyond the grave. This was wonderful news.

"Great. Would you like to see me for the rest of your pregnancy, or would you like…"

"You." This woman was the most normal she'd seen since hitting the Bay Area.

They set up a treatment plan. Cait got prescription vitamins and iron. She left euphoric.

A part of Thad survived! She had gotten pregnant on that wonderful last night! She'd have a baby in three months! She had no money, no job, not a pot to pee in. She was living in a place she didn't like with people she wouldn't like either.

Everything was wonderful.

When she got back to the guest house, she noticed her cell—which was courtesy of Jeffrey Hoagland like everything else—had a message from Dr. Morningstar. "Cait, I've just been watching your YouTube channel. I'm laughing aloud! You're hysterical. But I'd knock off anything with power tools. Chainsaws and so on. You could get away with that earlier in your pregnancy, but you're too far along for more heavy lifting. The baby doesn't show much, but it's there."

Shit! How could she do her show without demolishing things?

19

FIRE COMES IN MANY FORMS

E UPHORIC, CAIT FLEW into her guest-mansion and tossed the purse that Jeffrey's personal shopper had purchased for her onto the kitchen table. She wanted to dance and sing, until she took a good look at the table. A plate with a glass dome over it sat on it. It held a fancy sandwich on a croissant and a salad. The long toothpick skewering her sandwich had a gold foil seal with stylized H stuck on the end. Hoagland. A hand-addressed envelope lay next to the plate.

"Jeez, either she's got the best handwriting in the world, or she has a personal calligrapher." Cait opened it.

Mrs. Elizabeth Hoagland requests the pleasure of your company
In the Hoagland residence for supper at eight p.m.

It had the date and everything, like a wedding invitation. A formal invitation to dinner with Jeffrey's wife and child. Maybe him. Just on the other side of the lawn, for Pete's sake. That sounded like it could be from a foreign country.

Fortunately, Caitlin Cummins was San Francisco born and bred. How to respond to a formal invitation was branded into her consciousness before birth. She attended Cotillion and all that pre-debutante crap, though her parents weren't rich enough for her to come out.

Also, it would kill them to acknowledge "nineteenth-century, upper class, mating rituals," as her father referred to the city's annual Debutante Ball. Still, Cait knew the drill.

Mrs. Thaddeus Cummins accepts with pleasure the kind invitation of Mrs. Jeffrey Hoagland, for the evening of...

Perfect. Really perfect and showing the difference between a wannabe and a true well-bred San Franciscan: a woman is always referred to by her husband's name. *Mrs. Elizabeth Hoagland* was *incorrect*. Mrs. Elizabeth Hoagland was correct only if she were a widow or a hip divorcée. So, nanny, nanny, Elizabeth dipshit.

The butler picked up her response on a silver tray when he and the waiter took her sandwich plate on another tray. "Mr. Hoagland's assistant purchased a number of things for you to wear. They are in your closet. Dinner will be formal."

Cait wanted to mouth off to him, "So, that's white tie, instead of black?" She knew the rules of dress. This was so stupid. She couldn't resist a little poke.

"Did Jeff get knighted or something? Or maybe his wife? I don't think I know her."

"Mrs. Hoagland is from a fine East Coast family and is accustomed to living formally."

"Right." I'm just a San Francisco drudge. But I bet she doesn't have honors in literature, or an MA from Stanford.

"Do you have any power tools? Like a chainsaw?" Some people brought out the worst in Cait.

The butler stiffened. "I'll see if you may have access to Mr. Hoagland's workshop."

Off he and the waiter went. Two people and two trays to retrieve a plate and a piece of paper. Well, the Hoaglands were good for employment in the service sector.

"I almost didn't call you," she said to Jennie. "It's so crazy here." She told her friend up in the Delta all about her life in Atherton. At first, she wasn't going to tell her friend about the baby but figured she should. The baby would be "earthside" in just a few months.

A long pause, that Cait would come to expect. Everyone thought the same: how was *she* going to raise a child? "Oh, Cait! That's fantastic!" Another pause. "I mean, you are happy, aren't you?"

"If I was any happier, I'd be flying on a flagpole! Spinning around, screaming and bawling."

"Good. Good." That silence again. "Do you…"

"Have any idea how I'll cope? Absolutely none. There's some dribbles about a show for me, but my doctor says I can't lift heavy tools for the duration. I don't know how I'll put a show together without my chainsaw."

"Of course you do. Puppies. Do puppies. Everyone loves them, and you're great with them."

"I don't think puppies are allowed in Atherton. They might poop or pee."

"It's that awful?"

"Yep. I gotta get ready for dinner. I'm supposed to be in *Downton Abbey* at eight. But how are you?"

"Well, Cliff has a crew here working on the remodel of his brother's place that you started. You have a following out here! He has to shoo off housewives taking cell phone photos of your ideas."

"Say hi to him for me."

"I will when I see him. He's up in Magalia now, rebuilding our house."

"Really?"

"Yep. Home sweet home. He takes the kids with him, so they don't forget their old stomping grounds. Stays for a week at a time. I wish we could stay here. Magalia and Paradise will never be anything but the terror of that night for me. Our insurance paid us. We could buy a house here. But Cliff wants to rebuild up there. Make our place what it was, with all the trees and ferns."

Cait could barely stand to hear that. She felt sick thinking about Magalia. "I'm still waiting to see if we're covered and by how much. I will take the money and run. I'll never go back there." She put her hand on her belly and for the first time, really felt the baby kick.

"Oh, my God!" she squeaked. "The baby moved! Are you saying you don't want to go back, peanut? Or you do?"

* * *

Dinner took every ounce of what her formal San Francisco upbringing, her Stanford MA, and all the honors classes taught, and every bit of backbone she'd earned swinging her chainsaw. Jeffrey had a new wife who bore no resemblance to Diedre at all. Model thin, she wore a get up that must have come straight from French designer's runway. Cait wondered how she'd go to the bathroom in it.

Her cheekbones were so sharp, Cait thought they should be registered as lethal weapons. Her skin was smooth and white as Bond-o, the auto repair guck that dried hard as steel. Lips etched in red, brows etched in brown, to match her hair.

Elizabeth Hoagland sat at the foot of a magnificent, ripped-off-from-some-Hollywood-set table. Cait sat at her right, and the most miserable-looking child she had ever seen sat at her left. The girl hunched over her plate, holding her very ample arms to her chest. The child was obese and knew it. She barely looked at Cait. Her plate was empty.

Oh, boy, Cait thought. *They make the Addams family look cheery.*

A place was set way down at the head of the table, for Jeffrey, she presumed. The table was so long, his place setting was about a block away.

Elizabeth caught Cait's eye movement. "Jeffrey is so busy that we only get to see him for dinner occasionally. He did say he would try to make it. He has news for you."

Her insurance came through? Cait inhaled hard and grinned. "I hope it's what I've been waiting for."

"Experience has shown me that one seldom gets that, but sometimes what one gets is worth the wait." She indicated the vast room. "If different from planned. I lived on a horse farm in Virginia, for instance. No room for horses here, but infinitely finer cuisine."

Her voice was dry and grating. Cait didn't have the faintest idea what to say to her. She turned to the child.

"How do you like it here?"

The girl started. "Um. It's nice. I don't get to have a horse though. Or a dog…" She went back to staring at her empty plate. The butler served Cait an elegant plate with two of those thick small lamb chops that Cait could eat ten of, potatoes au gratin, and some fancy greens. *Elizabeth* had a similar plate, with one lamb chop and no potatoes. Cait ate slowly and glanced at the child, still staring at an empty plate. Did they feed her?

Elizabeth raised her eyebrows, indicating her daughter's plate. "Alexandra ate potato chips *and* ice cream at a friend's house this afternoon. Her dinner is being restricted. I *have* spoken to the girl's mother about Alexandra's dietary rules." To the butler, "Curtis, you may bring Alexandra's supper."

Half of a lamb chop, a mound of greens, and water.

Cait could hardly stand to sit there. The meal wore on, course after tedious course. Entrée, salad, cheeses, dessert. It took eons. No, double eons. Make that triple. Cait's stomach was in a knot when Jeffrey finally breezed in in shirtsleeves. He tossed a big manila envelope on the table and loosened his tie.

"See, I told you I'd make it for dinner, Liz. Curtis, move my place down here. I get to sit with the grown-ups!" He was ebullient, totally happy about something, or half-snookered. Jeffrey consumed about five of the lamb chops and a mound of potatoes. "Tell Patti she cooks better every day, Justin. She deserves an award!"

Elizabeth looked at him, mildly aghast at his gusto and, Cait assumed, because he spoke to a servant at dinner.

"Have I got a surprise for you, Cait!"

"What is it?"

"Took me the whole fuc— oops, sorry, Elizabeth, day to do the deal, but it's done. All I need is your signature. After dinner…"

Cait thought that she'd like to know what it was before signing. And pass it by Jason for a legal opinion.

Jeff had two helpings of *tiramisu*, then beckoned to Cait. "A little work before an early bedtime. You're on Brooke Burdette's show again tomorrow. The big guys…" He picked up the envelope and waved it. "…want another sample of the goods before signing. No problem, right? I'll have someone drive you."

They went into his baronial library/office. Looked like a place the Brits might use for Parliament. He tossed the envelope on a gigantic antique desk and pointed at a chair in a small seating grouping beside it. "Sit. Drink." He poured himself a three-fingered slug of scotch and about half as much for her.

"Well, ma'am, you're about to be relieved of your money worries. The producers and money people from a major cable network want you. You'll have a cable show first. When that proves out, you'll go onto the networks. They want to see one more example of your work before they set up your show. That's Brook Burdette's show tomorrow. Kill it like you did the last time, and you're set for life."

He took a healthy swig, smiling with satisfaction at the wonder of himself. "I was on the phone all day. I'll tell you, Ms. Cait. Busting my ass, I must say, for *you.*" She didn't like the way he looked at her.

"They looked at you on Brook's show, and then a dozen of you on YouTube, waving that chainsaw like an Amazon. They were practically drooling all over themselves.

"Drink, Cait. This is a seven-figure deal we're looking at. Ten million bucks over three years, maybe more. And maybe movie deals. It doesn't matter what your insurance company does, Cait. You're saved. I saved you." He leaned over and patted her hand.

"You are one sexy babe, little Cait. Lower your necklines a bit, shorten the skirt, you'll have men everywhere panting after you." She felt dirty. "Drink! Drink!" He poured some more for himself, and a splash into her glass. "Aren't you happy?"

"I'm amazed. A TV show and a few videos, and I get ten million dollars? I can't believe it."

"Believe it, girl. You got that because of your own talent and the fact you're represented by me, the best fucking lawyer in San Francisco. Drink! This is no time to be shy."

Cait felt like the Atherton version of the casting couch was about to appear. "I can't drink, Jeffrey. I'm pregnant."

"What!? *PREGNANT!* You can't be pregnant. Nobody wants to see a pregnant cutie waving a saw around. You *can't* have a baby. What will you do, *breastfeed* on the set?" He laughed riotously.

"Maybe. Maybe I'll do that. I want the baby. It's my baby and Thad's. It's all I've got left of him."

"Oh, God. Couldn't you just print out some more pictures of him? You can't *possibly* have a baby, Cait. This is a ten-million-dollar deal that could make you a star and give me the exposure I want in the movie business. I *worked* for this. *Get rid of it!*"

"No." She stood. "I'm keeping my baby. If that wrecks the deal, so be it. I'll get by."

"Get by—like you did playing house out in the sticks with that half-wit? You gotta admit it, Thad was no genius. Running your kennel wasn't getting by. It was slow suicide. You're wasting yourself—and you're not getting any younger, pretty girl. You have only so many years, and a new crop of funny bimbos will take over."

"That's it. I'm leaving. I'll find my own place tomorrow."

"After Brooke's show." He stood, weaving slightly. "And you owe me something." He moved so fast she couldn't get away.

Cait found herself plastered to Jeffrey Hoagland from her thigh to her mouth. He licked her, a scotch-soaked slobber. He was shoving his open mouth into hers, trying to insert his tongue. His hands flew all over her, grabbing choice hunks. He felt her belly.

"It's in there all right," he laughed. "You can't really see it, but it's there. For now."

"Get away from me!"

"Oh, no, little Cait. You're an investment." He was like an octopus, grabbing with eight arms.

"Let go!"

"What's going on in here?" Elizabeth Hoagland stood in the doorway, a clear view of her husband grabbing Cait's butt through her silk dress.

"What are you doing, you little tart? We take you in with nothing, and you try to seduce my husband. I knew you would. I know your kind. Cheap. Vulgar. GET OUT! GET OUT RIGHT NOW!"

"No. I don't have anywhere to go. I'll leave tomorrow. After I do my show."

"I hope you break your neck, you floozy."

"Thank you, Mrs. Jeffrey Hoagland. You've given me a wonderful example of upper-class morals. I think you need to take care of something, though."

"What?"

"Your daughter. That kid is dying, and you can't see it. Take care of your kid. And your husband. He's an asshole."

When Cait left the room, Elizabeth rushed to Jeffrey. "Oh, sweetie, what was she trying to do to you?"

"Cheat me. Cheat us. I worked my tail off for that contract. Now she'll make a fool of me with the studio heads."

"Well, darling. The little tart needs a lesson. She needs to know what daddy gives, daddy can take away." She smiled at him and moved closer, taking a bit of his lower lip between her teeth. "Show her your claws, baby. She insulted me in my own house. I'll be upstairs…" She sauntered out and turned back at the door to give him a provocative look. "You're never wasted on me, Jeffrey."

When his wife closed the library door, Jeff picked up the phone. "Brooke, Jeffrey Hoagland. There's been a change in plans. I want her to tank tomorrow. Show Caitlin Cummins as a lying fraud. Get her to say every rotten thing she's got in her head. Talk to Allison Chao—she's keeping a file on her. Now's the time to use it."

"Really. I thought you liked Cait." Brooke sounded bewildered.

"So did I. Big mistake. She won't work for the new show. But you might. If you can destroy her career before it goes any farther, you might find yourself with a nice cable contract."

"Me?"

"Sure, sweetie. Just show me you got what it takes."

20

BABBLING BROOKE, ROUND 2

JASON'S FACE WAS pale and drawn. Cait slipped into his Lexus next to him.

"Wow. I didn't expect the A team to drive me to the city."

"I don't know that I'm the A team anymore. I just quit Jeffrey Hoagland's cabal from hell."

"Really? Why?"

"Over what I'm about to tell you. Got your seatbelt on?" She checked. "Okay. Brooke Burdette has orders to take you down. Humiliate you. Air any dirt they could dig up. There's a little sleaze at the studio, Allison Chao, who hates you. Probably because she sees genuine talent in you. She's been digging up dirt."

Cait's jaw dropped. "Why? What have I done to her?"

"Jealousy. She hates real talent. Probably thinks you had it easy— all you had to do to get noticed by the press is lose your husband and everything you own. And there's the pretty blond factor."

"What?"

"Look at what the studio likes. Blonde, buxom Brooke. You, adorable and blond with blue eyes."

"I can't believe it."

"Believe it. Okay. This drive is a working trip. We need to discover your dirt and prepare you. Have you ever been unfaithful to Thad?"

"NO!"

"Told any lies about the dogs?" She shook her head. "Told any lies about anything?" Another shake. "I can't understand Jeff's switch. Yesterday, Hoagland would have taken a bullet for you."

"I'll tell you why. I'm pregnant." His eyes bulged.

"You don't look pregnant.'

"I'm thin, and it's my first baby. That's why I was fainting all the time. I'm anemic. Jeffrey told me to '*Get rid of it.*' I couldn't be a TV star with a baby. It would ruin the image he was setting up for me. Oh, he offered me a ten-million-dollar contract. Then he made a pass at me, but his wife walked in."

"And she called you a bunch of names…"

"How did you know?"

"Ol' Uncle Jason knows all." She stared at him as he drove. "He's done it before."

"To another woman?"

"Not quite…" He raised his brows suggestively.

"Really?"

"That's all I'll say. Jeffrey has a way of getting what he wants, no matter how. And his new wife is his true soul mate. But what can they use to hang you with?"

She remembered something.

"That would do it," Jason said.

"Yeah. But there's a way around it." She'd brought her laptop. "If I sent you some pictures and files, can you get the guys backstage to put them up on screens when I ask for them?"

"I think so. They're all in love with you."

"Okay. I'll do this…" She sent him an email with a couple of names and more instructions. "I'll tell the techs when to pull them up."

"Will do!"

Cait walked onto Brooke's stage like she was packing two chainsaws and a nail gun. Superwoman would have looked like a Girl Scout next to her. She took her place on the Styrofoam couch.

"Hi, Brooke! I understand today is 'This is your life, Caitlin Cummins.'"

"Why, yes it is." Brooke grinned idiotically. Cait thought she had her plastic mask on extra tight. "There's talk that you may have your own show. We wanted to send it off on the right foot."

"I'm sure you do, Brooke. Fire away."

"For those of you who missed our earlier show and don't know this young lady, let's welcome Caitlyn Cummins, survivor of the Camp Fire!" Brooke gawked at Cait.

"And oh, my! Aren't we wearing a fashion-forward look!" She stared at Cait. She wore ragged jeans, a torn shirt, and flip-flops

"Yeah, this is a special day for me. I'm wearing what I had on the day I lost Thad and the fire burnt up everyone's homes. This is the same kind of day."

"Oh." Brooke's expression said she didn't know what was going on. She expected Cait to be clueless about the show's content and the charming, feminine sprite she'd been before.

"Yes. Today's the day I start walking the walk."

"Are you an alcoholic? Don't they 'Walk the walk, not talk the talk?'"

"When they're in recovery, they do. My walk isn't that. I've been known among many people as 'really spiritual.' Like 'woo-woo,' because I can work with the puppies and dogs so well. Well, I am spiritual. I believe that something vastly powerful and loving runs the universe and cares for all of us. I believe it's right here, now, listening to what's going on and watching all of us. I believe it cares for those who love it and helps them."

"So, are you going to do a séance?"

"No. I don't believe in that. Since I lost Thad, I've depended on many people. Jennie and Cliff, our neighbors in Magalia, all their neighbors. Other people.

"This morning, I walked away from a seven-figure contract and a mansion in Atherton with the clothes on my back. I have nothing. On the way up here, my attorney told me that my insurance company had declared bankruptcy. I won't get anything from our farm or the loss of our valuable dogs. Or my husband's life.

"Now is my moment of truth. I truly have nothing, but that force lies beneath it all." She held her hands out palms up. "Okay, Universe, do your thing."

Brooke sat, flabbergasted. "Uh. Well, should we pass the hat?"

"No, I'm ready for anything. What do you have on me, Brooke?"

"Oh. Well, we sort of did 'This is your life,' as a deeper introduction to you. I understood you were going to have a show of your own."

"No, that's not going to happen."

"Oh." Brooke was derailed. "Okay. Well, does Officer William Mullany and October 7, 2013 mean anything to you? He's a voice from your past."

"No. I don't remember him."

"He remembers you." She nodded, and a screen came down. An attractive Asian woman spoke from the screen.

"I'm Allison Chao with a special report. Officer William Mullany, can you tell us what happened on October 7, 2013?" The camera panned to include a law enforcement officer.

"Yeah. I got hit by lightning." He was red faced and very paunchy. His uniform shirt strained at the buttons. Sweat dotted his forehead from the lights. "A little lightning bomb attacked me. Her…" He pointed at a mug shot of Cait projected on a screen. Her hair was a mess, with dyed blue streaks down the sides. She had a black eye. The officer continued, "I was trying to break up a fight in the homeless ghetto, and she turned on me. Packed a wallop. I got a bruise on my arm. I arrested her."

"Cait Cummins was arrested for assaulting an officer?"

"Yes."

Allison shrugged. "There you have it. The real Cait Cummins is a criminal."

"Well. I didn't know you'd run afoul of the law, Cait." Brooke batted her eyelashes.

Cait jumped up and pointed at the screen where Allison's face lingered. "I *know* her! She accosted me when I found out Thad had gone back to the kennel to save the dogs. She followed me all over the parking lot where poor lost people were grieving, trying to get me to talk, or *cry*, on her stinking camera. She's a vulture, feeding on death."

The audience, that had been mumbling disapproval during Officer Mullany's presentation, sat up and listened.

"You guys want to know what really happened?" Cait said. A murmur of assent, even excitement, came from the crowd. Cait went on, "Listen, I'm totally for law and order. But when that guy stole my Michael Kors handbag, I just went nuts."

Cries of "What?" "Who did?"

"Officer Mullany stole your purse?" Brooke sputtered.

"No, the *homeless* guy." The audience tittered. "I was walking by a homeless encampment, and this guy jumped up and stole my Michael Kors bag. It was the only designer piece I had, even if I got it at a thrift shop." The audience laughed flat out.

"I ran after him and jumped on his back. He fell, and I grabbed my purse, but he started beating me up. He kicked me a bunch of times. *But I didn't let go of my Michael Kors!* A bunch of other homeless people tried to pull him off me. It turned into a melee. Someone called the cops, but I didn't know that. I was fighting for my life!

"Somebody pulled my arm, and I let him have it. That was Officer Mullany. I didn't know he was a cop. I thought he was a homeless person."

"You'd hit a homeless person?"

"No. The homeless people were trying to save me. That bad guy cracked three of my ribs, gave me a black eye, cracked my tooth." She held her mouth to the camera and pointed at a tooth. "That one. It's an implant. I've got the most expensive teeth in the world.

"But he didn't get my Michael Kors!" The audience guffawed. This was the Cait they'd come to hear.

Brooke sucked in a deep breath. This wasn't playing right. The audience was amused, not outraged. "Well, I understand you have great relationships with your neighbors."

"Yeah. Mostly."

A screen revealed a large image of her in Cliff Madsen's arms. She was plastered against him, swooning into him. He kissed the top of her head. They looked like lovers.

"Wow. I wish I had neighbors like that," Brooke dished.

Tears welled in Cait's eyes. "That's my neighbor, Cliff Madsen. He took me to his family; he's got a wife and five kids… I stayed with them in his brother's house in the Delta over the winter. Well, can we have my video?" She addressed a tech off stage, and a big screen lit up.

It was a video of Cliff, Jennie, and all their kids up by the Delta house. "Hey, sweetie," called Jennie. "Way to go, Cait. We're all with you!" shouted Cliff. "Give 'em hell, Cait."

"That's Cliff. The photograph you showed of us was taken when I found out Thad had died. I fainted. He grabbed me and held me up." Tears ran down her face. "Such a good friend. So many of us, rootless, their lives ruined. Cliff caught me when I was falling.

"I learned why I kept fainting all the time a few days ago. I'll tell you in a minute. What else do you have, Brooke? Sock it to me! Do your worst."

She opened and closed her mouth, looking like a beached fish to Cait. "Well, we'll go to Allison Chao, who has an audio report from Magalia.

"Hello, listeners, this is Allison Chao with Herbert Watson, whose ranch is on the other side of the canyon from the Cummins' Charisma

Kennels. I was trying to get a complete picture of the Cummins as neighbors. What were they like, Mr. Watson?"

"Worst neighbors ever to live on the planet. Fightin' and swearin' all the time. Cursin'. Fight! They fought like demons. Filthy dog kennels. The two o' them runnin' around nekkid, day and night, doing it in broad daylight. Yowling like pole cats... Those dogs barkin' like they was bein' tortured."

Allison tsk, tsk'd. "Do you have any images of Charisma Kennels to share with us?

"Well, yes, ma'am. An' I consider it ma duty as a American to share them with you."

Cait didn't say a word, just let the video unfold. It showed aerial views and close ups of their farm at its worst. The kennels dotted with mounds of poop. The dogs barking at an out of sight delivery truck, which Cait knew was there, but none of the other viewers did. The video showed her and Thad having a pitched battle in the middle of the lawn. Followed, oddly, by them running around the lawn naked, laughing and making love. Parts of their bodies were fuzzed out for that one.

"Well, that about says it all. Anything else you think our viewers would like to know about the Cummins and their dogs?"

"Well, that Caitlin supposed to be such a dog trainer. She's not. She's never even touched that big gray one they had. The famous one. She's afraid of her. Should be. The thing has teeth like razors and a temper like a wild boar. Their dogs ain't much. *Doodles*. Who'd buy a dog called a doodle?" He laughed, wheezing from tobacco-infused lungs.

Brooke sat still, looking at Cait with amusement.

"That was great, Brooke," Cait said. "What did he promise you if you ruined me?"

Brooke blinked. "I don't know what you're talking about."

"Don't worry about it, Brooke. I'm a big girl. I can take what you can dish out." She turned to the audience. "The man who commissioned that tape and set up this show to destroy my reputation offered me a ten-million-dollar contract yesterday. That's right. Ten million bucks, over three years, to be his puppet." She pulled at her neckline. "Just a little lower here, a little higher in the leg.

"And, to get the money, I had to do something I won't do, which I'll tell you about when I'm done with Brooke and Allison. I'll save it for dessert."

"Let's go over Herb Watson's video. Thad and I had a bad year in 2018. We finally figured we weren't going to be able to support ourselves with the dogs. Turns out the expenses—vet fees, lab fees, food, the cost of the kennel, more vet fees—outweighed the costs of producing the puppies. And we spared *nothing* on taking care of the dogs. Well, maybe grooming. Thad took over grooming the poodles. He was terrible. He did the worst grooming jobs you could imagine."

"Could you show those pictures of our dogs?" A bunch of large poodles that looked like someone had gone at them with runaway clippers flashed by. "He didn't hurt them, but they wouldn't win any contests after visiting Thad the Groomer.

"That's what Herb Watson was talking about. And the images of us screaming at each other were all taken during that horrible year. We'd spent all our money on the dogs. We were in danger of losing the farm. We were stressed out, and we took it out on each other sometimes. Everyone here who's been married any length of time knows about *bad years…* "

She looked up and around the audience, ending by gazing straight into the camera.

"Okay. Can we play that video again, guys? I'll point out a few things."

The first part showed the kennels dotted with mounds of poop. "This is a cautionary tale, right here. If you move to the country, make sure you know *all* about it. We put the fancy concrete kennel in to make it easier for Thad—or me, I helped—to clean up after the dogs.

The idea is—see that big hose right there hanging on the kennel wall? The idea is you pressure wash the waste down the drain. Very easy.

"Except we were on a septic system. Whatever went down the drain went into our septic tank, where it clogged the whole friggin' thing. Twelve big dogs make a lot of poop. It jammed the house plumbing so we had septic water bubbling up our drains. All over the floors. Totally gross. Never move to the country if you don't know about septic tanks. Or wells. Or snakes. Varmints like coyotes, skunks, bats! BATS!" She held up her hands and mouthed, Ahhhh!

"So, we had to take an industrial-sized pooper scooper, fill the wheelbarrow, and bury the 'crappola' on the property. Guys, could you show that slide of the scooper I gave you?"

A screen filled with a giant galvanized steel tray attached to a thick steel handle. "Now *that* is a pooper scooper. One cleaning of the kennel filed it several times. And Thad just couldn't face it sometimes. But he did—he shouldered in and took it out. All of it, out. If you took a shot of our place just at the right time, it would look like that video, but most of the time, it was clean."

She pointed at the screen. "Look at these images. Forget about what they're showing, what's the same in all of them? Shout it out!"

"They're all taken from the sky," someone said, echoed by others.

"Yeah, they're taken with a drone. Drones are popular these days. I'm sure Herb had to fly his drone over the farm dozens of times to gather those images of it looking so rotten." People's brows went up, and mouths opened.

"Let's go through the rest of Herb's video masterpiece. A drone— spyware—took all of them. I don't know the law, but it must be illegal to fly a drone over someone else's property and use the image for blackmail—which is what this amounts to.

"Brooke, you did say you were vetting me for a show of my own, which I revealed as coming with a ten-million-dollar contract. Right?" Brooke nodded, looking pasty.

"My attorney is backstage." Cait shouted, "Jason, is what's

happening here illegal? Do I have cause to sue? Unauthorized use of illegally obtained drone images for the intent of harming a career?

"He's giving me the thumbs up. Two thumbs up! Great.

"Since you're showing all this on a public broadcast, the station is liable, as well as Allison Chao, *you*, Brooke, and whoever else was involved in the video production." The crew went silent, looking at each other. "There's more. Brooke and Allison said Herb lived near us. Across a ravine, so he could easily see and hear what we did. Guys, could you put that plot map up for me?"

A map of Thad and Cait's farm and the surrounding area appeared. "Okay. Here's our place. And here's Cliff's! It's a half mile from ours, over ravines and cliffs. To see or hear us screaming at each other, or making love, he'd have to have a good drone. An expensive one.

"Why would he need such a powerful drone? Well, the economies of certain rural areas run on weed. Marijuana. And meth, more recently. It's a rural tradition to have a grow going or cook some meth to afford the necessities of life. And, though I am not a DEA—Drug Enforcement Agency—officer, I do know that the DEA has visited Herb's ranch on more than one occasion. How do I know? By using drones? Spying? Gossip? No. It was in the local paper.

"Brooke, did you or Allison get any pictures of Herb? Why are there photos of our place and Thad and I, but none of him?"

Brooke's face was blank.

"I'll show you. This was taken at the county fair. I had it on my cell. Herb had a booth at the fair. Honey and hemp soap."

People gasped when they saw his face.

"A little rough, wouldn't you say?" Herb's ragged hair hung in greasy lumps down his shoulders. "See his teeth? Zoom in, guys." They were rotten stumps that showed bloody nerves in the center. "They call that a 'meth mouth.' Meth dries your mouth out, which causes the teeth to rot and eventually look like that. That's why his voice sounded funny, and he didn't want to be photographed. He hardly has any teeth.

"You know why he dissed my ability with dogs? He tried to steal Opal, our most famous dog. Poodles are incredible watch dogs. He got her out of her pen, and she went after him. She awoke the dead barking. When we got out to the kennel, she had him treed." Cait burst into laughter. "We had to help him down, a drug-dealing trespasser trying to steal our dog. And now this.

"He mostly had his drones so he could spy on the neighbors and harass them, as well as find any meth labs or pot grows to turn in the proprietors.

"We hear a lot about fake news these days. You're seeing how it's done. A little more real reporting would have revealed Herb as what he is. And not exposed the station to legal action.

"Okay, Brookie. You got anything else?" Cait looked at her watch. "We got time, even with my surprise at the end."

Brooke's mouth opened and closed like a tropical fish. "Uh, well, I believe we have a call on hold for you. Mr. Kenyan, you're on the air. This is a live interview."

A distinguished white-haired man appeared on the main screen. He sat in a wood paneled library surrounded by dog show ribbons and trophies. "I am Lyle Kenyan. Mr. and Mrs. Cummins acquired Opal through me on behalf of my employer." His face was more sour than a Dill pickle.

Cait took over. She jumped up and stood in the center of the stage, alternately facing Kenyan and the screen, and turning to the audience. "Hi, Lyle! I'm Caitlin Cummins. I never did get to meet you, but here we are. Did you call in to express your condolences on my husband being burned to death? Charred beyond recognition? Or are you sad about Opal getting lost? You have ideas as to how to find her? Huh?"

Kenyon's cheeks puffed out and puffed again. "No. Well... I am sorry, of course, about your loss and Opal, but..." He looked as officious and self-important as only a higher-rung servant of a rich person could.

"You can't get over the fact that Thad and I used *your* dogs to produce *doodles*. It just riles you, doesn't it?"

"How did you know that?"

"I'm not stupid, Kenyon. Everybody's on Facebook. You're the leader of the purebred dog believers, aren't you? You've got a page on it in Facebook. You rant and rave about the evil of mixing dog blood. Crossbreeding *anything*. Purity of blood. Superiority. Starts to sound like racist stuff, Lyle. You really should get someone to read your essays, so you don't shoot yourself in the foot. That might be actionable."

She turned to the wings of the stage. "Jason, you wanna check that out. His page is PURE BLOOD = TRUE BLOOD. Read that crap. Look it up, folks. You can get it on your cell phones. It's like what white supremacists say, before they kill people. Except people like Lyle Kenyon apply it to dogs.

"Lyle, I don't get it. They're beautiful, they're expensive, they're wonderful companions. They're *dogs*. By themselves, they'd breed all over the place. What's wrong with crossing a wonderful, totally vet-checked, personality/temperament checked Golden Retriever with an equally healthy, certified poodle? Where's the sin?"

"Well, you obviously don't know the years of work that go into producing a magnificent purebred dog. You don't appreciate tradition and breeding, the lifestyle it demands. You get an animal you can rely on at all times."

"Like Opal?"

"Yes. She is a magnificent example of what a purebred dog can be. Lovely beyond belief, proud, magnificent. And passing those qualities on to her offspring, a direct succession."

"Opal is a vicious fruitcake. You told my husband she'd bitten two people before you *gave* her to us. Those were the people who pressed charges and got paid off by your boss to drop them. You didn't know what a good researcher I am. Once I got started, I learned lots about her. I don't know how many people she's bitten, if you count kennel helpers and little people who can't fight back. I've never touched her, because I know she doesn't want to be touched. She's a mess.

"You also told Thad that she'd had three litters for you. In less than two years." Kenyan puffed and tried to break in, but she wouldn't let him. "Three litters in less than two years because all she was good for was the babies you could get out of her. She was unsaleable and vicious. Also, she might not be able to carry another litter, her organs were so messed up.

"Thanks, Lyle! That was a great gift. Our vet confirmed her reproductive problems. You pawned her off on a sweet, wonderful, trusting newbie who would have actually paid you thousands for a useless animal. You were going to put her down, weren't you, *Lyle,* if Thad hadn't taken her?"

His eyes widened, and the screen went blank.

"I'll take that for a yes." Cait faced the audience. "Thad and I loved Opal. She was our favorite, like a handicapped child can be a favorite. I've never touched her. She growled if I came close. She didn't want contact. I didn't want to be yet another person she'd bitten. But I love her." Cait looked up over the audience, addressing her dog.

"Opal, baby. Come home. I know you're trying. I can feel you, right here, sugar." Cait touched her chest. "I know when you come home, you're going to be different, just like I'm different. I'll give you a good life, baby. We'll be the pals you wanted to be. I could read your heart, sweetie. I know you love me."

Cait turned and staggered toward her place on the sofa. She took her seat and addressed the audience and camera. As moderator of the show, Brooke might as well not exist.

Tears streamed down Cait's face. "I'd walk off the stage right now, but I promised you a tidbit, dessert. I won't go until I've given it to you.

"I told you earlier that I'd just turned down a ten-million-dollar contract. I made a very wealthy, powerful man mad. All he wanted was a few changes in me. A little more skin in game, you might say. I wouldn't give in to any changes in how I present myself, nor would I give him or anyone else 'a little skin.' He wanted that, too.

"But the deal breaker was to get the ten-million-dollar package, I had to have an abortion." The audience gasped. "I'm six and a half months pregnant. I just found out. I'd been fainting. It turns out I'm anemic." She looked down, and a tiny smile touched her lips. "It was the last night with Thad. Heaven. I'll never forget it.

"Thad and I might have had our problems, but that night the night the baby was conceived, was…" She opened her palms to the audience as though releasing fairy dust. "If I had just that night for my lifetime, that would be enough."

"The baby is Thad's. And here we have people who would have you believe the baby belongs to someone else. To Cliff Madsen. To anyone.

"I don't understand how people can be so evil. That's why I asked Brooke, what did he offer you to take me down? A network show? The ten-million-dollar deal? What was it?"

Brooke was silent.

"I don't have anything now. Not even a freebie show like this one to appear on as a guest. I don't have a house, or my dogs, or my husband.

"But I've got the baby in my belly." Cait stood and hugged the little mound in front of her. "I will survive anything to have this baby and to make a good life for us." She raised both hands in fists over her head in a power salute. The audience rose, fists raised and screamed.

After that, Cait could have been a hit if all she did was paint her toenails in front of the camera.

21

HITTING THE BIG TIME

"WHAT SHOULD WE do now?" Cait asked. The day was young, and she was flying high.

"We should get to my office and file suits against Brooke, Allison, the station, and Jeffrey Hoagland. Ten million dollars each, plus emotional stress."

"Really?"

"Cait, they tried to screw you big time, and it's all on the video of the show. It's a slam-dunk. Jeffrey might be harder, but..."

"Would it help if I had a recording of what he said to me in his office last night? And his wife's contribution?"

"You've got that?"

"Yeah. I had a feeling something bad would happen, and it did. I had my faithful cell phone record it all."

"It's not illegal to secretly record yourself, so, we've got him. Let's go."

"I don't know, Jason."

"I do. They were throwing you under the bus. Jeffrey wouldn't pause for one instant if the tables were turned. Let's go to my new office."

They got in the Lexus, and Jason drove off, as ebullient as she was.

"What's this new job?"

"It's something I would have given my cojones for a year ago, and now I've got it—out of the ugliest stuff I've seen pulled in business. It's my dream job. I work for a rich capitalist, but not one like Jeffrey Hoagland."

They were driving through a section of the SOMA, South of Market, formerly the grungiest slum in San Francisco, give or take a few. It had been getting gentrified for years. The process was almost complete, except of a block covered by a decrepit galvanized steel-clad building covered with graffiti.

Jason pulled around a corner, ran a card through a reader cemented on a post by the building, and drove into the dumpy warehouse. Inside, an ultra-modern parking garage revealed itself.

"This is it." The space was pristine concrete, with stainless steel panels and murals on the walls: the most stylish, upscale parking garage in the world. One car was parked in it, a sleek…

"Holy shit, Jason, that's a Bugatti *La Voiture Noire*. It's worth a fortune."

"Yep. It's the car Jon drives when he's in the city. It's his town get-about."

"Who's Jon?"

"Jon Walker."

"The talk show host and king of late-night America? Also the world? Do you work for him?"

"Not for. With. Our boss is someone else. Jon wants to meet you. He's a fan. Let's go into the office." They walked across the parking lot to a doorway marked by geometric sculpture and oversized chains. The office had the same décor: somewhat disturbing nightclub drama.

Jon Walker had been a fixture of late-night TV as long as Cait could remember. She was twenty-eight years old. She remembered watching his daytime show when she was three. That's when he did family therapy on his morning TV show, like an ultra-gorgeous, gay, Mr. Rogers who could have been a comedian. Cait remembered that he had a PhD in clinical psychology. Now, he did ultra-grownup late-night programming that kids recorded and played when their parents weren't home.

"How do you do, Mr. Walker?" Cait was awed at first sight. He was very tall, thin, and amazingly gorgeous. Still. He had to be in his seventies, but he looked fortyish. His hair was dusted with gray, *just* dusted, not even streaked, and he had almost no wrinkles.

"You're a San Francisco native, aren't you? You know the proper way of addressing a new acquaintance." She blushed. "You'll fit right in. My mother-in-law is old school San Francisco. Knows every eating utensil ever made and where to put it." Jon was bright and affable.

"Boy, you really took those bitches apart on that show. I'd like to see you use a real chainsaw."

"I can't use my saw or lift anything heavy until after the baby."

"Pity, but I can wait. Would you like to be on my show?"

"When?"

"Anytime. But I'd wait a few days. We need to let the internet ferment a bit."

"What do you mean?"

"Have you looked at your numbers? You're trending on every social platform there is. The show has been dissected and replayed everywhere. You're a star, my dear. I'm going to let my publicity people work you a little. I'd say you'll have an audience of anger-crazed maniacs by Thursday."

"Crazed maniacs?"

"The doodles. People are taking offense at you breeding doodles." Jon shrugged. "It will be great TV, and I've already had an A+ list celebrity ask to do a cameo."

"Oh. Is that good?"

"Definitely. He's our boss." Jon turned to Jason. "Your office is over there." He pointed. "Why don't you get started subpoenaing people, or whatever you do? I'm going to take Caitlin for lunch. There's a guest suite next to Jason's office, Cait. You'll stay here until we can get you an apartment."

"Oh." Cait was getting pissed off. Didn't she get to say anything? Or decide anything?

"No, you don't." He read her mind. "Once we get you safe and settled, you can do wherever you want. You're not safe now."

"What?"

"You don't think sweet Jeffrey Hoagland and his lovely wife will let you escape easily, do you? Or allow you to sue him? This is a small town. Everyone knew that you were staying at Jeffrey's. They'll figure out who offered you a ten-million-dollar deal and dumped you because you wouldn't get an abortion. Do you think the Hoaglands will be happy?"

"People already have figured out who it was. Look at this," Jason held up his laptop. A group of panelists on an online blog was discussing Jeffrey Hoagland and his wife.

"They're some couple. Sort of a sexual tag team…"

"You better not talk about that. You could get us sued," cautioned a member of the panel.

"Slander is only slander if it's not true. One of my buddies got 'Hoaglanded' over a contract. They invited him to dinner and the guy got 'approached' by both them…"

"Change it. I don't want to see that," Cait said. She shook afterwards and had to sit down. Jon brought her some water.

"I forgot we had an expectant mom here. We'll take it easy with this stuff. Don't go on my show if you don't feel up to it. And know that my entire staff and I will protect you with everything we have. If you go on my show, your ratings will go beyond through the roof. You'll have international coverage. You'll be a star. Tell me why you'd want that—speaking purely from your soul?"

"I'd like to get Opal back. I know she's alive. She's in danger." Cait had been having visions of Opal the whole time they had been separated. Opal with the doctor who died. Being stuck with the meth head, saved by the bear. Just glimmers of insight, pictures of the dog struggling. "She's trying to get home, but she's in trouble. "I'd like to get her back alive and unhurt. And I'd like to keep her as long as she lives."

Jon patted her shoulder. "You're a real warrior, Cait. You didn't ask for a bunch of money or a show of your own. You want something for a friend."

"I'm a beat-up warrior. Could I take a nap in that suite?"

"Sure. And we'll go shopping after. Boho. That's your style. Bohemian. I know just the designer."

22

OPAL

O PAL ROLLED IN the sandy creek bank, moving her spine in an S shape, driving her shoulders and backbone into the pebbles. The warmth of the sun-infused rocks relieved the pressure in her belly and ache down her back. Her middle was swelling, and her teats grew tender. She knew what that meant. She had no way of tracking the passage of time, but she knew what was happening because of the changes in her body. She had felt all this before. The pups moved inside her when she tried to sleep. Her time with her mate had been fruitful.

She felt something else, too. Something ominous. Something wasn't right. Her insides didn't feel the way they usually did when she was this way. Opal was seldom afraid, but a pinching sensation and sharp pain said this time was different. This time she needed help.

Cait's face swam before Opal. *I need you, Cait. Help me. Save me.* She had never felt that way about a human before, but this felt natural and normal. She hadn't been friendly toward Cait before, but now she knew how desperately she would soon need her. She had to get home to Charisma Kennels. She saw it in her mind as it had been, the lawn and arching trees and all the charm Cait and her chainsaw could give it.

Cait. Cait. Cait. Cait.

She had to get home. She knew where the kennel was and could go directly to it, but it was getting more difficult. She was still in deep woods, north of Magalia. Most areas showed no sign of the conflagration. More humans were around, tromping through the brush and calling for *her*.

"Opal! Here, Opal! Come, Opal!" they called. They wanted her and knew her name. Why? How?

She would never go to these strangers. They made her chore more difficult. Having to listen and dodge took time. She knew where the kennel was, but not how many dark and light times it would take to reach it. She needed to do it fast.

Standing up, she shook the sand off her filthy, matted coat. Months had passed since she had been groomed. She'd never been in such an unkempt state but had gotten used to it. Except when her matts caught in tree branches, it wasn't a problem.

Opal looked and listened, then cautiously picked her way through the trees toward a clearing. A medium-sized, brown dog jumped out of nowhere, wagging her tail and licking at Opal's face. Opal pulled away in disdain. The dog was wildly in heat, swollen and attempting to get Opal to mount her. Opal growled, and the newcomer skittered away, only to return like she was attached to Opal with a leash.

She kept bothering her until they got into the clearing. Opal launched at her, growling ferociously. A pack of dogs appeared, bent on savaging her. She had no time to think.

The leader, a huge pit bull, charged her straight on. He intended to bite the back of her neck and shake her until it broke. Opal leapt to the side and came in under the pit's massive jaw, grabbing him by the throat right below the joining of the jaw to the spine. She bit and bit and bit, sawing away. The pit was well defined with muscle there, but it was a kill spot. All she had to do was hold on and bite. Her teeth severed his trachea and several large arteries. The pit fell, gasping his last breath.

One of the other dogs worried Opal's flank. She spun on it and attacked blindly and instinctively, harrying the animal about the front legs and chest. She tore the musculature and ligaments of the dog's forelegs, rendering it helpless. She turned again, like a machine, like the pit dog into which so many had wanted to make her. She turned on a third dog, ripping it along the flank, piercing its abdominal cavity. A loop of intestine showed and grew longer.

The other dogs of the pack pulled back, watching their leaders struggle for a single instant before running pell-mell into the forest. The little dog in heat circled in bewilderment, showing herself to Opal before Opal's snarl told her that ploy wouldn't work. She ran.

Opal staggered away from the killing field, exhausted. Her hip bore a jagged tear. She was bruised and shaken. Dogs had never packed up on her before. She didn't know they would. What world was this where creatures attacked their own kind?

Her soul cried out louder than ever, *Cait! Cait! I need you!*

Opal didn't dare stop. Other packs of wild dogs might be luring in this half-forest, half-farm area. She had to get to the kennel and Cait. Her belly ached, and her nipples felt like they might drip milk.

When the night came, she threw herself down behind rock outcroppings, lying in charred and collapsed brush from the fire. She moaned and whimpered in pain and despair, until coyotes howled. Then she bore her pain silently.

She found Charisma Kennels the next day. It was black ash. The concrete kennel's wire mesh enclosures were fallen. She stepped on the whiter ash of one, and it disintegrated. The house didn't exist. Nothing existed.

Worst of all, Cait wasn't there.

23

THE MYSTERY GUEST

"TIME FLIES WHEN you're having fun! It's hard to believe months have passed since the first time Caitlin Cummins was my guest." Jon Walker was using his combination "gay Mr. Rogers" and "Zoltan the Destroyer" persona.

He had developed this way of talking/being over his years as a talk show host. When the audience heard it, they went wild. It meant fireworks were coming, and if you grew rotten or unruly, Jon would bounce you faster than you could say, "That queer guy can really get mad."

Everyone was protective and on edge. It was the eighth of July, nine months to the day after Caitlin's baby had been conceived. This could be the day Cait gave birth. Maybe even on the set!

Jon spoke, "Caitlin has agreed to be here one more time because the online discussion of dogs and dog breeding has brought up issues she feels strongly about. We're taking calls from viewers, and we have a couple of guests later in the show.

"If this gets rough or Caitlin shows destress, I'm shutting this show down. If anybody causes trouble, you'll watch old Howdy Doody reruns for the rest of the year. Really. Manners matter!

"But that may not be necessary. All of you know that this show has a resident witch. Some of you have experienced her displeasure."

Jon's brows dropped, and he did his best warlock imitation. "I assure you she's watching today. Our witch loves Cait and *loves* dogs."

Jon's show had gathered legends and folklore over his many years on the screen. One thread of rumor said it was haunted, and *he* was haunted or a warlock or something. Sightings of ectoplasmic visitors were claimed. Some thought they'd been cursed for disagreeing with Jon. Others couldn't figure out how he looked so young. They counted his years from all the benchmarks that existed. He was close to eighty.

A tiny figure appeared on the edge of the stage. Jon rose, "Here she is, the star of the show. The rose of our hearts."

Cait had been on Jon's show three times over the weeks. She'd gained a rabid following and equally rabid set of haters. Seeing her in the flesh, even the most dedicated haters quailed. She was tiny. She was *huge*. The size of her belly was beyond the pale of possibility. She had her hair bound up in a scarf and wore her usual brightly colored ethnic caftan/robe over wide pants.

"Oh, my God, Cait, you're not going to have it here, are you?" Jon voiced what was on everyone's mind as he helped her onto the banquette where they'd talk.

"I don't think so, Jon. My doctor says a couple more days." She sighed and settled into the seat. "Boy, I'm glad you got these new sofas. The other ones were like planks." She fussed around, getting as comfortable as a woman two or three days from birth can get.

"Let's just do this. First question…" Cait was clearly uncomfortable. She grimaced and rubbed her side.

"Are you up for this?" Jon asked.

"As up as I'll ever be. Okay. The first question is…?"

"Uh. Poodles have been around for hundreds of years, bred by professionals for conformational and mental soundness. What makes you think you can improve the breed by crossing it with another breed? That question came from," he squinted, reading a prompter, "five hundred and fifty people. Poodle people. The Golden Retriever people numbered three hundred seventy-two, with the same point.

Though their comments were more direct: 'How could you breed a lovely, stable dog like the Golden Retriever with those fruitcake poodles?" And, "Why would anyone want a *doodle?*"

The audience growled, half happily, the other half getting ready to attack.

"No, no, no, people. You're on your way to Howdy Doody reruns," Jon held up his finger.

"I'm not entirely sure poodles have become perfect examples of strong conformation and mental stability. We need only look at our Opal, who is branded a vicious maniac by everyone who encounters her. She's a Grand Champion and incredible show dog. And beautiful. Is she an example of a perfect poodle?"

Someone called out from the audience, "Then why did you breed her?"

"We never bred her. She chased our two stud dogs off the farm. Beat them up. She didn't like them at all. No, no breeding for Opal. Lyle Kenyan, the man we got her from said she might have problems if bred. It could kill her. We didn't breed any animals that weren't delights to be around and very safe.

"Has anyone in the audience bought a dog from us? How did it turn out?"

A rustle was followed by a woman standing and saying, "Charlie is the best dog we've ever had. He's big, and we put a lot of training into him, as you suggested. He's sweet, never sick. A perfect dog."

"Wow. I'm glad to hear that. And you're a great owner. When we've had problems, it's been from clients who didn't invest in training. Good training. You can't just buy a big, active dog and turn it loose. It must be trained. When I'm back at work again..." she indicated her tummy, "I'm going to start a dog training business. Get these dogs behaving the way they really want to... as well-mannered companions.

"What's the next question, Jon?"

"Not about dogs. How do you mix your chalk paint? And where did you learn to use a chainsaw?"

"I've got the chalk paint recipe on my YouTube channel. March 16, 2016. You'll see it there. I'm going to do some writing, too. Put this stuff in print so you can refer to it. Chalk paint really has chalk in it, or you can grind up calcium pills, the kind you take for your bones. Or buy it in bulk…" That twinge was sharp enough for her to gasp.

"Do you want to stop?" Jon said. "I'm getting so nervous."

"This has been going on for weeks. It's end-of-pregnancy stuff. Chainsaw. Had to learn. Thad was a wonderful person. He was a computer geek. Totally unskilled with construction. A tree fell across our driveway. We couldn't get out until it was gone. Our neighbor Cliff helped us cut it out and showed me how to use his chainsaw. Later, I bought his equipment when he upgraded.

"Let's go faster."

"We have a visitor on our screen, our old friend, Lyle Kenyan, the guy who sold you…"

"*Gave* us Opal. Hi, Lyle! How do you want to insult me today?"

'Excuse me, ma'am, I have never insulted you." He sat in his library, surrounded by the trappings of upper-class dog fancy.

"I've read my comments online. It's a terrible habit, reading comments, you run into so many trolls. At least you identify yourself. You *have* insulted me, and my late husband, calling us bumbling do-gooders who think we can do better than generations of professionals.

"I'd say we have done better than many professionals. I've kept records of the dogs we've bred—follow ups. I used to be a teaching assistant at Stanford. I'm aware of research methods. Our dogs do better on all the health indices than either breed. That's called 'hybrid vigor.' They're healthy and if trained, they're great dogs. I can give you a report with all the data. How do your dogs do?"

"Well, we don't have the staff to do exhaustive repots…"

"I had one pregnant housewife, me. Took a couple of hours."

"Well, I'm sure our dogs are fine. We have *no* complaints…"

"That scares me. No complaints from an operation the size of yours says something's being suppressed."

"I beg your pardon!"

"Beg away! You should have *some* complaints."

"I've got a complaint!" someone from the audience yelled. "Our poodle, bought from Mr. Kenyan's kennel, bites. She's so nervous, we can't take her in crowds. She cost a [BLEEP] fortune. She shouldn't be like that."

"Did you report this to Mr. Kenyan?"

"No."

"Why not?"

"Look at him. Would you like to tell him that a dog he produced is a dud?"

Kenyon puffed. "Now see here, if you had made us aware…"

"You would have intimidated her like you're trying to now, and that's from a screen, not in person. I suggest you work something out. *Now.*" Cait was tough. She smiled at Kenyon's discomfort. "See, let women use chainsaws, look what you get." Cait thought for a moment. "I recognize that working out a problem on live TV is difficult. Let's do it like this:

"Ma'am, give the hall monitor your contact info, and we'll put you in touch Mr. Kenyan after the show. He'll make things right. Good deal, all?"

The crowd roared. Cait was a true-blue fighter and activist.

"Any more questions?" she held her side and grimaced.

"I think we need to get you a doctor…"

"No! I want to hear from your A+ list guest, then we'll do the doctor."

A big screen opened behind them. A beautiful mountain view covered the background, in the front, sitting on a deck overlooking the view was a tall, thin man with dead white hair. He was gorgeous, even on a screen and as old as he was.

"I'm Will Duane. Some of you may remember me. When I'm mentioned, people usually say, 'Is he still alive?' Yes, very alive. If you don't remember me, I started the computer revolution, founded and ran the world's largest corporation, Numenon, for twenty years. Then I started FISH, Inc. with my buddy Willy Fish. Now I'm doing stuff so classified, its classification is classified. I'm still the richest man in the world, despite what the magazine lists say." He smiled, the way you'd expect a wolf to smile.

"In my spare time, I save the world. Or selected portions of it that I can influence. I got interested in this conversation because of my dog. A purebred Labrador Retriever." The screen flashed the image of a beautiful black Lab with feet three times larger than you'd expect.

"Top bloodlines. Great attitude. Healthy and loving. Huge feet. A genetic flaw. I loved that dog. Duane Duane was his name. A little boy named him. He's been gone for many years.

"The dog suffered because of his feet, and yes, I understand that a genetic screw up can happen. But we traced this one to a line in his very purebred genetics. So, I'm interested in this breeding conversation.

"I'm interested in something else, too, that's underlying your debate. Freedom. Capitalism. Self-determination. The right to do what you want with your property without some [BLEEP] governmental or [BLEEP] quasi-government association or [BLEEP] [BLEEP] home-owner's association of other bunch of [BLEEP] [BLEEP] [BLEEP] sticking their [BLEEP] noses in your business."

He grinned. "They used to say I had a potty mouth. I don't think that's strong enough, and it isn't 'used to.'

"People have called me the biggest capitalist in history. That's true. I believe in market forces shaping existence and our economy. I believe that the world will do best under a capitalistic system—if its flaws are handled, which most capitalists don't bother with. You must take care of people who can't compete in the market. That's an integral part of the deal. It's called being a decent human being. But market forces should run the show.

"So, if Caitlin buys a poodle and wants to breed it to a [BLEEP] ostrich, it's no one's [BLEEP] [BLEEP] business. Get it? She owns both animals. If she can get them to breed, it's no one's [BLEEP]

[BLEEP] business—unless she hurts them doing it. Or *they* don't want to.

"I'm a big animal welfare activist these days. Some people remember me as a shark, out for whatever I could get. I've grown. I'm only a shark when someone gets in my way. You, Mr. Flashy Suit over there, if you sell something or give it away, it's NOT YOURS. Your right to say what happens to it is GONE. Deal with it.

"Crossing different types of compatible animals often produces superior results. They call it *hybrid vigor,* and it creates bigger, stronger, healthier, sturdier animals, assuming it's done with care—the way Caitlin and her husband did...

"So, all of you can shut the [BLEEP] up now and do something useful with your time..."

"Here's something useful. I just love Cait Cummins. I'm a real fan, Cait. I've watched you on Jon's program, and I've seen most of your YouTube videos. I want to help you.

"*LISTEN UP: THIS IS REAL.* I'm offering a reward for the person who brings in Opal alive and well. The kind of reward that people need: if you bring Opal home to Cait, I will send your first-born child to college. Any college he or she can get into, free of cost. All four years.

"Is that a motivator? *Now go find that dog!*"

Cait jumped up, clapping with joy. "Oh, my God! I can't believe..." She grabbed her belly and screamed. "Oh, it hurts..."

Jon leapt to his feet. "Is there a doctor in the house?"

At least forty people jumped up and ran to the stage.

"I want *my* doctor," Cait wailed. "I need to walk, Jon... The doctor said to walk. If it's false labor, it will stop."

Jon took her arm and put his other arm around her waist, such as it was. "What do we do?"

"Walk. And I'm supposed to breathe."

"Me, too."

24

BIG CAT

O
PAL'S FEET WERE covered with black soot when she left Charisma Kennels. She had no idea where to go next. She stood silently. The wind brought something: the sound of voices and children laughing. She knew those voices. It was Cliff and his pups. They were friends of Cait and Thad. They would help her.

Rather than trot up the street to the place where Cliff and Jennie and their pups lived, she circled back through the woods. Too many people had been calling for her recently. She didn't understand why they called for her by name and why they wanted her so much. She didn't want to expose herself to them. She could reach the Madsen farm just as easily going around the back through the forest. Most of the forest wasn't burned back there.

Opal loved the forest and had become as quiet as any predator in it. She padded along silently and stopped when she saw Cliff's pups. They were Kent, Emma, and James. She knew their names from all the times they'd come to Charisma Kennels. Those were Jennie and Cliff's smallest pups.

When they came to visit Thad and Cait, the human pups fed her treats when the grown-ups weren't looking. "They say she's so mean, but she's not." She wasn't, to those pups. Opal loved them, they'd run around and play tag with her. They'd be outside her kennel, and she would run inside. They could let her out; she wouldn't have been mean to them. But they didn't know that.

She watched them playing at the edge of the forest. They had a swing and a thing that went up and down. They laughed so happily. Opal wanted to join them, but they might think she was still mean and run.

Her stomach lurched and pulled from inside. It hurt. She needed to show herself to the pups, and they would get Cliff. He would help her. She needed help.

Stepping out of the forest, Opal remembered the one great rule of the woodland: look up. The cat was up there, eyes fixed on the children playing. Only its tail twitched. It launched from the tree, claws open to take James, the smallest.

Opal acted without thought, leaping forward. She hit James with her shoulder, knocking him aside, and then she flipped on her back, the only way she could kill the cat. If it bit her on the back of the head where her head met her neck, she would die. If she bit it in the throat right behind the jaws, she could kill it the way she had the pit bull.

It would kill her, of course, with the horrible claws on its front and back legs. Opal got a good bite, a killing bite, and the cat did what she knew it would. Tearing at her belly with its hind legs, the cougar tried to disembowel her. Opal pulled her legs up to guard from the cat's raking blows. Soon, blood covered her belly. Her rear legs were red ribbons.

It reached around her body with its front claws and tore at her back and shoulders. They turned red as though they'd been drenched with paint. But it was living blood, life blood.

Boom! A shotgun went off. The cat tried to flee, but Opal, in a killing rage, had it by the throat and wouldn't let go.

"Run, kids! Get back to the house." Cliff ran up the incline to the play yard with his gun. "Get out of here, you stinking cat. Get! Get!"

The cat did run. It was a predator, not a warrior. It would attack but run if it didn't get its prey. The cat ran, throat drenched with blood and a stream trailing from its gullet. It ran when Opal stopped biting it; it ran when Opal let go because she was unconscious.

"Oh, my God!" Cliff threw himself down next to savaged dog. "Oh, my God." He felt her neck for a pulse. He could feel a faint throb. How could the dog survive this?

"Dad! Dad! Opal saved us. She saved James. The mountain lion was going to eat him."

"She knocked James out of the way and attacked it."

"Kids, get some blankets. We need to do what you learned in Scouts. Major first aide. Kent, Emma, press where the blood is coming out. Don't worry about your hands. Blood washes off."

James was crying. "Honey, it's okay to cry, and it's okay to be scared. But we need to do it later, after we've saved Opal. Let's you and I get blankets to wrap her in. We're going to take care of her."

Cliff drove like a maniac, stopping only to get his shortwave going. He gave his call letters and summoned his bowling club. "Commandos, this is Cliff Hanger. We have Opal! We have Opal. She's really hurt. Saved my kids by fighting a mountain lion. We need a good vet. Help. We need cffing UC Davis."

"You okay, kids?" he called into the backseat. The children held the unconscious poodle across their laps. She was wrapped in old blankets and out cold. They applied pressure where any blood flow called for it.

"We're okay. But I think she's going to *die*, dad. Her gums are *white!*" All three were crying.

"She's not dead yet, honey. And the Commandos are helping."

The next call came fast. "Cliff. This is Sheriff Boroughs. You have the dog?"

Opal Saves the Children

"Yeah, but she's going to die if we don't get her help fast." Cliff surprised himself. His ribs pumped, and tears came out of his eyes. "She saved my kids," he sobbed. "Damn dog saved my kids from a mountain lion. Attacked it on purpose. All three saw it. It ran off behind the play yard at my place. The SOB was stalking them in their own backyard."

"Don't you worry about that, Cliff. Do you know about the reward?"

"No. What reward?"

"Some rich old guy took a fancy to Cait Cummins and wants to help her get her dog back. He offered four years of college for the oldest kid of whoever brings her in. But the dog has to be alive."

"I don't know how she can live. She needs an Army Medivac. Surgeons. Blood, everything."

"I'll call this Duane guy and see what he can do. You keep driving. A sheriff's escort is on its way. They'll clear the road for you. We gotta get Cliff Jr. that scholarship!"

Cliff realized what the sheriff had said. Four years of college? He could never afford to send his kids to college. But thanks to a stranger, Cliffy would be able to go. If they could save the dog.

Squad cars pulled up on all sides of him, and the caravan headed toward UC Davis and its world-famous veterinary school. They didn't stop for anything, but they'd never get Opal help soon enough, even with that kind of assistance.

"Sheriff, she needs blood," Cliff cried. "She needs a super vet like they show on TV."

"One's on its way. You're on highway 191, right?"

"Yeah."

"Go to the Paradise Airport. You'll be directed there. Sheriff and National Guard teams are on the ground and a medivac helicopter and staff."

"What?"

"This Duane guy is a big cheese. I remember him from a long time ago. He must be almost a hundred now."

A scream interrupted them. "*Dad! Dad! She's got* puppies *inside her!* There's a hole in her stomach, and you can see them.*"

"Holy shit. Are they alive?"

"Some of them are. Some of them, the mountain lion killed." The boy started to cry.

"Don't look at that, pull the ones that are alive out and dry them off with a towel. Sheriff, do you cut the cord of puppies whose mom may be dying?"

"I don't know, Cliff. I'll call for that information. Keep them alive."

Cliff wondered if the sheriff was thinking what he was: If Opal died, some puppies would qualify for the scholarship.

"How many are there, guys?" Cliff said over his shoulder.

"Three are dead. They're torn up."

"And eight are alive. That's all of them."

"Keep them warm. We're almost at the airport."

25

BREAKING WATERS

THE EMERGENCY SERVICES guys arrived amazingly quick. Maybe they'd been watching the show. They tended to stick around since the show where that guy in the audience swallowed a wad of bubble gum and almost choked to death. This time was even more dramatic. And the cameras rolled.

They got Cait strapped on the gurney on her back, even though the baby resting on her spine in that position hurt her. A birth coach in the audience jumped onto the stage and shouted orders. "Let her lie on her side with her knees up."

"We can't strap her in that way."

"Yes, you can. Just do it."

"JUST DO IT," roared Will Duane from the screen. "You're torturing the poor woman!"

"Oh, no!" wailed Cait, as a small river of fluid splattered off the gurney.

"GET HER TO THE HOSPITAL," Will bellowed. "Don't worry, sweetheart. I'm sending my doctor to you. You'll be fine. She takes care of me and look how I look."

Cait didn't get any of that, being busy wailing and saying, "Oh, my God. My water broke on national TV. AHHH!"

Indeed, it did, helping to push the episode's ratings above all conceivable levels.

* * *

"Oh, God, it hurts!" Cait was in a bed in the maternity ward of the most prestigious hospital in San Francisco. Also, the closest to the studio.

Jon and Jason accompanied her into her delivery suite, as she didn't have other companions or coaches. "It's okay, Cait. We're here."

They were putting an I.V. in Cait's arm when Jon whispered to Jason, "Do you know anything about this?"

"Absolutely nothing," Jason whispered back. "But as her attorney, I'll watch out for her interests." He said the last bit in a normal volume voice.

He might have said, "I am a demon from hell and will sue the wonkers off anyone who messes up."

The doctor attending Cait stepped back and said to her, "You're fully dilated. Do you feel any urge to push?" She shook her head, then squealed horribly. "How tall is your husband?"

"Was. He died. Six foot two inches."

"And you're…?"

"Five -two."

The doctor grimaced and looked at the nurse in the room. "He's way too big for her pelvis. The baby can't get out. We'd better prep for a C-section."

"Wait a minute," Jon said. He knew from his "Having a Baby in San Francisco" series of programs that if she had a Cesarean, she might not be able to have a natural, vaginal birth at a later pregnancy. Also, they hurt a lot and recovery was longer. And that because of the number of lawsuits slapped on doctors when a natural birth screwed up, docs were now inclined to do Cesareans when they might not be totally necessary.

"Jason, go out in the hallway," Jon barked. "Okay, everyone. I'm just a talk show host. I don't know Shinola about law or babies. The lawyer's in the hall. So, relax."

They couldn't relax; they were set to cut. The idea of anyone cutting Cait's cute tummy made him sick.

"WAIT!" Jon yelped.

"We can't wait. The baby may be brain damaged."

"Stop, Will's doctor is on the way. Just wait a minute."

Two orderlies and a nurse lined Cait's bed up to be taken *somewhere* in the vast hospital, her guts cut open and the baby pulled out.

"No! No!" Jon cried.

"STOP RIGHT NOW. TAKE THAT WOMAN BACK INTO HER ROOM. *STAT*!" A tall, gaunt woman about fifty stood in the way of the gurney. "Back into her room. Then leave, all of you."

"Who are you?"

"Will Duane's doctor, Dr. ..." Something. The word garbled so that no one recognized it. Still, they heard it, and they knew a megadoc's voice when they heard one.

"What instruments do you need, doctor?" A nurse pulled out forceps. Jon thought he'd faint. They'd used something like that in his high school metal shop class.

"None. I need you to leave." Cait moaned. They left, including Jon.

The three and one-half minutes spent standing in the hall were the longest of Jon's life. He heard a baby cry. He, Jason, the doctor, and nurses lunged at the door. They saw Caitlin holding her baby to her breast with the tall, scary, older lady doctor next to them.

"A healthy baby boy, delivered vaginally. No tearing of the mother's tissues. Mom and babe are perfect. The placenta is whole and presented immediately." The stern lady smiled, and stroked Cait's cheek. "Well done, my dear.

"Now, I must go help a dog in distress, *if* you people can manage to clean the baby off and diaper him without killing him. You, the *lawyer*, watch them."

She walked out the door.

Jon looked after her, but the corridor was empty. He fell back against the wall, heart racing. That's why he loved working for Will Duane, though he did feel hysterical and faint often.

26

OPAL IN DISTRESS

A BLACK UNMARKED HELICOPTER approached the Paradise Airport. Cliff held the limp Opal wrapped in blankets and a towel. All were soaked with red. Sheriff Boroughs carried the puppies, also wrapped in a blanket, in a plastic crate improvised to hold the bunch of them. Every patrol car in the valley surrounded them. Military vehicles were parked in a circle around the landing area. The approaching mysterious chopper added to the surreal mood. Police officers watched, awed and perplexed.

"That's a military aircraft," the sheriff said. "It's UH-60 Black Hawk helicopter or I never served in the Army. I thought they were sending a veterinary copter. That's a military medivac chopper. But it's not marked."

They landed and a spry, tough-looking lady dressed in a long black dress got out. She looked about fifty and was as no-nonsense as a high-ranking officer. "Get the dog and pups in the helicopter. In the rear, please, the separate compartment. Mr. Madsen. You and the children may ride in the front compartment. When I've seen to Opal and her pups, I will attend to you. You are about to go into shock."

They climbed in, and the chopper lifted immediately, leaving Paradise behind.

"Where are they going?" the sheriff cried. "UC Davis is the other direction." He waved his arms, trying to tell the pilots they were headed the wrong way. "What's going on here?"

No one knew, and they wouldn't know for a long time.

When they were airborne, the old woman took over. "I'm Will Duane's doctor. Also his veterinarian. I use unorthodox methods that work far better than traditional ones. Now, put Opal on this secure platform in the rear and the box of pups on the floor. Go sit in the passenger area.

"You will never speak of what you see or hear on this flight. Sit!"

The woman unwrapped Opal. "Oh, you poor darling. You are the bravest dog I've ever seen. Let's get you healed." The dog's hind legs were shredded, and her belly laid open in ribbons. Hideous gashes from the cat's claws covered her back. The flesh was white, she'd lost so much blood.

"They'd amputate your hind legs, darling. Not needed at all." She took a needle and thread from a bag at her waist and stitched up the dog. "Nice and tidy. Don't die, darling, you have a full life left. Of course, if you die, I can deal with that. And now…"

A wave of a wand that found itself in the woman's hand, an incantation, a puff of smoke.

Opal's eyes opened.

"That's a girl. I need to get you some broth. That will bring you right back." She addressed the other compartment. "Gentlemen, there's a carafe of broth in my container. Could you pour some of it into the porcelain bowl. It's in the same container. Opal is thirsty. She needs to build herself up."

Moments later, she joined the others.

"Is she…?" Their white faces said they feared the worst. Little James' face was covered with tears. "She saved me," he said. "She jumped under the cougar on purpose."

"Alive? Of course she is. She's nursing her pups now. Nine, as it turned out. I wasn't able to save two."

All of them froze. Three of the pups had been dead. They knew what dead looked like. There had been eight living. What did this woman do?

"She's fine. You know, children and gentlemen. There's a place in the world for magic. Without it, things sometimes would be too horrible, too awful. If you can fix things with magic, why not? The world doesn't have to be so painfully real. Just a pinch, that's all."

Jerking as he remembered, "How is Cait? They said she went into labor on the show."

"She did indeed! Gave all those entertainment junkies a thrill. She's fine. Has a bright baby boy."

"Where are we going?"

"We're going to Will Duane's ranch in Montana. He wanted to meet you. Cait will be there when she's up to traveling."

"Who are you?"

"Ah. Someday, I'll be able to tell you, but not today." The wand appeared in her hand again. "And now, all of you—except the pilots—will fall sound asleep. None of you will remember what happened here, except that Will Duane's vet saved Opal. The pilots will remember an ordinary flight."

And so it was.

27

ALL THE NEWS

NOT ONLY DID the internet go crazy over the events surrounding Cait Cummins and Opal, the regular news media did, too. Many people in the studio audience caught Cait's impromptu and *watery* exit from the studio on a gurney on their cell phones. Cait's departure splattered the TV news across the country and provided headlines in prestigious newspapers such as the *Wall Street Journal*, that normally only wrote about serious things, like money. Of course, Jon Walker was an internationally known figure, used to creating headlines, but this was spectacular, even for him.

People normally interested in commodity futures and world economic forecasts became fascinated with the little woman with the big belly, as well as the things she did. They found themselves watching YouTube as Cait made chalk paint from crushed calcium pills and color-rejected paints from the hardware store.

They admired pictures of her Victorian mansion in Magalia, before it burned down. People loved her adorable taste. As well as her. The redo of the Madsen family's summer cottage on the Delta was a smashing success. WSJ readers thought it would transport to the Hamptons fine.

Cait's future as a designer was foregone, if anyone could figure out where she was. She seemed to have disappeared from the hospital with her newborn son.

The world wasn't just worried, it was *hysterical*. First, she left the studio so spectacularly, and then she *left*, period.

Jon did appear on his show the next day with multiple pictures of a beaming Cait with her adorable baby boy. She waved and blew kisses on video.

"Cait is having a little vacation to enjoy her child. They call it 'maternity leave.' She's entitled to it, especially after you *people* spread your vids of her *water breaking* all over the world. That's why we had you sign agreements today, to keep what happens in here in here. That was Cait's *lawyer* handing out what you signed.

"If you're lucky, she'll get over the embarrassment in this life-time, and we'll have her back on the show. And all of you who have requested design consultations with her will get them." Jon could be very stern. "But you'd better shape up."

"And now today's guests, a troop of Schutzhund-trained Chihuahuas…"

Opal's story caused even more furor, if that's possible. The Comman-dos, Thad's bowling team, all had stories to tell of their pell-mell race to the Paradise airport surrounded by sheriff's vehicles and search and rescue, and every other emergency vehicle the sheriff could command.

"That dog—she's a hero's hero. How many people has she saved since the fire? She's a superhero."

The Madsen kids appeared stair-step, from little James, to bigger Emma, to ten-year-old Kent. The Commandos had been unable to resist recording their story while they were waiting for the helicopter to save Opal and her pups. The regular press showed up right behind them so what happened while they were waiting for the chopper was very well documented.

James' tear-stained face filled screens around the world. "She pushed me away and then jumped under the mountain lion and bit it in the neck. It was going to eat me! Opal saved me!"

Emma and Kent piped up, "It was going to eat all of us!"' "It scratched Opal so bad." "Dad shot his shotgun and it ran off." "But it hurt her so much. Blood…" Then they all started crying. "She had puppies inside her. The lion killed three of them." "It scratched them to death." By which time, all the people doing the videos and the three kids were sobbing.

"I am so grateful to that dog," Cliff Madsen said. "They were *in our backyard!* Who expects a mountain lion in their backyard! The fire has made everything crazy."

A multitude of images showed Cliff clutching bloody blankets wrapped around Opal. Sheriff Boroughs was right next to him with a crate of puppies,

From there, the reporting got sketchy. Some people said a private helicopter picked them up and went to the veterinary school at UC Davis. Some said that military personnel and vehicles were all over. Some said just sheriff and emergency vehicles. None of the photos or videos of the scene came out, oddly.

One guy said the military was everywhere, and it was a Black Hawk helicopter that got them. It flew in the opposite direction of UC Davis. Everyone hooted that one down as absurd. The only professional that reported that story was Allison Chao, who had been working for the Lodi Alternate News Press since her disastrous televised reporting about Opal and Cait. The Alternate News refused to publish her story about the Black Hawk flying away from Davis; it was so far out and substantiated by no one. Allison was demoted to garden editor.

Opal's whereabouts remained a mystery until a young attorney no one had heard of, Jason Bridger, appeared on Jon Walker's show with an announcement—in photos and videos. People in the audience exploded into applause and tears.

"I represent Caitlin Cummins and her son, Benjamin Thaddeus

Cummins, and the dog Grand Champion Opal's Elegant Masquerade Contessa, known as Opal. Cait wants me to tell everyone that she's resting and enjoying her baby. Her babies. Opal is recovering well from her injuries with her nine puppies. The vets were unable to save two of them from injuries inflicted by the mountain lion. The rest are alive and well, and so is Opal."

A short, tightly edited—*no one* could tell where it was taken—slide and video presentation showed Cait hugging a *huge* red-headed baby that waved and smiled, looking more like a six-month-old, truth be told. Thad's picture was shown; the baby was a stamped image of him, to the red hair.

"Thanks so much for your love and support." Cait blew kisses.

And then Opal stole the show, sitting up, and grinning at the camera. Not walking but sitting fine. The puppies were being fed by what looked like vet techs. Opal wiggled with health and happiness.

"We'll post more of Opal as she heals. And we have DNA matching this dog with the lost Opal: this is Opal."

And then, in the most dramatic moment of the video, the entire Madsen family–Cliff, Jennie, and all five children–was front and center in the camera. Will Duane walked onto the stage, amazingly gorgeous for a hundred years old. He waved at the camera, obviously no stranger to being in the spotlight.

"On Jon Walker's show, I committed that I'd pay for the college education of the first-born child of the person to return Opal alive and well. She was a little tattered, but she's going to be fine. And for Cliff Madsen Jr., I have a certificate to cover your education. Room, board, the whole shebang. I'm going to be in your life, young man. I want to make sure that you make good choices. I might even help with some other stuff your family needs, too." He winked broadly.

"I've got a few other goodies that should come in handy for your family." Will's eyes turned to Cliff Madsen, Sr. "I can't tell you how grateful I am for bringing Opal home. I figured you could use some help on that rebuilding up in Magalia you're doing. I've got a crew ready to go up—under your command. And this should cover materials." He handed Cliff an envelope. "Don't open it now. Just know that I'm grateful."

"OPAL KILLS MOUNTAIN LION!" was the biggest headline of all. Sheriff Boroughs and people from the Forest Service and Fish and Game grouped solemnly behind a podium for the local and national newscast.

"Our trackers and scent hounds followed Opal's trail. She came out of the forest to the site of her home, Charisma Kennels, which was burnt to the ground by the Camp Fire. Seeing it was gone, she backtracked through the woods to the Madsen residence, where she prevented the mountain lion from attacking the children.

"The kids describe her as diving under the cat and biting it in the throat. Given the cat's musculature and size, that's the only way she could stop the animal. A large amount of blood was at the scene, mostly Opal's.

"We tracked into the forest in the direction Cliff Madsen said the cat ran. An eighth of a mile into the woods, we discovered the body of the cat. It's throat was ripped out, and it had bled to death. We've done DNA testing: Opal was the killer.

"This was a juvenile cat of about 120 pounds. Opal weighs about sixty-five. She couldn't kill a full-grown cat, but it's an amazing feat that she was able to stop and destroy a cat even this size."

The rebuilding town of Paradise nearby Grass Valley and Nevada City had OPAL DAY parades. Cait could have charged anything for those pups.

28

BOY, ARE WE
IN TROUBLE

JASON SAT AT his desk in his large well-appointed office in the grungy warehouse in San Francisco. He was the only occupant of the space. It was weird and lonely and scary. It echoed and felt empty.

He expected to be bored now that Cait and her babe and Opal and her pups were safely sequestered at Will Duane's ranch in Montana. But he wasn't.

The lawsuits claiming Opal had bitten people kept pouring in. Given the number of lawsuits and their originating jurisdictions, Opal must have chewed her way from one side of the country to the other. Dog bite injuries carried serious penalties to the owner, and especially the dog, which could be euthanized as the result of a legal proceeding.

Cait said that Opal had bitten a couple of people, but the cases had been settled. That had been revealed by Lyle Kenyan, the manager of the kennel they got Opal from. She and Thad suspected she'd bitten more—kennel helpers and others without the resources to fight.

Videos of Opal playing with her pups and giving Cait big kisses came from Will's estate daily, sometimes hourly. Jon Walker featured them on his program, along with the Madsen family and the Commandos. Everything about Opal and Cait and their broods was a thing in the news, online and in print. Opal was still being hailed as a hero, but for how long?

Jason called Cait. She needed to know what was happening. "Is she a vicious dog, Cait?"

Silence. "Maybe. I had never touched her before we got up here. She did nip at me and growl. I figured I'd give her space and let her come to me in her own time. That seems to have worked."

"You never touched her when you had her in Magalia?"

"No."

"Did she attack any of your other dogs?"

"The poodles, no, though she wasn't friendly with them. She would have torn the two Golden Retrievers we had as stud dogs apart if we hadn't hosed them—*her*—down."

"Would you call her a vicious dog?"

"No. Well, we kept her locked up in her kennel except when Thad shaved her. She was good with him when he groomed her. What's this about, Jason?"

"So far, I've gotten fourteen affidavits and claims against Opal by certified mail, another five by a process server. The plaintiffs all claim Opal injured them, some severely."

"That doesn't sound possible."

"Not to me, either, especially since the pictures of you and Opal playing have been circulated. Keep those coming. I'll make sure Jon gives them big play on his show. 'How cute Opal is. Sweet dog. Good with kids.' Though if you do feel she's dangerous, keep her away from your baby."

Cait paused. Jason thought he could hear her gulp. "Opal is fine. She's totally changed by everything that happened to her. I'd trust her with my baby." No shadow in her tone.

"I have to deal with this. Opal is how old, now?"

"She was six when we got her. We had her for three years. She was missing for nine months. So, she's almost ten. Why?"

"The statute of limitations on dog bite injuries in California is two years. Could she have bitten anyone while you had her? There's an affidavit from," he checked the name, "Herbert Watson. He's your neighbor who was spying on you with drones. The meth head. Did she bite him?'

"Well, he tried to steal her when we were gone. She had him treed when we came back. Thad had to get the ladder for him to get down. I didn't see any blood on him, but he screamed bloody murder about her being vicious. Her kennel was locked. He cut through the chain link fencing to get her out."

"He was trespassing. That nullifies the suit. He's not a credible witness from what you say, but still… Statutes of limitation are all over the place in other states, usually one or two years, but up to six in places like Maine and Minnesota. Since you had her for three years with no incidents, I can toss the affidavits whose statutes have expired. That's a lot of them. What worries me, Cait, is the ones that say she attacked them when she was running free."

"The last nine months?"

"Yes."

"That's ridiculous. She's saving people on the one hand and attacking them on the other?"

"It doesn't make sense, does it?" And then it did. It was Will Duane. He also realized why Will had hired him and put him up in this warehouse. Duane wanted to keep him at a distance from the other law firms he used. He used the biggest and best legal teams in the country. Why would he want a junior guy from a less that nationally known firm? That had bothered Jason all along.

He had been out of his mind with joy when he got the phone call from Will Duane offering him a job. He remembered Will as the historical figure he was—singlehandedly kicking off the computer revolution in the 1950s. Changing world culture forever. Founding and running the gargantuan Numenon, Inc. for twenty years? Thirty? Then getting tossed out by jealous subordinates. Losing half his fortune and earning it back. Starting FISH, Inc. with an unknown Native American genius—who wouldn't jump at the chance to work for Will Duane?

He was an up and comer at his previous job with Jeffrey Hoagland of Hoagland, Moore, Cassavetes, Peters, et. al. in San Francisco. They promised the stars, if he just kept doing everything Jeffrey sic'd him on for the rest of his life. But when he found out some of the sick stuff Jeffrey was into, Jason couldn't work for him. That was just the *sick* stuff; the illegal stuff scared him to death.

So, he went to work for Will Duane.

"You'll have your own office in San Francisco and all the support you need. I'm putting you directly under me in 'Special Projects.' We'll start small, and then get bigger. First off, I want you to rescue Cait Cummins before your old boss and his wife have her for dinner."

Which he did. He realized that his first assignment for Will was helping Cait. He was more into tortes and subpoenas, but he figured he could babysit for a while. He was, after all, regarded as the 'widows and orphans' man. He was the guy who appealed to juries and judges emotionally and creating sympathy for his clients, even in the attorneys on the other side of the case.

He thought Duane would give him another assignment when Cait was wrapped up. He didn't, and now Jason could see why. Cait wasn't wrapped up. She'd never be able to live peacefully.

It was association with Will Duane that did it. Duane had stepped out to defend her when the anti-breeding doodles people attacked. He defended Opal and offered—and gave—that amazing reward for her. Cait was clearly one of his people.

The dark side of what he'd heard about Will came to him. That he was cursed by some evil power. That he had to stay hidden to survive himself. People who were his favorites came to personal harm or disaster. He'd used magic or dark science to look so young. There were old stories from back to the late '90s. A guy named Doug Saunders, a top MBA, went absolutely bonkers after attending some Native American retreat with Will—going ballistic in court and never seen again. And Melissa Weir, another star MBA and old name in the history of Silicon Valley, dropped off the map mysteriously. Were there other lives and careers ruined after a few years with Will Duane?

Was he in for the same?

The dog bite suits and affidavits came directly after Will publicly awarded the scholarship on the Madsen boy. The timing wasn't coincidental. Why would someone want to destroy a hero, even a dog hero? Really destroy her: they'd put her down if the court said she was vicious. Figuring that out was his assignment.

Some of the suits were outside the statues of limitation. Those he disposed of. Others were obviously bogus: a guy in Florida saying Opal bit his kid when they were at the Everglades. Another guy, same time, saying Opal bit his mother-in-law in the Olympic Forest in Washington. They could be debunked easily. The descriptions of the dog were hysterical: one plaintiff showed a picture of a white poodle, show groomed, running in a field. Or a black hairy thing in an inner city.

Other cases, biting that Opal did while running around the Gold Country, needed more work.

How did you get rid of a lawsuit? You fought it and won in court, or you threw money at the plaintiff until he went away.

Jason called Will and told him what was going on. "Do I have a budget for paying those people off?"

Silence. "I don't like to play that way. I like to destroy whoever comes after me. But Cait deserves some peace. And Opal's the sweetest dog I've ever seen. We romped all over the yard this afternoon.

"Your budget is: whatever it takes. Just make them go away."

That's what Jason would do, until the case with the little kid whose face looked like it had been chewed off, came in. Usually, affidavits didn't come illustrated. A few had, like Florida show dog, but this was so horrific that it would sway any judge and jury. And it was near Magalia during the period she was running loose. Opal could have done it.

He picked up the phone. "Will, I need to meet Opal." He had to see for himself whether this dog was capable of that kind of carnage.

29

WILL THE REAL
OPAL STAND UP?

J ASON LOOKED OUT the window of the private jet taking him to Will's Montana ranch. FISH was written along the whole side of the plane in wild colors, rimmed with still wilder colors. Psychedelic and then some. Will Duane owned a controlling interest in FISH, Inc. Flying in this plane meant it was true: he was Will's employee going to his boss's wilderness outpost. The possibility of doing that had sounded so mysterious and glamorous to Jason when he'd signed on. Now his stomach clenched.

They flew over miles of pristine wilderness and mountains. Is this where Will had to hang out to be safe? The image of that kid's chewed up face haunted him. Wondering what happened to Will Duane's missing associates roiled him more. Would *Opal mangle him*? Would he disappear? Jason was scared stiff.

He got off the plane on a private airstrip. "God's country," he whispered. The scenery was breathtaking; flower-dotted meadows ringed by tall mountains, most still snow topped. The trees—cedars, he thought. Maybe pines, looked like first growth. Insects hummed and birds twittered. They seemed louder than at home.

"It's impressive, isn't it?" A tall, lanky, older man approached him across the tarmac landing strip. "I'm Billy Jack Abernathy. This is my spread. Will said you'd be coming and to carry you to his place. He's my next-door neighbor, but you'll be staying with me." He grinned at Jason and winked. "It's weird, but it's how we do things here. My helicopter is waiting."

An unmarked helicopter sat a short distance away. Turned out Jack was an accomplished pilot. "An airplane or chopper is a man's best friend up here. I'd never see Will, but for this," he indicated the whirly bird.

They flew over more green wilderness and first growth trees. Jason couldn't imagine having a place so big that he had to take a helicopter to visit his neighbor. When they landed, Billy Jack gave him a pep talk.

"Will owns 450,000 acres in Montana. Seemed like he wanted to buy the whole state at one time, but he's slowed down. The main ranch house is here. You'll be visiting it, and Cait's cottage. Everything else is restricted—and I mean restricted. Step out of bounds, and commandos will pop up out of the ground. I'm going to have some coffee while you're with Cait and Opal." He shook his head, "Boy, are they a pair. And those puppies!"

Jason stumbled out of the helicopter, staring at Will's house. It was the biggest, most magnificent log house he'd seen. Not that they were too common in the San Francisco Bay Area, but even fancy country living magazines didn't have houses like this. The logs were two feet across each, and the building spread out, wing after wing. Way in the background, he could see a barn made of the same logs. There were pens for horses and cattle.

"C'mon in here, partner. Will's in his office. I'm heading for the kitchen." Billy Jack took his arm and led him through a log cathedral furnished with priceless Western artifacts. "Right in there. That's Will's hangout."

Jason walked through the double doors into an office that shouldn't have been a surprise, given how huge and oversized everything else was. It still was a surprise, though.

Will nodded from his desk. "Hello, Jason. Give me that report." Jason handed over an envelope containing the information about the suits against Opal. The picture of the kid with the chewed-up face was on top. Will looked at it and said, "Hmm.

"Cait's just walking up the path. I'll talk to you later. Make sure you get all your questions answered." He went back to looking at the photo.

"Hi, Jason! It's good to see you." Cait gave him a one-armed hug, the other arm holding her baby. "I never thought a baby would keep me so busy. It's given me a *ton* of ideas for shows. *Easy baby. Baby shortcuts, decorating for baby that* works!…that sort of thing. Let me show you my house."

It was a log house of a simpler and finer cut than Will's, but as cozy as Cait's old home in Magalia must have been. Lace and eyelet curtains swayed with the breeze. "I've done a few little projects here, but I don't have time, between Benny and Opal's puppies."

"How are the puppies?"

"Come and see." She took him through the living room to a screened porch on the other side. The luscious aroma of the meadow and trees wafted in.

Jason didn't see her for a moment. She lay in a big box with low sides. She could get out easily, but the puppies couldn't. He jumped. He'd spent the last week reading affidavits to the effect that Opal was a killer. Actually being near her was a shock.

She raised her head and looked at him. Her eyes were *black,* and the rest of her a cropped short gray/silver. They'd had to shave her matted hair. He'd never seen such a sweet expression on any animal, or human. She radiated contentment and happiness. She was lying on her side, with a few of the puppies suckling. As he approached, she raised her top leg, as though offering him one of her teats or asking him to rub her tummy.

"That's a sign of submission. She's telling you that you're the top dog. She'll do what you say."

He'd expected her to snarl or try to protect her puppies. "Oh."

"Yeah. She's totally different from the way she used to be. Whatever she went through worked a miracle. Would you like to feed the puppies? Her tummy got scarred up by the cat, so she lost a few of her mammary glands. And she's still healing, so we help her by feeding the pups."

Jason looked at the dog's belly. It looked like it had been rototilled. Her back legs had stitched scars like zippers. He caught his breath. "You poor thing. You had a bad time." Jason reminded himself: she threw herself under the mountain lion to protect Cliff's kids. All three said the same thing. She bit its throat so effectively, it bled to death. The Forest Service confirmed that.

Opal was a hero, not a killer.

"Here, hold the puppy like this and then tickle its lips with the bottle's nipple until it grabs hold."

It did, sucking away like a little demon. Or baby. Cait's baby made the same noises as he nursed. Jason sat there in this female empire, feeding a puppy that seemed like a curly, hairy sock, a wiggling, very alive sock. They were all black and looked pure poodle, not that he knew what tiny pups of different breeds looked like.

They were silent feeding the pups and babe, the warm air moving in and out through the screens. Sucking sounds coming from first one, then another. He fed four puppies! Jason had never done anything like that. The femaleness of it. The maternal love. He felt something beguiling him. Enchanting him. He could stay there forever, reveling in new life.

Insects buzzed. Time slowed. The flat light of late afternoon filled the porch. Cait was asleep, head bent over her babe's. The baby slept, too, a thread of drool escaping his lips and falling on his mother's breast.

Something nudged his hand. It was Opal, standing next to him, her pups sleeping in the box. She nudged his hand again, insistently, wanting to communicate something.

Care for us. Keep us safe. We are the mother, the babes, the pups, the pack. We are your home and your family.

Jason jerked awake.

"Hey, Jason, Will wants to talk to you before we fly back," Billy Jack's voice drawled, a whisper. He got up silently and patted Opal's head. The dog licked his hand and stared at him.

I'll save you. I'll do everything I can to save you and Cait and your babies. I will not let anything hurt you. It was like a prayer, arising from inside of him.

"They're something," Billy Jack said as they walked back to the main house. "I've never seen anything like it. I could sit with them forever. I'd do anything to keep them safe."

Will was stern as he sat in his office. "That's not a dog bite on that kid's face. I sent it to an expert, and she said that positively wasn't made by Opal. It's obvious, too. Look at this—see the width of the bite between the puncture wounds made by the canine teeth? That must be five inches. No dog has a jaw that wide. A cat did that, a full-grown mountain lion." His gaze diverted. "Or something else."

"What else?"

"Oh, something much nastier. I've faced it before. I'm going to hand this to my wife. She's an expert and will know what to do. Meanwhile, you work on the other cases. Find out the ones that don't make any sense: the dog's wrong. Two attacks are at the same time in different places. Anything that's fishy. Document it all. We'll see if we can get a summary judgement and have a judge dismiss the whole package. Except this one," he indicated the envelope. "That, we'll leave to my wife."

Jason didn't know Will had a wife.

"I have a wife," he said. "I've been married three times. Being married to me has proven dangerous to my wives. This go around, we stay apart much of the time. She has children to care for and her own responsibilities. I have to stay here for my health, and to run this." He spread his hands to indicate everything around him. All 450,000 acres, Jason understood. "There's a lot more here than meets the eye. But I am married, and I love my wife."

That was the end of the conversation. Billy Bob took him home in the helicopter. Jason spent the night enveloped in dreams of cottony maternal love and puppies.

He went home to his husband, whom he'd given short shrift since meeting Will. He remembered the puppies and Cait's sweet affection for her baby and made love that tenderly.

The ranch hidden in the wilderness was good to remember. A place of love and peace and sweet breezes, hidden from the viciousness and duplicity of the outer world. A magic Shangri-La out of sight of ordinary eyes.

He would do anything to defend it—and Cait and her little one, Opal and the pups. Will and Billy Joe.

The next day, Jason dove into the paperwork of the affidavits. He'd punched holes in all of them by midday. All but the one with the chewed-up kid.

Will's wife would take care of that.

30

ALL MAGIC ISN'T MAGIC

"OH, GOD. I thought it was all happening again." Will's voice cracked. He held the phone away from his mouth for a moment. His ribs rose and fell, pounding with the emotion running through him. "Oh, Vanessa, I thought it was…"

"No, darling. It wasn't the Dark Lord and his demons coming after you."

"Her, that's the problem. All of them, Cait and Opal and all the babies. I thought…" His head slipped forward, his forehead resting in his fingers. Tears fell on his slacks. "I can't stand it again."

"Will, you've got me. I've got you hidden. You *are* hidden. They won't come for you or anyone you love."

"Did I make a mistake, coming out, Vanessa? Should I have ignored everything and stayed hidden?"

"I don't see how you could and be a human being, Will. It was a risk, and you took it. But let me tell you what I found. It was nothing supernatural. It was *evil*, but ordinary evil that humans create." She paused. "Drugs are the scourge of the universe. This country seems to be facing a plague from them.

"It was a full-grown mountain lion," she said. "You were right about the canine teeth being too far apart for a dog. The lion Opal killed was young, but the full-grown ones are huge. Over two hundred pounds. It's a wonder that poor child survived."

"What happened?"

"His uncle kept the cat to guard his meth facility. It was in the woods, in an area that didn't burn in the fire. The animal was usually locked up, but it got out. The child was just *there*. It ran, and the cat got him. His family saw his injuries as an entrepreneurial opportunity, knowing the reward you'd given for Opal's return. They decided to…"

"Make me pay though the nose to protect Opal."

"Right. But they were stupid bumblers. They didn't think the neighbors—or the whole mountain— knew about their pet mountain lion. And the meth lab. I don't know why the sheriff didn't pick them up. That's another story. They managed to keep the attack quiet, because if it got out, it would have shut down their drug business."

"Did the kid get treatment?"

"No. The grandmother patched his face up. No plastic surgery. He's stuck like that the rest of his life."

"How could they do that?"

"They're all meth heads, Will. Mentally impaired. And evil. Some drugs access parts of the human brain that shouldn't be accessed. You don't need supreme evil to do horrific things. Regular evil is enough."

"Are any of them worth saving? Is that child ruined?"

"I think the child can't be worked with, if we intervene right now. I don't think he's ruined, but he needs psychological and spiritual care as well as physical mending. He doesn't have much going for him on either the nature or nurture scale. But I think he's worth a try.

"The investigation Jason and I did shook up the whole mountain. The child is in public custody. Animal Services is holding the mountain lion, pending court action. It will be put down. What it did to that child is obvious evidence of its viciousness. What a shame, the animal was as distorted as the people around him. The sheriff has shut down the meth operation, obviously."

"Was he crooked?"

"If he was, he isn't any more."

"Vanessa! What did you do?"

"Oh, a little this and a little that. Nothing that will kill him, though he will be the straightest sheriff in the back country for the rest of his life."

"Vanessa…"

"I can't help myself sometimes." She was about to change subjects, "Will…"

"Yes, I agree." He picked up her thought and responded to it. "We should help him. He's a candidate for our program."

"I'll start Jason on the paperwork in the morning. Jason is good, Will. He's getting what we're about and wants to be part of it."

Will chuckled. "I keep fantasizing about him and Cait."

"Not going to happen, Will. Jason is very gay. His husband is a nice man. I met him. And so have you. I'm coming up to visit this weekend. You've been alone too long, shouldering the burden."

At that, Will wept. "I miss you. You're the only one I can tell everything to… And I miss *you…* "

"Same here, darling. We have these crazy lives. One day, we'll be able to live together all the time."

But not now, he thought as he hung up. He heaved a huge breath. It hadn't been the Dark Lord, just the evil that we do to each other. He didn't relax.

31

NEXT!

JASON OPENED A letter from a law firm he'd never heard of. His eyes widened with disbelief as he read the writ of replevin. Replevin was one of the oldest forms of common law, aimed at recovering personal property taken legally or illegally by someone with an inferior claim to it. Rather than monetary compensation, a writ of replevin was aimed at regaining the object itself.

In this case, Opal.

'Holy shit! It never ends." He called Will right away.

"Some guy named Matthew Thibeau claims to be Opal's rightful owner. His grandfather bred her and named Matthew as heir to his entire estate. Opal is in that estate."

"But she's been owned by a half-dozen people!"

"That doesn't matter if the original sale wasn't valid. It's as though you bought a building, but the title wasn't clear. It is owned by someone far back in the chain of ownership, not the person selling it and purporting to own it. You can lose the property if the title isn't valid in the present."

"How could that happen? She was registered to Cait and Thad with the AKC. They had a bill of sale, though for a zero price."

"That's why we have title companies in real estate, to keep this from happening. The person behind the writ claims the signature on the original transfer of ownership was forged."

"How could this happen? After all this, some stranger steps in and takes Opal? Is this another attempt to shake me down?"

"I don't know, Will. I'll do some research and get back to you."

Jason did, with a heavy heart. "I've done some sleuthing in the world of show poodles." Jason couldn't suppress the smile in his voice. "It's *something*, Will. Different. But everyone I spoke to recognized Matthew and Michael Thibeau. Michael, the grandfather, bred Opal and several fantastic dogs. He was very prestigious, but not well-heeled like many of the other owners of fine dogs.

"Matthew was his grandson, a young man when the grandfather died. He originally trained and showed Opal, and started her Schutz-hund training, which everyone on the show circuit disapproved of. Including his grandfather.

"People assumed that Michael Thibeau didn't leave Opal to his grandson because of that. Instead, he sold her for a fortune to one of the wealthiest people in the dog world. Matthew was booted as her trainer and disappeared.

"He's come up with evidence that the sale wasn't consummated legally, and the transfer of Opal's registration at the AKC was bogus. He is the grandfather's rightful heir, and Opal was in the estate."

"Is there any merit to his claim?"

"Maybe. I'm deposing him in two days."

Jason deposed Matthew Thibeau in a law office in Stockbridge, Massachusetts. Thibeau was an East Coast guy. He lived near the charming colonial town of Great Barrington but didn't want to hold the deposition at his house or disclose his address. Odd.

His home address was easy enough to find using the court records of his grandfather's estate. Jason didn't even need that. Google was enough. Michael Thibeau owned an eighteen-acre farm/kennel on the edge of town. It was a beautiful pasture rimmed by verdant woods. He'd left it to Matthew, who still owned it.

Jason got there the day before the deposition and drove by the place. The greenery of the East Coast always flummoxed him, even though he'd lived there for years. He did Yale undergraduate and Harvard Law School. Jason had all the bells and whistles that Will Duane required of everyone he hired.

He'd done his homework at Harvard Law School, inhaling their negotiation coursework. "Know your opponent" was key. He made his way past the farm, which was almost stereotypical East Coast rural: Rolling pastures and a cute house that Cait would transform into a masterpiece of hominess. He leaned forward, peering out the window. So, this was where Matthew Thibeau lived.

He hadn't been back for long. Jason was able to find clear records of him until his grandfather died. Then he disappeared, as in vanished from every public record and the many private databases he could get to through Will's influence. There would be more on him if he'd died.

That could be explained in words of three letters: CIA, FBI. A bunch of clandestine governmental ops. He could be in some branch of military not recorded on the books.

Why should he want a dog so much after eight years? Opal had been two when the senior Thibeau sold her. She was almost ten now.

The next day, Jason walked into the Stockbridge law office of his buddy from Harvard Law School. He borrowed the conference room to depose Matthew Thibeau.

"Hey, Len," Jason said. "Nice digs." Len's office was a poster-perfect eighteenth-century building, manicured to the nines.

"Yeah, law's treated me well. How about you?"

"Can't complain." The whole town had seen him arrive in a FISH, Inc. jet the day before. "Is the video tech here? And the court reporter?" A court reporter was standard at a deposition; the video tech was a bit above.

Will Duane wanted to see the deposition. Something about his health required him to stay on his estate in Montana. Jason didn't understand it, but if the guy could look that good at age eighty-seven, he'd stay in Montana, too. He'd done the math on his boss: He started to lose control of Numenon in 1995. That was recorded. He was sixty-three then. It was 2019 now—twenty-four years made Will eighty-seven. He didn't look fifty.

"Boy, that video tech is the most compulsive guy I've met," Len said as they walked to the conference room where the deposition would take place. "He's got this place wired for everything but heartbeat."

"He may add that," Jason said, smiling.

"Seriously?"

"Yeah. It's Will. It's the way he is."

"He's really alive?"

"Definitely. I'll see him tomorrow with all the video and the deposition." Jason checked everything and sat at the conference table.

"Do you mind if I sit in?" Len asked.

"Not unless you're representing Matthew Thibeau."

"No. Definitely not."

"Okay. Are you billing?"

"Ah. No. Old buddy's favor."

Be still my beating heart, Jason thought when Thibeau walked in. Jason's heartrate (fortunately not visible in any way) cranked up, along with his breathing and body temperature.

Matthew Thibeau was a stone-cold hunk. About six foot two or three, built like Ironman, short-cropped hair, chiseled face—but manly. He had a small scar below his left eye and longer one down his cheek. They added to the guy's overall allure and impact. He had perfectly trimmed nails, perfectly groomed everything. He moved with the grace and power of an athlete. Command presence, Jason thought. This guy personified it. Matthew Thibeau was as military as he could get.

"Uh," Jason said coherently. This was the one disadvantage he could see to being gay, being blindsided like this. But Thibeau had the same impact on women.

"Well, why don't we get to work. I'm Jason Bridger, representing Caitlin Cummins in the matter of…" He rattled off the case number and some identifying facts about the case. "Let's swear you in…"

"Why do you think you own Opal? We'll refer to Grand Champion Opal's Elegant Masquerade Contessa as Opal."

"Because I do. My grandfather never signed the contract for Opal's sale. He was never compensated for it. I know—I'm his heir. $250,000 was supposed to be transferred into his account. It never was. I have all his financial records.

"I'm his heir, I own his house and everything in it. I have a copy of what was submitted to the AKC to change Opal's registered owner from my grandfather to the man who said he bought her. If you look at the copy of the papers submitted to the AKC to transfer her ownership, you'll see that the signature looks nothing like my grandfather's.

"I've got a copy of the document here. And I can supply dozens of examples of my grandfather's handwriting. I've brought ten."

Jason hadn't been able to get the original registration transfer from Michael Thibeau to the original new owner from the AKC. They'd have to subpoena it. That was time consuming, and Cait was a wreck over this thing, as was Will. Jason wanted to wrap it up.

"Let me see that." The old owner's signature on the registration transfer was clear, in large block letters, and different from the spidery handwriting in the many documents that Matthew laid out.

"My grandfather was old. He had cancer when he sold Opal. His handwriting had been shaky for years before that." He indicated the AKC document. "He didn't sign that. He didn't sell Opal, and he didn't get paid for her. He would never sell her—he wanted her for me. She was the best he'd ever bred, and he wanted me to have her."

Every time he looked at Thibeau, his heart jumped, but Jason mushed on. "Why did you wait all this time to bring this up? Opal is almost ten now. She was two when this paper was signed. Why wait eight years?"

Thibeau looked down and cleared his throat. "I haven't been back stateside for long. When my grandfather died, I was devastated. One of the richest men in this country said he owned my dog. I never saw the paperwork, but he had a platoon of fancy lawyers." Matthew jerked his head, indicating Jason and Len. "I had no way of fighting them. I was twenty-two. I'm an orphan. Grandpa was all I had. And Opal. They said they'd give me a job, but not as her trainer. I didn't have the name, and they didn't think I was good enough to 'get everything she's got' out of her. I did what any kid in my circumstances would do."

"You joined the Army."

"Marines. It ended up being a bit different than that. I can't say anything about what I did, except that it was overseas."

Everything that Thibeau said rang true—a saint singing at the gates of heaven wouldn't speak in more convincing syllables. He was telling the frigging truth. Jason began to sweat.

"Why did you wait until now to come forward?"

He snorted. "I've been busy." In a war, obvious, but unspoken. "I just got back and decided not to deploy again. I saw all the stuff about Opal and—*Cait*—online and on the TV. I finally knew where she was. I had no way of finding her before—either access to information channels or even a cell phone over here.

"I decided it was time to go for justice. Opal is mine, and she's never been anyone else's. I want her back."

Len's jaw rested on the table. Jason blustered, "Do you know what Cait and Will Duane—and *Opal*—have done to get her safe where she is? Do you know what the whole community has done?"

"Yes, I do. She's still my dog."

"You intend to go forward with this suit?"

"Yes, I do."

"You know that Will Duane wants to keep Cait and Opal together?"

"Yes."

"Do you know that he's probably *still* the richest man in the world? That he can pour all the assets in the universe against you?"

"Yes, I do. I've been in this situation before. When that guy *stole* Opal from me, I was a kid. I feared how rich he was and what he could do to me. I'm not a kid anymore. And I'm not scared. I'll fight with everything I've got. If I must sell my grandpa's farm, I will. If I end up on the streets to get my dog, I will."

"Damn it," said Will. "He's telling the truth, isn't he?" He and Jason were talking in Montana the next day after watching the video. "He's clear as a bell. We need to get a copy of that registration transfer from the AKC, as due diligence.

"But I believe him. What the hell are we going to do?"

32

SURPRISE!

"AREN'T YOU A *clever* girl!" the tall, thin woman petted Opal's head and then swooped down and grabbed a puppy. "No! Don't do that," Caitlin cried, trying to avert an incident. "Opal…"

"Don't worry about her, we're old friends." She weighed the pup in her hands and then held it up over her head. "Whee! You're flying."

Opal not only didn't react at a stranger picking her pup, she wiggled all over and grinned from one side of her face to the other.

"Oh, Opal, you had your secret, didn't you? You are such a naughty one, out there in the woods with everyone worrying about you and having the *fling* of a lifetime." She bent down to the dog, who flopped on her side and then showed her tummy. The older woman rubbed Opal's belly. "Do tell darling. Was your lover wonderful? To die for?" The woman stopped talking and became serious.

"Oh, I'm so sorry. He left you for his pack. I understand that would be dreadful, even if he did invite you to come with …"

Cait was mystified. "Are you talking to her?"

"Well, yes, it's skill I have. And Opal is intelligent," a knowing smile to the dog. "None of them know, do they?" Opal did her dog grin and wiggled, wagging her tall furiously.

The old lady laughed at Cait's mystified expression. "Well, I shouldn't keep you in the dark. These are not *dog* pups, they're *wolf* hybrids. Their father was a full-blooded wolf, the charismatic pack leader. These are going to be peerless animals, if dangerous and hard to tame. That's what you'll have to do, teach them, not train them.

"Oh, look. There's Will!" She waved heartily. "Over here, darling. I have a wonderful surprise." Will Duane walked across the lawn, heading toward Cait's cottage and the display of pups on the lawn.

"You're Will's wife," Cait said.

"Yes. You may call me Vanessa. I'm going to stay for a while. It's been too long."

"You're also the doctor who helped me when I had Benny."

"Yes. You picked a lovely name. My son is also named Benny."

"Oh. Are you the veterinarian who saved Opal?"

"Yes, I helped Opal. Brave creatures, the two of you."

"Are you a doctor?"

"Yes, certainly, though not a MD. I'm a theoretical physicist. So much more useful in healing than all that nonsense about disease."

"Oh."

"No, I'm not licensed to do what I did with either of you. Do you mind? Do you wish I hadn't?"

"No..." Cait felt dizzy. Will approached them cautiously.

"Here you are, darling!" Vanessa leapt toward Will and embraced him passionately, planting a kiss on each cheek. She was as tall as he was and similarly thin. "I've missed you so much! I can stay a whole month!"

"Barring fires?" Will looked as delighted to see her as she was him.

"I think the fires are tamed for now. I've just given Cait some fantastic news. I knew when I touched them when they were born, but I thought I'd wait until they'd grown a bit before announcing it.

"Opal's mate was a wolf! Full-blooded and very dominant. His DNA is superb. Those cubs will be winners in every way, if there was a hybrid poodle/wolf competition of any sort. Opal was devastated when he left her to go back to his pack, but she's a dog and needs human companionship. Although she hasn't shown that aspect of her character until recently."

"Are you sure they weren't sired by a local dog? Does that make a difference?"

"All the difference in the world. For one thing, we need to look up regulations applying to hybrid-wolf ownership in Montana. Do you need a permit to own one? Are they subject to a hunting season? Are they owned by some ridiculous government agency? Are they government property, or some nonsense?"

"On, no!" cried Cait. "No one owns them. No one can shoot them!"

"Not on this ranch, I'm sure. And fortunately, it's large, but if they got out…" Vanessa mused. "Training may be a problem, and they'll need training. They'll be huge, due to hybrid vigor you know. Crossbred animals tend to be larger, stronger, and tougher than their parents."

"Tougher than Opal?" Will whispered.

"Oh, yes. Some of my dogs are twice the size of their parents. They'll also be more intelligent and cannier. We'd better find a real pro to work with them…"

"I can do…" said Cait.

"I'm sure you could do better than anyone we know to train them, but they aren't dogs. They can already see that you can be manipulated…"

"What?!"

"Oh, yes. They talk about you, and the rest of the humans here…"

"That's ridiculous!" Cait was becoming annoyed with this know-it-all visitor. "How can you know what they 'say?'"

"I shouldn't have been so direct. I should have allowed them to teach you a thing or two, but we need to be prepared. Prepared for human reactions to them, too. Have you had them on your YouTube show? I know you've been taping from up here."

"Yes, I showed them to everyone."

"How did Opal take that?"

"She didn't like it at all. She moved them out of our house. Her daytime lair is in the forest now."

"She knows. And she loves those babies. These will be her last—that mountain lion destroyed her reproductive system. I've promised her that she can stay with her pups as long as she lives. You agree, don't you?"

"Yes. I'll stay with them, if I can live here. Can I Will?"

"I hoped you would want to, Cait. We'll have to figure out a way to manage your career from here, but the cottage is yours for as long as you want."

Cait, teared up. That's what she had wanted, a settled home for herself, her son, and her dogs. Wolf/dogs. Will just had given it to her. "I'll work. I'll do whatever you need around here."

Will laughed. "I just want to see you use that chainsaw, Cait. Your career is in broadcasting. We'll make it work."

"Let's go inside and have some tea," Vanessa suggested. "We need to discuss Matthew Thibeau and the AKC. And laws pertaining to keeping wolves."

They sat in the breakfast room of the great log mansion in a surprisingly cozy nook. Cait sat with little Benny on her lap. He looked around, big and startlingly alert.

"He seems to have hybrid vigor, too," said Vanessa.

"Yeah. Though his dad was very athletic, for a computer jock. What about the AKC?"

"Jason has seen Opal's original transfer certificate, transferring him away from Michael Thibeaux and to his new owner. It's the same as the copy Matthew told us about—the handwriting doesn't match Thibeaux's at all. The AKC people hemmed and hawed about it, but no one can controvert that big signature and Thibeaux's actual weak writing. Jason asked how the slip up could have happened. They said they were just getting computerized eight years ago—or their system went down, something. The bottom line is, they don't know how it happened. They handle millions of transfers a year.

"Matthew has a copy of the bill of sale, which isn't signed by his grandfather. He can show bank records that indicate his grandfather never received a large amount—or any amount—of money from the buyer."

"So, it was fraud, pure and simple. How about the buyer? Did Jason contact him?"

"He died a year after 'buying' Opal, and his kennel was disbanded."

"The rest of Opal's owners assumed they were buying a dog with a clear title. Everyone knew that second owner by reputation, and by his other dogs. Opal was the brightest star, but not the only one. No one would question her provenance; her owner was too prestigious."

"Why would he do that?" Will asked.

"Why would people attack Cait for doing innocent things? Evil, Will. It exists to tear people down. Maybe that rich dog owner saw a young man, Matthew, who appeared to be shining too brightly. Maybe he wanted to take him down a few pegs."

"This is hard to take in."

Cait bounced her baby on her knee. "I know one thing, no one's taking Opal and her pups away. I will do anything I have to do to keep them." She looked as though using her chainsaw was foremost in her thoughts. "No. one. will. ever. have. them."

"We agree on that. But we need to get Matthew to agree as well."

"How?"

"Oh, I think we should have him up here," Vanessa said, "and have a little visit. I'm sure we can tempt him with something."

"One thing I'd do is have them groomed like poodles," Will said. "That will keep people from figuring out what they are."

"Until they drag off someone's cow," Vanessa drawled.

33

MATTHEW, MEET CAIT. ALSO OPAL

MATTHEW KNEW EXACTLY what this Duane dude was trying to do. Make him feel like an inconsequential piece of crap. It was working. A big black car with a chauffeur picked him up at his grandfather's house. *His* house. He had to remember that. He was a property owner and had been for years. His rental agent had kept the place cleaned up and rented while he was overseas. Now he lived in his own house.

He'd been talking to that lawyer, Jason, by phone every day. He said that Will Duane wanted to have a talk—at his ranch.

"We'll pick you up at your place," Jason had said.

"I'll meet you in Great Barrington. Don't worry."

"I'm not worried, Matthew, except about why you're so secretive about where you live." And then he rattled off his address. Matthew's face flushed. He was glad Jason couldn't see it. "I drove by your place when I was back there. It's cute. Cait would have a ball with it."

"Why are you so surprised that I know where you live? Haven't you heard of background checks and Google?"

Matthew was shocked. The online world wasn't such a big deal when he left the States eight years before. Now anyone could know anything about him. No, not his previous life. He was under a cover so deep, nothing could penetrate it.

"Why do you need to know so much, Jason? I'm just a guy trying to get his dog back."

When he said that, Jason drew so deep a breath, Matthew knew he would never get Opal back. But he would try.

"Okay, you're going to Will Duane's ranch and meet Opal. We'll see if she remembers you. You'll talk to Will about what happens next. You'll meet Cait so you'll know Opal's owner and *mom* now. Then you'll come home."

He didn't have to spell out that Will Duane was one of the best negotiators on the planet and had made business history as far back as the 1950s. He must be ancient now, but still had his marbles. Matthew was able to get that much with his limited Google skills. It would be David against Goliath if he met Duane. No, an insect against a battleship.

"I'll get a ticket from Boston to…"

"No, this is Will Duane's party. We'll pick you up. You'll fly in a FISH, Inc. jet to Denver, deplane, and take one of Will's jets to his ranch."

"Where is it?"

"Nowhere, Matthew, unless you need to know, which you don't."

He'd felt like a termite since that conversation. He did what he always did—worked out, shaved, got a haircut, and stood tall. Fake it until you make it. He wished he could wear his uniform.

The car smelled of new leather. They went to Boston's private airport, where he boarded a corporate jet. The FISH, Inc. terminal swarmed with activity and those crazy-painted planes with the cartoon fish covering the whole side. They made Matthew smile, though, which was what they were supposed to do. "I'm FISH, Inc. You've never seen anything like me before. I'm business. I'm innovation. I'm fun."

He got on the plane, feeling weird about not going through security. Or maybe he had; maybe they were so sophisticated that he was screened and didn't know it. Private travel was a ton different from commercial. People lounged around in the cabin of the plane. There was room enough to do it. Some of the seats were row style, like a normal plane. Some were arranged in a circle, like to have a meeting or play poker, which a few of the passengers were doing. The plane looked about half full.

Matthew snooped around. The cockpit door was open, which made him nervous. He couldn't stop himself. "Federal regulations require this door to be closed and locked," he said to the pilot.

"While we're in the air. But, duly noted. What's your name?" He gave it to him, and the pilot wrote it down and smiled.

"Do you mind if I look around the plane?"

"Not if you do it in the next five minutes."

Matthew did a quick surveillance. A meeting room. A couple of bed chambers up the wall like they had in Japan. Everything looked in great shape. He looked around for a place to sit. That group of guys playing poker took up the center of the cabin, making a racket. They sounded a little high or buzzed. Matthew didn't like that, but as long as they weren't behind the wheel, he wouldn't complain.

He sat toward the rear, crossing his arms and pretending to sleep. He felt his heart race and breathed carefully. Long breath in, long breath out. It wouldn't happen. Not here. He had his meds with him, but breathing worked better. Long breaths, in and out. Let go of the thought. Let go of the sound. The explosion and thud of bodies. Blood. Bruno.

His eyes popped open, and he jumped. Someone had sat next to him.

"Whoa, compadre! I'm not the enemy!" The guy put his hands up, which was funny because Matthew didn't meet people taller than him very often. This man was, even seated. Nor had he seen anyone decked out like this guy in *any* setting. Yes, he wore a sport jacket and slacks, but they seemed more like a bearskin coat and buckskin leggings. If his beard had ever been trimmed, Matthew couldn't tell. His hair stuck out in fingers of dreadlocks, blond dreads; the guy was white, beneath his tan and what had to be *dirt.* He didn't fit in this world, at all.

"I'm Doug Saunders," he held out his grimy hand. "I don't get into town much, so I'm a bit rusty. Who are you and where are you going?"

"I'm Matthew Thibeau, and I don't know where I'm going."

"Hah!" The stranger guffawed. "I like a man who tells the truth. Where are we going? That is the big question, compadre. I've been working on that all my life."

"Have you gotten anywhere?" Matthew racked his brain, trying to remember who Doug Saunders was.

"Oh, yeah. I've gotten everywhere, which is where we're going."

That didn't make any sense at all, so Matthew nodded and pretended to go back to sleep. The poker players became more raucous. Doug got up.

"Hey, guys. You're on the train to riches and a better life."

"You better believe it!" Someone pulled out a flask and offered it to Doug.

"Oh, no, buddy. If you're going to work for Will Duane, or Willy Fish, or anyone in their universe, you better put that shit away. An' don't stick anything up your nose. Those are big no-nos in FISH Land."

"That can't be true. I know how the tech world is."

"But not how this tech world is. This is FISH. Put it away, boys, or you'll never make it to San Jose."

They looked him up and down, unkempt slob that he was.

"How do you know?" "Who are you?" "How can you tell us what to do?"

"I'm the hall monitor on this flight. I'd say my name is Doug Saunders, but it's really Captain Wonderful." *He* seemed more stoned the longer the conversation continued. Doug got up to go back to his seat by Matthew.

"Doug Saunders! You were big in Numenon in the 1990s! You were Will Duane's right hand!" one of the card players shouted at him.

"Yep, boys. And look what happened to me." He raised his hands. A smell of a wild animal spread in the cabin. A bear maybe. "Got to be my true self. You listen to what I said, now. You get one chance here, one only."

They were silent for a minute, but flasks came out, and the game continued.

Doug crossed his arms over his chest, dropped his head, and went to sleep, just like that. Matthew stared at him. Doug Saunders had been Will Duane's top honcho back in the days—the twenty years' worth of days—when Numenon, Inc. had been the biggest corporation in existence. Matthew remembered the old stories and headlines about him going crazy and bursting out in a federal court, attacking a judge. Disappearing forever. Except he was here. He was the *hall monitor* of the flight?

Matthew felt himself drifting asleep and then pulled into a place he didn't want to go. His friends' frantic voices. Explosions. Sounds that left his ears ringing, but incapable of hearing. Dust, bricks, timbers flying. He and Bruno couldn't walk side by side because so many little red flags indicating bombs were stuck in the ground. Crimson death alerts flapped in the breeze. Gunfire. Screaming. He was screaming. "Bruno. Oh, no. *Bruno*."

He awoke, panting. He loosened his tie. Shit. Doug Saunders was looking at him. His eyes didn't miss a thing. Sweat ran down his face, wetting his collar. It had happened again. It wasn't supposed to happen. He was supposed to be well. Fit to work. Fit to be discharged into the general population. He looked down. Blood on his hands. Bruno lay there, guts hanging out of his belly.

"Take a deep breath, buddy." Doug said in an almost inaudible voice. "You're okay. You made it. You're here. Your life is going to get a whole lot better very soon. Deep breath." Doug ran his hands over Matthew's head and shoulders. "I'd do a full healing, but I can't do it here. Will's wife will take care of you when you get there. She's almost as good a healer as Grandfather was."

Matthew felt dizzy. Something had happened to him, but he wasn't sure what. He felt in love with Doug. He wanted to cry.

"Let me get these yahoos off the bus, and I'll clean you up a little."

They landed in Denver.

"Okay, boys and... *boys* ... this trip. We don't have any women this run. We've reached the end of our time together. You, you, you. The four of you playing cards. The rest of you in the back... go out the front exit. Your plane will be leaving in five minutes." They left, chattering and oblivious. They would be going back to Boston, not that they knew it. They were "the bad pile."

"The rest of you," Matthew and three other guys, "will deplane with me. Matthew, come with me. You guys, a FISH representative will meet you at the terminal and direct you to your next flight. Congratulations, guys! Welcome to FISH, Inc. You passed muster."

"We made it?!"

"Yeah. Your training as a FISH employee began when you stepped onto this plane. You were smart enough to realize that if a guy stinking like a bear and looking like me tells you he's the hall monitor, he means it. I wasn't on the flight for fun. I wasn't asleep in the cabin. I can tell you every word every one of you said, and I know you'll be good additions to FISH, Inc.

"That's an honor. You should know what Willy Fish and Will Duane and the rest of us diehards are about with FISH. We're saving the world. We're remaking this planet into the paradise it should have been before greed and evil screwed it up. That's our mission, and it will be yours, if you stay with us. That and having fun. FISH is about fun. Say 'hi' to Silicon Valley when you get there."

Doug led Matthew through the private terminal to wherever his next plane departed. He got to a deserted alcove and pulled him over, embracing him like the daddy of all bears had him in a mortal grip. Matthew wanted to fight but couldn't; he was dumbstruck and immobilized. He felt something enter him from Doug, like a force from Doug's heart had flowed into his. Then he felt dizzy. Tears leapt to his eyes.

"See you later, buddy," Doug said. "Everything's going to be okay. You're with good people." Doug looked around. "I gotta get going back to my wife. She only lets me out for my wilderness jaunts occasionally." He stepped back from Matthew and took a sniff of his armpit. "Ripe. Better hit a shower before I go home." He waved as he walked away. "Sayonara, compadre. Remember: your life is about to begin."

Someone led Matthew down a corridor and onto a small jet. It was black, unmarked. He was the only passenger. The woozy feeling he'd had since Doug hugged him intensified, along with a pain in his chest. He wondered vaguely if he should tell the attendant, but he fell asleep before he could.

When he awoke, they were landing. He had no idea where he was. He'd missed the majestic Montana scenery and the wildness of Will's ranch from the air. He saw a landing strip, a big one, jet sized, ringed by trees. Pines?

He grabbed his bag and walked down the jet's ramp, nodding at the attendant and pilots. Noting through his fuzziness that a private jet, two pilots, and a stewardess was a lot to get one person to an unknown location in the woods.

A white-haired guy in jeans stood next to an SUV. Matthew thought he was a driver until he recognized that face. He wasn't too young to forget Numenon and its historical management fight back in the '90s. He mostly read about it in old news magazines, but his grandfather said it was the battle of the century.

That was Will Duane, one-time richest man in the world. Still one of the most handsome.

"Hi, I'm Will Duane," the guy confirmed, stepping forward to take his hand. "I assumed you would want to see Opal, so I'll take you to her. You'll be staying with my neighbor Billy Jack Abercrombie. I'll have a chopper take you there after you visit with Opal."

They drove a ways. He could see a magnificent and gigantic log house in the distance. They drove up to a little log cottage that reminded him of his house in Great Barrington, except his wasn't logs.

"Cait and Opal are just inside the woods. We built a little corral for the pups in the shade. They're getting so big; they needed some room. But we bring them in at night. The forest is wild and alive at night."

As they disembarked, a golf cart drove up. It must have been modified; Matthew had never seen a cart go that fast.

"Cheerio, everyone!" A tall, five pounds short of gaunt, middle-aged woman climbed out. She wore a long, black dress trimmed with black braid and tucks. Matthew did a double take. She looked like a witch, not that he would say it.

Will didn't seem to be the slightest bit perturbed. "Good to see you, darling." He pecked her cheek. "Matthew, this is my wife Vanessa."

"I had to be here for the reunion. What has it been, Matthew? Eight years? Let's see what Opal remembers, having run wild for nine months, surviving an historic fire, and having a love affair with a wolf!" Her smile was so gleeful as to unsettle him as much as Doug's hug had.

He saw a movement inside the forest and recognized the dog's outline.

Matthew stood away from the others, put his fingers to his mouth, and delivered a shrieking whistle.

Opal put herself between the newcomer and her pups, growling.

"It's okay, Opal," Cait said. "We're safe. Will and Vanessa won't let anything happen to us."

Opal heard the whistle, froze, threw her head up, and then jumped the puppy enclosure's fence, running straight for Matthew. Her ears flopped, legs scissored, and her tongue lolled. She ran for Matthew like he was the king of Dog Heaven. Two strides from him, she leapt into the air, throwing herself against him with her front legs around his neck and back legs grasping his waist. She grabbed him like a little kid would its long-lost dad and buried her long nose into his neck. She whimpered like a child taking refuge in the arms of a lost parent.

Matthew hugged her back just as hard. "Oh, baby, I've missed you."

"I think it's safe to say Opal knows him," Vanessa said in her dry voice.

"Yes, definitely," Will responded.

34

LOVESONG

CAIT SAW WHAT happened and froze. Her face went white and rigid. As the hug went on, she crumpled, becoming even tinier than her five-foot-two frame. She spun and headed for her cottage, anything to get away.

Matthew and Opal embraced for a while, then Opal wiggled, wanting to get down. She barked, taking Matthew's fingers and pulling him toward her pups and Cait. She tugged insistently.

Cait didn't see the dog trying to lead Matthew to her. Her back was turned as she fled the sight of their loving reunion. Before reaching the cabin's front door, Cait stopped and spun again, her eyes narrowing. Her mouth compressed, and she shot forward, running at Matthew the way Opal had, but with a different intention.

"If you try to take my dog, I will *kill you.*" She stood in front of Matthew, quaking with rage. She pointed at him as though brandishing a sword. "Try to take that dog, and you are *dead.*"

Will and Vanessa jumped forward. "He won't take Opal, don't worry."

Cait shot a furious look at them, took a breath, and fainted, falling like rough-sawn timber.

All of them leapt to help her.

Cait felt herself falling, but rather than a jolting landing, something soft enveloped her. Something soft and loving conferred a sense that everything was all right, had always been all right, and would continue that way. She was in heaven. The hands holding her gave everything and promised everything. Pleasure surged through her body, pulsating as an opalescent cloud suffused her and everything around her.

She opened her eyes. That *Matthew* crouched over her, holding her in his arms. She struggled to get away, but he held her tight. "What are you doing! Get your hands off me! What did you do? Push me down and do *that* to me? What kind of creep are you?"

"I didn't do anything. You fainted, and I caught you. You could have been hurt. I don't know what *that* was." He looked nonplussed and held out his hands as though they were radioactive.

"Right, bozo, trying to butter me up so you can steal my dog! Thief! Thief!"

"She's *my* dog, not yours. She always has been legally…"

"Liar!" She was on her feet, flaming out of control. "You lured me here so you could steal my dog."

"What?! That doesn't make sense. You were already here, I came to…"

"To steal! And you knocked me down.…"

"You fainted." He swung his arm toward Vanessa and Will. "They saw it. Tell her. I just caught you."

Cait was in the same state she'd been in when she slugged the police officer—enraged and out of control.

"Yes, dear," said Vanessa. "You fainted." She paused. "Oh, dear… You aren't … "

"Pregnant? You think I'm *pregnant,* and I *fainted* because of it? Not a hot chance in Hades I'm pregnant! How can you…"

"You're very unstable, you know," Matthew said. "You aren't making sense at all."

"*What*!?" That was the nuclear trigger. "*I'm* unstable. You come in here and steal my dog. She *ran* to *you*..."

"And then ran back to you..."

"She ran to you, and I..."

"Fainted. I grabbed you to keep you from getting hurt when you landed."

"Right! That's what they all say." Why did her arms throb where he'd touched her? She swore she could hear angels' voices in her ears, singing so beautifully. And her body vibrated with pleasure. "Why did you come here and *do that?*"

Before anyone could answer, Opal made the most chilling sound they'd heard a dog make. A combination of a howl and a shriek, it was a cry of agony. She stood, looking from Cait to Matthew as they argued. Her two pack leaders were snarling at each other, destroying her world. Their fighting filled her with pain and terror.

"No, Opal, it's okay. We're okay," Matthew held his arms out to the dog, but it was too late. She ran, making a wide circle on the lawn with her amazing speed. She threw herself down and bit her legs and sides, unable to cope with what was happening.

"Opal, no!" Matthew ran to her and wrapped his arms around her, preventing her from savaging herself. "No, sweetheart. We won't fight anymore." He looked at Cait and the others. "She did that when my grandfather died, and when they kicked me out of the kennel."

Cait was right behind him. "She did that because we were *fighting*. Oh, no, I'm sorry, Opal. I was being an idiot. I thought he was going to take you away. We won't fight anymore."

Her eyes widened, as though she had cracked one of the secrets of the universe. "Thad and I fought all the time. We had screaming fights right in front of the dogs. As though they couldn't tell what was going on. In front of *Opal!*

"Oh. I'm a terrible person. I fought with Thad. I hurt him. Oh,

Opal! I'm so sorry to subject you to that. We just had such a bad year the last year. But when we went away the night before the fire, we made up. Really, we decided to cut back, but keep the kennel going. We figured out how to do it. And we realized we loved each other more than anything.

"Oh, my God. I bet you wanted to bite yourself when we fought in front of you. You didn't because you were too frozen then. I'm so sorry, Opal." She looked around, a hysterical glance, and ran toward the puppy pen, past it and into the forest.

"Oh, my heavens!" Vanessa gasped. "Things are quite out of control. I'll go to her, Will. You take care of Matthew and the baby." She handed the infant to Will.

Vanessa followed Cait, reminding Matthew of a praying mantis at full gallop. Opal followed her.

"What just happened?" Matthew said.

"Hard to say, Matthew. It's part of our culture." He was referring to what transpired when Matthew grabbed Cait. He saw it, Vanessa saw it, and they felt it—the heavenly release of divine energy that came when soul mates touched for the first time. It swirled around them, making Will and Vanessa intoxicated and ecstatic. What it must have done to the couple was surely much more intense.

Matthew responded from a different angle. "Screaming at people and calling them liars and thieves is part of your culture?"

"No, not that part. Cait has a real temper. She thought you were… being inappropriate. She always fights back. You need to watch some of her YouTube videos where she's got a chainsaw, to see. Well, you need to hear her commentary with it, too. She's usually funny."

"Funny? She's a raving maniac."

"Maybe in this case, but not usually." An older woman drove up in another cart. Will said, "Oh, hello, Mrs. Naughton. Did Vanessa call you?"

"Yes, she said that baby was all but forgotten in the ruckus here. You needed my help."

"Thank you. She was right. Here." He handed over the baby, his shoulders dropping as the weight went off them. "Poor kid was getting forgotten."

Then he turned to Matthew. "Do you want to go to the main house? Vanessa and Cait need some time. You want a beer?"

"No. I don't drink."

"Me neither. Well, how about some coffee or a smoothie? I'm good at those."

They rode to the big house in Will's SUV. He made a call while they were driving. "You're off the hook, Billy Jack. He's going to stay at my place. Kind of an emergency. Yeah, and would you call Reverend Bruce? Tell him it's another one."

They arrived in the main hall. Will talked while Matthew gawked. "My neighbor usually hosts guests that aren't close to me, but I think we'll be close by the end of tonight. Things usually speed up about now."

That was as close as Will could get to explaining the way things went with the spirit warriors. When they touched their soul mates, a countdown was initiated. Meaning how long they could last in the torrent of physical, sensual, sexual attraction that would continue to arise between them until their love was consummated—which would happen after they married.

He and Vanessa kept the same rules that Grandfather had: You had to be legally married before you hit the hay. A sensible rule, Will thought, given the consequences of the many unmarried, and married, transgressions *he* had perpetrated in his younger days.

He wasn't about to tell the staggeringly straight-arrow, gorgeous Matthew all that. He looked like he stepped out of a Marines recruiting poster. Probably thought spirituality had to do with séances, which it did, sometimes. Vanessa could brew up a hell of a séance.

But that wasn't the point. True love was the point, and what would happen when a soul met its perfect match. It was about perfection in human relationships and human being. About love beyond infinity…

How could he tell a guy who came to the ranch after being bilked of all his wealth, spending years in the most dangerous of active military duty, and who was just trying to get his dog back what he had walked into? He couldn't. No one could explain this place, not even those who lived there. It was an anomaly, a crack in the rules of existence. Miracles not only were possible on the mountain, you had to beat them off.

They went into the gigantic kitchen with its miles of rare granite countertops and sat at a breakfast bar. Matthew had unbuttoned his sleeves and was looking at his forearms like they belonged to someone else. They were reddened. Blisters were coming out. "What is this?"

"Do they hurt?"

"No. The opposite. They feel good. What is this? What's going on?"

Will stalled, then started talking, motor-mouth fashion. "It's actually a very deep, esoteric Native American experience—though I've learned that cultures all over the world have similar experiences and traditions. It's just that I first learned of it from a powerful Native Medicine man named Grandfather. His American name was Joseph Bishop… Turns out that Vanessa knew him, too. He was a divinity student in Berkeley when she was there getting her PhD in nuclear physics."

Will jabbered as he sliced mangoes. He had already cut up a pineapple for their smoothies. He sliced and talked compulsively. "So that's the origin of it, a Native spiritual experience which only the bravest and purest spirit warriors can have. And do have, when they meet their soul mates. It's simple, you see."

Matthew looked at him, face screwed up in a mask of disbelief. "That *thing* that happened when I grabbed Cait is something that happens to ancient Native American spirit warriors?"

"Yes."

"I'm not a spirit warrior…"

"Like hell you aren't. What were you doing in Iraq and Afghanistan all those years?"

"You're not supposed to know about it. It's classified."

"I've got a top-secret security clearance. I know exactly what you did and why they really let you go."

Matthew's cheeks flamed, and he jumped to his feet.

"Sit. I know all about PTSD, personally and from half the people that come through this place. You don't get to play in my world unless you're a little whacked. You met Doug Saunders."

Matthew had. He thought Doug was crazy, and the most empathetic human being he'd met. He didn't understand what happened when Doug hugged him, but he knew he was better for it. "Doug said you and Vanessa would be able to help me."

"Oh, yeah. Vanessa's the real expert; she healed me. That's when I finally realized she was my soul mate. We'd known each other forty years! Crazy. But that's how spirit is. It picks the time and place you wake up; the people involved have no say.

"You and Cait are soul mates. You might as well face it. You're meant to be together. She can heal you better than anyone on the planet. You should marry her."

"What!? I came here to get my dog. I didn't come to be the *soul mate* of a crazy, raving lunatic with temper like a …wild animal."

"You didn't? You didn't watch Cait's videos when you found out who had your dog…"

"*My* dog. You said it."

"Yeah, your dog, and Cait's dog. Opal's not a *thing* like a sack of flour. She's a living creature with a soul and an identity. Losing either of you will tear that dog apart. You saw that. Not to mention the puppies. Eight gigantic puppies. That wolf she mated with must have been a monster."

"Wolf?"

"Oh, yeah. Those are half-wolf pups. Beautiful. They belong to

Opal. I would never ask her to give them up. They'll need a big yard when they're grown, too. Like my backyard: 450,000 acres of mostly wilderness. No one will shoot them or trap them. I have security you wouldn't believe."

Matthew's eyes narrowed. "Do you know the state and federal statutes that apply to owning hybrid wolves?"

"No idea."

"I know some of them. Some states restrict ownership of part-wolves, some require permits. Some let hunters shoot them on sight. They're damn good dogs, I know that." Bruno's beautiful form flashed before him. Heavy dark coat, powerful body. The eyes of an old soul. A nose for scent work like no other animal.

Matthew felt his world shake as the image came back. Bruno. So brave. They were together for five years. His dog saved thousands of lives with his ability to detect explosives. Bruno was a legend and remained a legend in death.

Matthew clutched his chest. "Oh." The images came back, more real than the fancy kitchen around him. They were in a trap, a ruined village that looked like it might hold survivors. There was a half wall in the rubble. He couldn't see behind it, but Bruno knew. He moved in front of Matthew and charged around the wall. The bad guy nailed Bruno, but not him.

Eyes clenched tight, jaw even tighter, Matthew tried to fight back the tears.

"They killed Bruno." He choked and tumbled off the barstool.

"It's okay, son. I've got you." Will bent over him, placing one hand on Matthew's heart, the other on his forehead. "I've done this before."

When Vanessa and Cait came in, Matthew was out cold on the floor with a blanket over him. Will was drinking his smoothie, looking satisfied.

"I did okay, Vanessa. I think I really helped him. You may have to clean up the edges, but he should be a lot more comfortable." Will turned to Cait. "He told me a lot. Matthew was the head of a unit of men and dogs that sniffed out explosives in Iraq and Afghanistan. He did that for six years, in severe combat situations. He lost three dogs in the first year, and he partnered with Bruno for his last five years. The dog was a part wolf/part German Shepherd. When he lost Bruno, it broke him. They furloughed him to get treatment, but it didn't work. He's on a medical discharge for PTSD.

"I asked him why he kept redeploying all those years. He said because of Bruno—he was government property, not his. The service wouldn't allow him to be adopted and put back into the general population; he was considered dangerous. Matthew said he wasn't as long as *he* was there. But they wouldn't let him go. He had nothing but the dog—well, his grandfather's farm, but no people.

"He said to me," Will's eyes misted, "that he kept reenlisting so Bruno wouldn't be alone. He figured one day, they'd step on a mine Bruno missed, and it would be over for both of them. They'd be free."

"Oh, no!" Vanessa cried.

"Yeah. Brutal. When Bruno died saving him, Matthew flipped out. They discharged him.

"This trip was his last hope, He wanted to find Opal because she's the only thing on this earth that he loved. He thought he could save her, and himself. And make up for what happened to him as a young man. The dog was stolen from him by a billionaire 'dog lover.'"

Cait looked stricken. "That's so sad. He's not a bad guy."

"Not a bad guy at all. And, yeah. It's sad. He's a hero. I'll go over his military record with you, when he gives permission. He's the real deal."

She looked at Matthew lying on the floor with his eyes closed, then at Will. "I was really out of line yesterday, Will. Crazy. I thought if Opal liked him better and went with him, I'd die. I have the baby, but I don't have any grown up partner, either. I couldn't see that she loves us both."

"We don't have to get into that now. We can discuss it tomorrow. Now I think we should try to get some rest. You can sleep here tonight."

Cait's eyes bulged. "Benny! I've forgotten about my baby."

"Don't worry dear, *I* didn't," Vanessa said. "I brought a friend from home, Marjory Naughton. He's been well cared for during the recent... *drama*. They're at your cottage."

Cait rubbed her back and side where Matthew had touched her.

"What's the matter, dear?" Vanessa asked, her eyebrows raised, and mouth pursed.

"I just feel so weird since Matthew grabbed me. Kind of..."

"Happy?"

"Ecstatic?"

"In love ..."

"Yeah. I guess." But underneath the surface, something dark was stirring.

35

GRIEVING

CAIT STOOD CHEST deep in the freezing gray ocean. The waves were a light chop, not enough to throw her off her feet, but they kept rising. A ferocious storm whipped the wind and made lace-like streamers of foam that danced off the saltwater.

"Thad," she called into darkness. "Thad, come back. I'm *here*. *Thad…*" Her shouts increased in intensity and desperation. *"THAD! I'M HERE! COME BACK!"* He was gone, disappeared. She waded farther out into the sea, waves jostling her as she stood on tiptoes. "THAD! IT'S GOING TO BE OKAY! WE WORKED IT OUT, REMEMBER? REMEMBER LAST NIGHT?"

The wind howled and rain pelted her, stinging; it was almost like being flogged. "Thad. I won't be a bitch anymore. I promise. I'm changed. I'm different. I'm *sorry* I was so rotten.

"I'm sorry. I've learned. I can handle my feelings. I've learned how to talk about what I feel… OH, THAD, PLEASE COME BACK…"

She heard Benny howl from the shore. "We have a *baby*, Thad. He's beautiful. He looks just like you. He's perfect. He learns stuff every day…"

She was screaming. The water overwhelmed her. She clawed to

keep her head above the sea that was claiming her. Sucking her under. She was all but gone.

"*THAD,*" she screamed, one last cry. A bleak watery world took her, pushing her into its depths, tossing her. Water entered her mouth, filled her lungs…

"Cait! Caitlin! Wake up, darling. I could hear you screaming in the big house. Wake up, you're dreaming." Vanessa was there, holding Benjamin, who looked around, solemn and wide-eyed.

Cait clawed her way out of the nightmare, just as she had fought her way out of the devouring surf.

"It was so real," Cait told Vanessa about the dream. "It was awful. Oh, I feel so bad. I was so mean to him." She looked around the room, lost and bereft. "I miss him. He was such a nice person, and I was such a bitch.

"Do you know what the fire captain told me?" Vanessa shook her head. "He said that Thad didn't suffer. A burning branch from a giant falling tree went through the van's roof and into Thad's head. He died instantly, as did the dogs when the tree smashed the van and burned them up.

"If that isn't suffering, tell me what is? My husband was killed by a branch piercing his skull! And our dogs died when that monster tree smashed them, before burning them to ashes. How bad can it get?

"I mean, I guess Thad could have been lit on fire, and run down the street screaming in agony…

"Oh! I can't stand this. I don't know what I'm going to do. I don't want to be everyone's cute dolly, cutting stuff up with a chainsaw and making benches out of old beds. What am I supposed to do, Vanessa? I'm depending on your charity, and Will's. I need to stand on my own feet."

"Oh, darling. One thing at a time. You need to get over Thad before you plan your life. Have you grieved like you did in that dream before?"

"No. I cried. I sobbed, but never like my soul had been ripped apart." Tears came again, and Vanessa balanced the baby on her long thighs while petting Cait's back.

"You need to do a lot more of that, Cait, before you pick up your chainsaw or anything else. I happen to think you're talented and have future in entertainment. Not as a dolly, as a funny, wise woman who can help others, especially women.

"But that's later. Now, we must get through the night. Would you like me to stay with you?"

Cait's blue eyes were huge and solemn. She nodded and said, "Yes," in a tiny voice.

Vanessa put the slumbering Benny in his crib and curled her bony body around Cait's.

"Sleep, little angel, tomorrow is another day." She smiled when Cait's breathing became long and regular. *You may be surprised, little one, what sleeping with a witch with my powers does for your soul. Tomorrow will be a* different *day.*

36

A VERY DIFFERENT DAY

ANESSA AWAKENED BEFORE Cait, with the sun barely risen. She dressed quickly in her black walking dress and boots. She had plans for the day that she didn't want to share. Looking back, she saw the pale, beautiful Cait sleeping like a child angel. Beyond her, a very awake baby Benjamin stared at her with his bright-blue eyes. He didn't miss a thing.

"Benjamin, I need to work with the pups," she whispered. "And your mother needs to sleep. I'm going to call a dear friend to stay with you. Let your mother sleep as long as she can." She jotted a quick note and left it by the bed for Cait, then walked out the front door to the screened porch where Opal and her pups waited.

"Good morning, Opal. I trust you and your brood had a good night." They moved the mother and pups into the screened porch every evening. Their outdoor enclosure was at the edge of the forest. Wild things of all persuasions lived in the shadows and came out at night.

Opal stood quickly and cast a wary eye at Vanessa before bursting into wiggles as she recognized the tall woman. The pups just wiggled.

"I see you're ready for a new day." Vanessa addressed the dog and pups as though they were human. "Opal, would you like to come on an adventure with me today? You and your babies?" Opal's whole body wagged. "I thought so."

She turned to the door of the porch. "Oh, Marjory, I'm so glad to see you. I didn't see you last night, but I'm glad you were here."

The erect, rounded form of Marjory Naughton stood before her. Mrs. Naughton was Vanessa's chief housekeeper and confidant from her estate in the mountains of the San Francisco Peninsula. "I came as soon as I could. Things sounded in such a muddle."

"Indeed, a muddle. But sortable. A couple of witches should make short work of it." She reconsidered. "A trio of witches. Will is coming along nicely. I need you to stay with Caitlin and her baby. Benjamin is fine. His mother is healing from her husband's death and the loss of their farm. She's still grieving. Poor thing." She brought Marjory up to date on what was going on.

"Oh, dear. I hoped you and Will would have some peace and quiet on this trip. Some time together, a little romance…"

"Plenty of time for peace and quiet and romance when we're dead, my dear. Now, I want to take these puppies," which wiggled around the feet of the two women, "on an adventure. Time to get them out of the shallows and into the woods." She grinned at Marjory's reaction to the pups.

"Oh, my God, Vanessa. They're wolves!"

"Half wolves, and half Grand Champion poodle. The *best* Doodles—the *Woodle*. Won't those uptight old farts freak out at that!"

They laughed, only cackling a tiny bit.

"Now, little ones…" Vanessa took Opal and the pups outside the pen and addressed the little ones formally, "It's time for a new order. *Your* order as grown members of the community. Find your pack ranking, and form rank." The pups lined up from most dominant to least. With one exception. Even as a pup, her body radiated composure and power.

"Ah. There she is," Vanessa remarked. One pup stayed away, not because she didn't understand; the rules of the pack didn't apply to her. She didn't feel like obeying, either. "You're the outlier, aren't you? Like your mother. You don't conform. You think for yourself. And when you're complete, you'll be a perfect work of nature. A miracle."

Chills flashed through Vanessa as she led the dog and pups into the forest. She didn't need to say that *she* was the alpha. Even the insects buzzing in the woods knew that.

"What you are going to do today is learn who you really are. Your mother and I already know—we are hunters. Carnivores, predators. The only time you'll be happy is when you are being who and what you are. You can be tame and mannerly indoors as the situation calls for, but you will need to revert to your identity or perish. Let's go."

Vanessa raised her face to the motes of light permeating the tall evergreens and howled, the sound coming from deep within her and reverberating as it moved outward. The pups and Opal jumped, then joined her howl, bonding with each other as the sound filled the forest. The column moved around a bend and disappeared.

"*Who* are you?" Cait awoke feeling shaky, only to discover a peculiar, but maternal, woman holding her baby next to her bed.

"I'm Marjory Naughton. I'm Vanessa's chief housekeeper from her Woodside home—I run the domestic side of the estate while Vanessa handles business and her physics experiments. She called me to help last night. She said things were in a muddle. I took care of Benjamin for a bit."

Cait drew a long breath. "That's right." Her dream of the night before glimmered in her mind, followed by the sting of tears. "*Now, give me my baby.*" She held out her arms, fierce and protective even if half awake and grieving.

"Of course. I've raised many a child, ye… *you* … should know. I have a good hand with them." Which was obvious: Benjamin went to his mother but held his arms out to Marjory.

Cait's eyes narrowed. "He's *my* baby."

"Of course. Vanessa just wanted ye to have some rest and help while she worked with the pups."

"What!? Those are my pups…"

"Oh, I think you're cutting them a bit short. Those are miracles. They could change the world."

"*You* could see that? I knew that from the beginning."

"Of course. So could everyone who watched them being saved on the tellie. Half the world knows they're special. They should be dead, killed in their mother's belly by that cat. Killed by the fire before they existed. But they're not."

"They're here. And *I'm* here. But why?" Cait's brows pulled together as the intensity of the question took her. "That's what I can't figure out. *Why* am I here? *Why* didn't *I* die with Thad?"

"Ah, there's the heart of it. Why are you here, in this place? Vanessa said you were a smart one. Why didn't you die with your husband?"

"I took a sleeping pill that morning, or I would have gone with him. Or talked him out of going. But I wouldn't have been able to do that, I know… We both would have gone for the dogs, and we both would have died." She felt stricken, crumpling. Trembling, she let Marjory take her baby.

"That's why Vanessa called me, to let you have time to discover what you need. You took a sleeping pill, but that isn't the reason you're here. Many things have happened to you since the fire. Since your husband died. You could have ended up anywhere, but you ended up here, on the top of the world."

"What do you mean?"

"Look at this place. Look around you…"

Cait looked out the windows. "It's heaven."

"Yes. And more than that. It's a place of miracles. Do you know how old Will is?"

"He has to be in his nineties…"

"Yes. And what about the others around him that look so young?"

She thought of Jon Walker, who had to be in his seventies but looked forty. "Jon? That's not all plastic surgery because he's on TV?"

Marjory smiled. "You've landed in heaven, and you've been through hell. That's the characteristic of people who end up on the mountain. This mountain, and the heights anywhere. There are more people here, and stories here, to explore and learn from. You will meet many of them, if you choose to stay. If the mountain accepts you, and you accept who you really are, you'll be invited to stay. The invitation may not come from a person; it may come from the mountain speaking to your soul.

"Will and Vanessa are soul mates. It took them—*him*—a long time to learn that. But now they're a team and finally able to begin their lives' mission. They're very wealthy, more than anyone knows. You can research who's the richest person on earth and never see their names on charts and magazine articles. Do you know what their mission is?"

Cait shook her head, chills running over her. Her teeth chattered.

"They want to save the world. Person by person, country by country. They want to make a planet where love is king." Marjory chuckled. "Long ago, there was an old Native American holy man, a dear, saintly person. Will and Vanessa knew him. He spoke of a world where love is king. A world where goodness, kindness, generosity, and healing expressed through everyone. He lit a flame. Everyone who met him felt it.

"Vanessa and I have our own traditions, but they melded with Grandfather's. We've become a people, Grandfather's people, our people, the people dedicated to love and understanding. And righteousness. "

Cait stared at her. "Oh."

Marjory chuckled. "I expect that Vanessa called me here to tell you that. She doesn't like to impart the sermon, ye know." She dandled the baby before her. "This one is already famous, comin' into the world the way he did. On the tellie. Also famous for what's in his pants right now. Can I change him? Then we can go to the big house for breakfast."

"Yes. I'll get dressed."

"Good, you'll want to be dressed, as Will has that good-lookin' man with the scar up there."

"Oh, shit! What's his name?"

"Matthew."

"Matthew. Shit."

37

WORLD PEACE

MATTHEW AWAKENED IN a strange room. He didn't recall where he was or how he'd gotten there. His arms, chest, and belly grabbed his attention. He pulled up his T-shirt and looked at himself. His appendages and torso were bright red, as though he'd gotten a sunburn beyond anything he got in the Middle East. He looked fried. It didn't hurt; it screamed.

"Cait! Cait! Cait!" His belly and forearms shrieked. He wanted her. Matthew was a self-controlled guy. He didn't lust after women, or anything. Control was his middle name. Also his first and last name. The Marines hadn't been disciplined enough for him. *This* was impossible.

Matthew got up and splashed water on his face and the flaming rest of him. What was he going to do? He didn't even like Cait. She was a shrill, vicious shrew who threatened to kill him repeatedly. Will had said she was just upset.

He was about that upset himself. What he felt for her was insane. He walked out of his room into a magnificent corridor in a log house. Each of the logs was two feet across. The ceiling of the corridor was spanned by bigger log beams. Paintings of Indians and cowboys hung at tasteful intervals. He'd seen all of them in books and museums. He didn't care.

Half-running along a fancy rug in the hallway, he turned left into a huge room. A kitchen. That was about all he could process. Matthew wanted to scream, "Cait? Where are you? Let's get married."

But that was stupid. He didn't like her, and strongly felt that people who'd hated each other on sight should not get married after knowing each other just a few hours. Especially since her death threats had been the major topic of their conversation.

"Oh, there you are. I was about see if you were okay." A man with white hair. Will Duane. This was his house.

"I'm okay. Where's Cait?"

"She's in her cabin with Vanessa and Mrs. Naughton. Why?"

"Because I'm insane." He held out his forearms to Will. "Look at this? What is this? I haven't been in the sun." In addition to the redness, his skin was pocked with juicy pustules like poison oak.

Will smirked. "Does your belly look like that, too?" Matthew nodded. "Every place you touched Cait. I was afraid of that. I'm not as good at healing as Vanessa. Mine didn't last. I'll have to try again. You won't be able to see Cait for a while."

"Why?" He couldn't keep the belligerent tone from his voice.

"Because she's still mourning her husband. He died in the Camp Fire. I thought you knew. She's in seclusion."

"Yeah, I heard." Everyone heard, but this kink in his plans, stupid though they were. "How long do you think she'll need to grieve?"

"I don't know. It took me years for my first two wives. I don't know if I could get over losing Vanessa, if I lost her."

"Oh." Shit.

"Lie down on the couch, and I'll see if I can back off what you're feeling."

Matthew did, and Will put one hand on his belly and the other on his forehead. Matthew immediately blacked out. Or something. He saw an old Indian, sitting cross legged and holding a peace pipe. He seemed real, realer than anything around him. Will Duane disappeared from his mind.

The old Indian waved the peace pipe in a circle, while taking a puff occasionally. He sang in a foreign language, which had to be *his* language, Matthew realized.

"My son," the old man said, "this must be very confusing to you. You've entered a realm different from the world you know. This is a world of spirit, a world of the soul. I'm certain you belong here, but you didn't receive any of the early training and education my people get. Don't worry, Will Duane was the same way, and look at how well he turned out."

Even semi-conscious, Matthew didn't get that. Will was already the richest man in the world when he met Grandfather, who he recognized as the old Indian he was communicating with. Back on their plane ride, Doug Saunders had reminded him that Will lost control of his giant corporation and half his wealth after he went on retreat with this old Medicine man. How was that turning out well, other than looking fiftyish when he was ninety? *That* was good.

"Oh, my son, Will was the most miserable man on earth. He had money, but nothing else. Now he has true love, spiritual power, a home, and more money than ever. Plus, lots of friends and *visions.* Most men would kill to have Will's visions. Most of them involve new ways of making money. The rest are just ecstatic, wild, full-color *trips,* like with mushrooms, but without the mushrooms. He experiences the Great One directly."

This conversation was getting weird to Matthew, even at the low level of awareness where he floated. Strange and trippy. The old man seemed stoned. Matthew had refrained from indulging in the types of psychoactive substances available in the Middle East, but he'd seen them used. This old Indian dude was farther out than... Matthew felt like giggling. Guffawing. Rolling on the ground hysterically laughing. This was so funny.

He came to this place to get his dog or die. He had been threatened by a beautiful woman maniac with a chainsaw. He found the richest man in the world in an enchanted mountaintop kingdom. Matthew was sure this was where he was. Will's wife was a witch, Matthew knew that. But it was funny. Everything was funny.

Balloons and iridescent bubbles carried him aloft. The old man acted like an anchor.

"The best thing would be for you and Caitlin to get married immediately, but her husband's unfortunate death makes that impossible. She's not interested in a new life or romance." The old guy peered at Matthew. "Though I can see *you* are interested in both. Well, you must wait. Do what Will Duane says in the meantime. He's your teacher.

"You will make an outstanding spirit warrior. Look at Will Duane. He was a mess when he came to me. Worse than you. The Great Spirit should find you in, oh, two or three hours. Then you'll know what I'm talking about." The old man faded.

"Come back," Matthew called. He felt so good around the old man, even as he floated before him in his mind's eye, peace pipe and buckskin clothes taking on various psychedelic colors randomly. Matthew wanted to laugh. He did laugh.

"Once you've found me, I'm hard to get rid of. You will be a great spirit warrior."

"But I don't believe in God, or spirit, or anything. I have flashbacks of people and dogs being blown up. I can't sleep. I don't have any friends, or a job. I don't believe in anything."

"Wonderful! Those are great credentials for a spirit warrior. When the Great One finds you, you will think you are going crazy. You're not—you are going sane. Now, go with Will all day and do what he says. Tell him the truth.

"Goodbye, my son. Dog Warrior. That is your name."

Poof. The guy was gone, and he was lying there with Will's hand on his belly and forehead.

"That went well," Will said. "Usually I get one of the minor warriors, not Grandfather himself. How do you feel?"

"Uh." Stoned off my ass. He was supposed to tell Will the truth. "Stoned off my ass."

"Wow! I've never gotten that before. The people I heal usually just feel better, and happy. Stoned is advanced. I must be improving. Well, let's get some breakfast and head out. I have a full day planned."

Will turned around and said, "Cook, you can come in now. We'll have that breakfast you fixed for us."

A very round woman with forearms bigger than hams appeared behind a kitchen island with a huge stove embedded in it. "Certainly, Mr. Duane. George Yeoman is here, ready to fly your helicopter."

"George," Will called toward the room's rear door, "come in and eat with us."

A stubby, almost dwarfish, older man in a green wool tunic and pants entered the room. "Ah et already, but I canna say no to one of Mrs. Cook's breakfasts." He seemed like he might have morphed from a Teutonic fairy tale.

"Vanessa brings her own staff when she stays here. Can't stand the inefficiency of my mine. I think my people are fine, but she has her standards. I must say that Mrs. Cook is the best cook in the world, and George Yeoman is the best overseer a property owner could have."

They beamed, and Matthew felt bewildered. These people were so odd, they could have been from a comic book.

The breakfast took care of that. An omelet so fluffy, it could be a cloud. Cheese sauce. Fried potatoes with crispy outsides. And best— homemade biscuits. Those *were* clouds.

"You'll be needing my preserves with those. Or the honey from the Woodside estate." A beaming Mrs. Cook brought them over. "I love to see a man who enjoys his food. I'd beef ye up a bit, were ye here for good." Matthew had carefully maintained his Marine physique since his discharge. The thought of anything but muscle on his frame terrified him.

"Thank you, ma'am. This is good." He couldn't help stuffing himself.

"You come back for dinner, and I'll do you better."

Matthew didn't know what he was doing for dinner, so he nodded and wiped his mouth.

"Speaking of that," Will said. "I need to talk to Matthew privately for a while." The two retainers exited, and Matthew was alone with the richest man in history. Things were about to get serious. His palms tingled, and a light sweat covered him.

"What did you imagine would happen when you came here?" Will asked him, eyes sharp and hawkish.

The old Indian had said, "Tell Will the truth." So, he did.

"I thought you were going to schmooze Opal away from me. Maybe give me what her first owner said he would pay my grandpa for her. Maybe not. Maybe say the proof I had wasn't conclusive. I thought you'd pitch me out with nothing, most likely."

"Nah. I would have given you something. I'm not that mean. But, yes, that's about what I intended. And what would you have done?"

His mouth tightened. "I would have proof of what I believed, that life was shit, and justice didn't exist. I would join the starving vets on street corners. Or taken up drinking, or something else, to hold the flashbacks down. I'd probably be dead within a year."

Will nodded. "I figured that, too. When I saw your military record, I realized I couldn't let that happen. I thought of offering you a job somewhere. I've got businesses everywhere. None that involved dogs, and that's what you're an expert at.

"Tell me, what would you like to do in life that you haven't been able to do, so far?"

"I wanted to go to college. My grandpa sold Opal to finance that, but…" He shrugged.

"Uh-huh. That's something we can work on. But since you've been here, I've realized a need I didn't know existed. You and Opal's pups can work into it. I want to show you this place and tell you more about what we do here. I think I said on Jon's TV program that even the classification of my projects is classified. That's true, but only to an extent. My major projects here on the ranch are so classified, the *government* doesn't know they exist. *My* security makes the feds' look like kids' science projects.

"George," Will called. George came into the breakfast room with some papers. "You need to sign this nondisclosure agreement to go any farther."

Matthew didn't like it, but he signed.

Will stood. "Off to the heliport. We're going to survey the ranch. Four hundred and fifty thousand acres is big. You'll see the problem I face."

They flew for hours, stopping for fuel in a mountain outpost that looked like it came from an FBI thriller. All concrete and steel, sunken into the ground. Mostly, they flew over pristine mountain wilderness, interspersed with brilliant sapphire lakes. And occasional tearer-downer settlements that looked like hobos' camps. While they flew, they talked on headsets that made theirs a private conversation.

"Those are camps on Indian land or transients' settlements. The feds have an outpost or two, as well. Fish and Game. Forestry Service, those kinds of agencies. My head security guy said keeping this place bottled up is like trying to plug the holes in a sieve. The ranch is a checkerboard of my land, federal government land, and Indian land. The boundary is a crazy jigsaw.

"It's so far out, the Indians don't bother building permanent settlements. They've built fishing camps, really. The feds aren't doing anything we can see. If they knew what was going on, they'd be swarming on our borders, and we could pick them up on our instruments.

"But, we have hunters, fishermen, prospectors, industrial spies, regular spies, and runaway kids trying to go back to nature, traversing this place, as well as fruits and nuts who think it's a spiritual haven. And anyone who's curious as to why I'm living out here and look fifty years younger than I am. As well as the curious residents of a half-dozen towns that border my property, trying to figure out why we consume trainloads of *everything* with an invisible population.

"In short, all that keeps the ranch from being overrun is my security force. I won't show you that now. Not until you've 'drunk the Kool-Aid.'" Matthew looked at him quizzically. "Signed on as an employee."

"Me? What would *I* do?"

"That is the genius of it. Or *me*." Will smiled with pure self-satisfaction. "When I saw those pups, I thought what a perfect additional security force. I've got all sorts of surveillance, drones, helicopters, every kind of stuff. But I can't stop the breaches. How about a nice wolf-force patrolling? If everyone knew they were out there? You're a dog expert. You could train them. And we can breed as many as we want."

"Wait a minute. All those ranchers and yahoos trying to get into this place would hunt them down for trophies. They would be an added incentive to breaking in. And you don't train wolves, you enlist their cooperation. You teach them."

"We can make them safe from poachers. I have the technology for that. And these aren't wolves per se; they're half Standard Poodle, one of the smartest breeds that exist. And not just Standard Poodle, *Opal*, probably the most skilled survivor in the canine world."

"How can you make them safe from guns?" Matthew scoffed. "Bullets cut through any intelligence difference. That's why our great warriors don't carry swords anymore."

"How about if we have stronger weapons that no one can breach?"

"What? Magic?"

"No. My wife."

Matthew was silent. Stunned. But not for long. "You're saying your wife can overpower a bunch of crazed gun maniacs intent on a nice wolf pelt for their game room wall?"

"Yes. She can give Opal and the pups protection that nothing can breach. My wife and others up here that you haven't met."

"Who?"

"That's what 'you haven't met' means. You don't know them yet. And now isn't the time."

Matthew was getting pissed off at this preposterous discussion. His face grew red and his belly itched.

"Look, you just got here. I'm not going to spill our secrets to you," Will said. "Just consider the idea of settling here to train and maintain the 'Wolf Force.' You can manage the breeding program. Outcrossing our hybrids and more poodles with fresh wolves so the Force doesn't get inbred. Maybe trying other dog breeds."

Will grinned. "I know lots about breeding animals. My first wife had champion horses. 'Best of the Best' was the barn motto. She won a ton of prizes at shows."

"What if that's not enough for me to do?"

"Oh, you'll run the wolf missions around the property. Patrolling 450,000 acres is *plenty* to do." He leaned over to George Yeoman. "George, take us to the main airport and land. I want to give Matthew the introductory tour of our main facility.

"Cait hasn't seen this yet, so you're one up on her." Will's grin was devilish. He knew they would compete, just knowing them the little bit he did.

Matthew found himself standing outside an airport more modern than any in a small city. Only a part of it showed, the terminal part being underground. What showed could have been taken for a landing strip for a large ranch. But the runways were much bigger than any ranch could require. Hangars in the background showed that multiple large aircraft could be stored there. Mathew's eyes narrowed. This was a good camouflage of a big aviation facility. Why?

"We're going to the first level of the facility, George," Will said. "We'll see you in a while." Will took off down a concrete path on a beautifully landscaped meadow. "Don't wander off the path, Matthew. You may break a leg."

Matthew pulled back, noticing multiple depressions in the lawn.

Leaning over, he could see a glass skylight built into the ground. The pattern of depressions showed hundreds of skylights must exist in the acres covered by the field.

"You're standing on top of a research facility bigger than anything in Silicon Valley. Bigger, more modern, more powerful, with more potential for changing the world. That's what we're doing here: developing tools that will save the world. I have contacts who know the way history will turn out if someone—us—doesn't intervene. It's bad.

"I also have people who work with me—Willy Fish, for one—who are committed to the world working out right. Chaos *is* coming, if we don't stop it. The Russians are planning another revolution, one that will wipe out democracy worldwide. It will be in this century, if we can't stop it."

Matthew wanted to get his dog and go home. He finally croaked out, "You're telling me you not only know the future, but also when nuclear Armageddon will happen?

"Yes. We know from unimpeachable sources that Russia will have a revolution in 2096. Another one will occur about two hundred years later. The whole planet will be blown up then. In the one in 2096, the Russians just take over the world and establish martial law. And reestablish the monarchy and tsar."

Matthew took a measured breath. "Will, this is interesting. Can I go home? Maybe have visitation rights with Opal or something?"

"Oh. You don't believe me. Well, why should you? Let me show you what we have. Here." A cubic building that Matthew initially thought was a piece of sculpture proved to be an elevator. Will clicked a control on his belt, and the door opened.

"I'm going to take you to the first level of our facility and show you part of the reason we know the date of the meltdown."

The elevator door opened into a huge white world partitioned into workspaces. People in white lab coats wandered around. Screen displays covered the walls.

"This is the least secure part of the facility. Would you like to see Caitlin? Here she is."

A screen showed Cait and Mrs. Naughton sitting on the patio by her cabin. Benjamin played happily by their feet.

"Don't eat that, Benny. I don't think caterpillars are good for you," Cait said very clearly.

"Would you like to eavesdrop on someone a bit farther away?" Will asked.

"Sure." He had been unaware of any surveillance devices at Cait's house.

"How about this? Want to know what's going on in Russia? Check this out."

The screen showed Yuri Petronov, the president of Russia, in his office talking to his closest aide. They spoke Russian.

Matthew startled and then leaned toward the screen, frowning.

"Do you speak Russian? What are they saying?"

Matthew nodded, then burst into a grin. "He just said that President Thurgood is an idiot, and a monkey could outmaneuver him."

"Hah! That's what I think, too," Will chortled. "Though that's not for public presentation, his or mine."

"How do you do that? That's his inner sanctum!?" Matthew was mind-blown, yet again.

"I've got FISH Inc's resources *and* Willy Fish. I have the best tech minds on the planet at my disposal. We can tell when Petronov farts and what he and his mistress do in the bedroom."

"You can do that?"

"I said, this is just the lowest level of security. So, do you want the Wolf Force job and whatever else we can think up for you? Being able to speak Russian is a plus. You'll get compensated fairly and have a nice cabin like Cait's. And you'll see Opal all the time."

"Okay. Is there a contract?"

"Of course there's a contract. George Yeoman will have it in the helicopter. We can shake on it though." They shook hands. Matthew noted that Will's hands didn't have the papery texture of age. They were strong, almost young.

Before Matthew could think more about the fountain of youth operating on the mountain, the lights went up in the lab, signaling the arrival of evening. It looked almost night on the screen that showed Cait, Mrs. Naughton, and the baby outside her cabin.

"It's dark. I'm getting worried about them," Cait said. "Vanessa has had the pups and Opal out in the forest all day. I wonder if they're lost or something. What could she be doing?"

Mrs. Naughton also looked and sounded concerned. "She didn't say what she was doing with them, but I can't imagine taking puppies out that long. They mostly sleep all day. I wonder if we should notify Will?"

Cait stood, holding the baby, and peered into the forest. "It's really dark in there. I think we should call Will."

Will jumped and turned to Matthew, eyes widening. "Oh, shit. Vanessa's had the pups in the forest all day? She didn't tell me about that. It's dark… Coyotes…"

Matthew choked. "They've been out *all day*? They're babies. They can't handle that much exercise. Their bones and tissues aren't formed enough yet. She could have ruined them!"

"Let's get back!"

38

BLOODIED

GEORGE SET THE chopper down in the circle in Cait's driveway. They were out running before the blades stopped turning. The forest was in a state—lightning flashing and thunder booming on top of them. All sorts of animals howled. They ran for the cabin.

They found Cait behind it, heading for the puppy pen and forest beyond, holding Benjamin and looking stricken. Mrs. Naughton ran beside her, distraught.

"She's had the puppies out all day! They're too young for that!" Cait cried.

"That's right. They're too little for that much exercise. What's the matter with her?" Mathew spat out, as outraged at Vanessa as Cait.

Will jerked at that, holding his hands out in a gesture of calming things down. "Vanesa usually has a good reason for what she does. Let's not…"

Howls erupted from the forest. Cait ran into it, holding her cell phone and its flashlight in front of her with the baby clutched to her chest. Matthew was behind her, holding his cell the same way. They didn't penetrate the trees very much; too many odd animal noises wafted back at them. The forest seemed alive and ready to attack.

"Hi ho! They're *searching* for us!" Vanessa's voice crowed, a little too close to a cackle to give comfort. No one could see them, but they could feel the pups and Opal's vibrations disrupting the forest calm. Vanessa led a group howl, then another round.

"We are warriors! Today was a total success! They're bloodied, every one of them. Mighty hunters!"

Vanessa burst into view, her black dress a mess. Blood trickled from the side of her mouth and her lips were rimmed with it. The pups jumped into the light, covered with gore. They were jubilant, running to Matthew and Cait in a state of frenzied puppy ecstasy. They looked larger and stronger than they had that morning.

"What did you do to them?" Cait flared, temper about to explode. "What's the matter with them? They're covered with blood. Did you hurt them? You had no right. These are my pups!"

"That's right." Matthew was as furious as Cait. "But they aren't your pups. You had them out far too long. You might have damaged their ligaments and tendons."

The forest went still, like the instant before a viper strikes. Will waved his hands, trying to diffuse the situation. "They don't mean, Vanessa. They don't …"

Vanessa walked up to Cait, towering over her. "I appreciate your spunk and fighting spirit. Your willingness to take on powerful adversaries is admirable. But you lack discipline. You must learn when it's wise to express yourself, and when you should hold your tongue. You should *always* hold your tongue with me."

The forest shuddered, trees shimmering as though struck by an invisible force. Frost formed everywhere. Their feet crunched on it. Cait felt a sensation of terror, something she had never felt. It moved like a cyclone from Vanessa, the kindly witch-like woman who had sheltered her the night before.

"Never speak disrespectfully to me. Never forget who and *what* I am."

Cait found herself bowing to the older woman. Matthew did the same.

"I'm not the cordial old lady you think I am, not by a long shot. I carry some of the oldest blood in Europe. I am a predator and a killer—and a witch. Never question my judgment—until your powers are as strong as mine."

Snow swirled. Cait clutched the baby tight. He opened his eyes wide, taking in breath for a scream. Cait felt every terrifying thing rush through her. The branch piercing Thad's skull. The dogs burning. Being stalked by that awful lawyer in Atherton. Opal dying. The pups. Matthew. All dead.

"I'm sorry. I get carried away sometimes, when I feel wronged. I didn't mean to…"

"You certainly did, Cait. You intended to level your puny rage on me. You didn't count on *mine*. You weren't much better, Matthew. Not a good showing for a subordinate officer." Matthew ducked his head.

The forest disappeared, swallowed by red-hot flames, spinning ashes and cinders. Cait held Benjamin as tight as she could and prayed to survive the maelstrom.

"I'm sorry, I didn't know. Who you were, what you could do…"

Vanessa raised her proud head. "And now you do. That was the barest taste of my power. Pray that you don't feel all of it.

"Now, these are not *your* pups. They are not even Opal's, though she has a greater claim to them than you. They belong to the universe. I won't allow them to be coddled and turned into hothouse flowers.

"They are wolves! And poodles! They were heroes today, showing the woods who was dominant. They're bloodied—every one of them made their first kill! Opal brought down a mature deer! It was glorious! And…"

The outlier pup crept into the light, holding the limp remains of a rabbit. Vanessa pointed at her. "This one… this one is an avenging angel! She killed two rabbits and a squirrel."

The pup growled furiously, shaking her dead bunny. She dropped it and headed toward the group of humans. She stopped some distance from them, peering at them with curiosity and no fear. She was changed since that morning, coming into the fullness of who she was.

She approached the group gingerly, legs stiff, body ready to attack. Zeroing in on Matthew, she came close enough for him to touch her. No one moved and no one spoke. Raising her muzzle, the outlier stared at Matthew. She walked to him stiff-legged and defiant and poked his leg with her nose.

Then she whirled and headed back to the other pups, proud as the Queen Mary pulling away from the dock. She squatted and urinated, then returned to her family.

Matthew whooped with laughter. "*I guess she told me!* Oh, my God. It's Opal. That's how she was as a pup. Arrogant, snotty, and knowing full well she could get away with it. That people would beg to see her show off. Opal the Queen. Oh, what a pup."

"I think she gave you a nice F— you, and also picked you for her master. You may begin working with her tomorrow," Vanessa said, as imperious as the puppy. "You might want to think of a name for her. One that she approves."

After a few moments of silence, Mrs. Naughton said, "I made a nice stew today. And my best apple pie. Maybe we could put all this behind us and eat a bite." It was pitch black out by then.

"Oh, Marjory. I can't eat a thing." She wiped her bloody mouth with the sleeve of her dress. "I've been stuffing myself all afternoon."

39

BONDED

VANESSA DIRECTED A slow, meaningful look at Will. "After a day like today, I'd like to spend a quiet evening at home," she said, her voice purring, nothing like Matthew had heard from her before. "Will, would you take me home?" She was coquettish. And sexy.

Will responded instantly, moving to her side and putting his arm around her. "That's just what I was thinking." He nuzzled her neck. "Let's make it an early night."

"Wait just a minute. You can't tell me you won't be hungry soon. An' I'll not see my cooking go to waste." In no time, Marjory Naughton had packed up dinners for Will, Vanessa, and George Yeoman. They climbed into the helicopter, Will and Vanessa entwined like moonstruck teens. Then they were gone.

"Well, it's just us for my stew and apple pie." Mrs. Naughton said to Matthew and Cait. She brought out a tureen. Cait's cottage had a charming dining alcove, just the right size for the three of them and the baby in his carriage. Cait and Matthew were a little shaken after Will and Vanessa's romantic display.

Mrs. Naughton laughed at them. "It's the blood and the hunt that got her goin'. Vanessa is a passionate woman. Most bloody passions run into th' primal passion—an' they do in Vanessa, fer sure. Ye ought t' see her and Will at the big house in Woodside," Marjory said. "Like squirrels running up and down trees in spring. Know each other for forty years, and then *wham.*"

Matthew had never thought about old people having sex, but that was obviously what they had in mind. Seemed weird and a bit gross.

"Oh, jus' because they're old doesn't mean they're dead, young man."

Matthew reddened, embarrassed that he had been so easy to read. And because of what the old couple were doing.

"Oh, you're blushing!" Mrs. Naughton was merciless. "This is a retreat site, but it isn't a nunnery. You should see…" She stopped, "Well, I won't go into that. Do you have any questions for me, now that the grown-ups are gone?"

"Well, yes… Are you and Vanessa really witches?" Cait asked.

"Of course. And Will is coming along very well, too. Vanessa and I come from ancient lines of witches. Her lineage is German; mine is English. Very old and proud."

"What she did, when she was mad at me…"

"Was nothing to what she could do if she was *really* mad at you."

"Oh. But she doesn't use her power to hurt people. Does she?"

"Not good people. To tell the truth, I've *never* seen what she could do if truly vexed." Marjory shrugged. "I'm off to bed. It's been a roller-coaster day. Would you like me to put Benjamin in his crib?" The baby slept peacefully in his pram, the only one unaffected by the events of the previous hours.

"Yes, that would be great. Matthew and I will put the puppies away."

Matthew realized he had been left at Cait's house without a ride back to Will's big house. He was stuck with Cait, who hated him. He would have walked back, but it was several miles through a black forest, home to predator animals, and marauder ghosts. He felt the hair prickle down his back. He didn't really believe in witches, but Vanessa had done *something* when she rebuked them.

"Don't worry, Matthew. It's a three-bedroom house. Your room is right there," Marjory Naughton pointed. "All made up. *I'll* not bother ye." She nodded significantly.

Matthew bolted onto the rear porch and out the back to the dog pen to bring in the dogs. "Okay, Opal, get them in for me. No fooling around." Fortunately, Opal and her brood were tired and followed him into the screened porch, which he locked behind him.

"Hi." Cait stood with a tray containing a pitcher of lemonade and glasses. "I thought we could talk. We got off to such a bad start. *My* fault, I must admit. I threatened to kill you.

"Do you want some lemonade?"

"Yeah, sure." The attraction he'd felt for her was tamed down, but still there.

They sat and sipped lemonade for a while, relaxing and getting used to each other's company. Opal and the puppies settled in their bed. The puppies wheezed, snoring.

"They're so funny," Matthew said.

"Yes, adorable," Cait answered. "It's too bad Opal can't have more puppies. She loves them so much."

"Oh. She can't have any more?"

"No. The cat ripped her up inside. It's a wonder she's alive. Vanessa had to take out what was left of her reproductive system."

"That's a shame. I think what she likes best is being a mom."

"Yeah. I think that's true. But, how are you doing?" Cait asked. For once, she seemed like a normal person.

"I'm okay."

"What are you going to do in the future? Are you staying here?"

"I think so. Will made me a job offer today, security." He didn't want to tell her it was managing the Wolf Force. That would make her blow up. "That's something I know about.

"What are you going to do, Cait?"

"I don't know. I thought I'd take Opal and my puppies somewhere and resume with my YouTube channel. Will has mentioned things like a cable show, but he hasn't made any offers. Probably after he saw my performance with you, he thought twice of hiring me." She looked down, eyes watering.

"Oh, I think he'll be good on his word. Give him time. I thought I'd go off to my farm in Massachusetts with Opal and the pups. It's clear they're not going anywhere with either of us. They're here for good."

"Yeah. And it's right, too. The wolf pups need this place more than anything we could do for them. Opal needs them. And they need protection. We got a different outcome than either of us imagined."

"I've got a farm back east. Eighteen acres on the edge of Great Barrington, Massachusetts. When I left the service, all my friends said to sell it. Pull up roots and move somewhere without the history the place has. I don't want to sell it, even if I'm out here. It's been in the family for generations.

"Would you like to see it? My grandfather left it to me. I've had it rented while I've been overseas." He pulled out his cell phone and flipped through photos of a sweet Victorian farm with barns and outbuildings.

"Oh, my God! It's adorable! A Victorian with all the original trim. And all those acres of green around it. Oh! I love it."

Matthew laughed. "I thought you might. I've watched your show a few times." Every episode, including early archives. "What would you do to it?"

"Hmm." Her brow knit. "I'd do a lot, but I wouldn't change any of its bones. Or trim. *Don't sell it, Matthew!* It's a treasure."

"Yeah. But I don't know what to do with it if I'm here, and it's on the East Coast."

"Something will come up, don't worry. Don't sell it!" Her brows pulled together, the famous "Caitlin is thinking" expression. "Is there more land around it for sale?"

"Yeah. Old farms turning over."

"Buy them. Get a loan from Will and buy them." She rubbed her forehead. "I'm seeing your brand. What was the kennel's name?"

"Thibeau Kennels."

"No. Not good. How about… Valkyrie Farm? I like that. A sign with ancient warrior goddess cared in bas relief. With… what was your grandfather's name?"

"Michael."

"Okay. Matthew is better. Bottom of sign: M. Thibeau, Proprietor. And the date it was established?"

"A long time ago. Post-Civil War, when my ancestor came back from fighting."

"Okay. We got it: Valkyrie Farm, M. Thibeau, Proprietor. Est. 1873. When we get the graphic down, your brand is made…

"*Or…* we could do Opal's Farm, with a bas relief of Opal carved on it, if you wanted to breed poodles again or just because it's funny and charming. Opal has super brand recognition."

Tears sprang to his eyes. She ignored them and went on.

"Or—what about Opal's Nest? Or Opal's Den? Those would be great. Let me think more about the name.

"Okay, as you know, making a living with a kennel is hard. I'd advise developing a holistic farm and even a spa/health retreat on the side. Organic veggies, herbs. You can make a fortune on fresh herbs for restaurants. You could open a restaurant, too. With a B & B, you can keep full all year. And have several streams of income. Think big.

"Yeah. I'd go with the poodle and Opal instead of Valkyrie. You teared up when you heard Opal's name. Other people will, too. If you want, I'll draw up a sketch of the signage and logo for you to give to Will. I could even manage it for you, if you want. I know how to do that. All it took was losing everything I've got to learn what not to do."

He started to object, mostly because she'd seen his tears, but realized her plan was brilliant. "Wow."

"I know Will won't be paying you peanuts if you take his job, so you'll be able to afford to fix up the place. It will be better if you can go full on with a brand, the big way, but if he won't loan you anything, I can do my show from it. I can live there with Benjamin and transform it. *Don't* sell it. I can see it for your family…"

"I don't have a family."

"Oh, me neither. But, you can *create* a family of friends and customers and have Christmases there. Easter. Every holiday. Forever. You can make it a memory for *lots* of people. Make Opal's Nest a tradition."

He was dazzled by her. He sat silently, jaw quivering. "I've got PTSD and have flashbacks all the time. I never can tell when they're coming. Makes it hard to get or keep a job."

"Are you getting one now?" She squinted at him.

"No!" He laughed. "I just wanted you to know that."

"Okay. Now I know. What do you think about the farm?"

"I think it's the most wonderful idea I've heard since Will offered me a job. You're so creative—and fast. You even have a sign designed in your head, don't you?"

"Yeah. I want to get my sketch pad." She looked down, preparatory to getting up to get her notebook. "Look," she whispered. Opal was laying between then, her rump by Cait's foot and her nose touching Matthew's shoe. The puppies were gathered around her, some sleeping, some nursing.

"Oh, my God! Look at that." It felt like a miracle. "Remember what she did when we met? And I was screaming at you?"

"Yeah. She bit herself. I've seen her do it before."

"Whatever we do, we mustn't fight. Not in front of her, or anywhere around her. It would be a sin."

He nodded. "Yes, a terrible sin." It clicked for him; this was Opal's dream, what she'd wanted her entire life. Sitting with her family in the evening. No dog shows. No training and honors. Just love. And peace. And puppies.

"Let's leave them there and go to bed. They're so serene."

They slipped away, unnoticed except by the outlier, whose head popped up and bright eyes found Matthew's. He put his finger to his mouth, and she went back to sleep.

He had to think of a name for her. Opal was the only one that fit, but it was taken. She was the same multi-color silver as her mother. He thought, *How about Pearl? She gleams like a pearl.* That was it: Opal and her daughter, Pearl. Precious gems.

40

SLEEPWALKING

CAIT MOVED THROUGH the chamber, parting silk draperies that barred her way. A lute played, and a violin. She was enchanted. Her leg bumped against something. Her eyes shot open.

"Oh, my God!" She jumped back. "I'm so sorry! I didn't know where I was. I sleepwalk sometimes. Oh, I'm sorry. I'll leave."

She'd walked into Matthew's bed wearing her nightgown. It was a torn T-shirt that barely covered her behind.

Startled, Matthew jumped out of bed wearing less than she. She saw him in a flash: the wide shoulders, those pectorals, the taut belly. Hairy chest—which was much more masculine than those shaved boy-babes on book covers. His *six-pack,* for God's sake! Thighs. And in the darkness, hanging …

Matthew jumped back into bed, but it was too late. His physique was branded on her consciousness forever. Also on her subconscious, ego, id, dominant and inferior psychological functions, and various internal states posited by numerous psychological theorists. She was done for in a hot minute.

"Excuse me, I'm sorry." Cait shot out of the room.

"No! Don't leave," he cried. The door closed. "Damn it!" He felt like an idiot. First, flashing her, and then her running away when she saw him. Did he look that bad? He had some scars that embarrassed him. And he'd never been much for wooing women. Maybe she didn't like him.

She seemed like she liked him that evening. They had a normal time, talking about the future. She came up with that plan for his farm. He couldn't let that end. He pulled on his jeans and ran to her room, knocking lightly and then entering.

Cait was bent over Benjamin's crib. Her short nightgown exposed the beautiful, rounded curves of her buttocks. Peach-colored pearls were imprinted on his mind forever.

"Oh, excuse me." Matthew pulled out of the room. Damn it! Why was he the way he was? PTSD or not, he'd always been shy with girls.

Cait opened the door, a silk wrapper over her gown. "Matthew? Are you okay?"

"No. I'm not. You show up in my room and run away." Panic rose inside him. "Look, I know we got off to a bad start, but don't hate me!"

"What? I don't hate you. I think I'm in love with you, but I keep remembering Thad and feeling guilty. I can't sleep. I'm a mess. I don't know what to do."

For once, Matthew did. He jumped forward and embraced her. His mouth found hers.

"Oh." That was it for quite a while. They migrated to the living room sofa.

Marjory Naughton heard them and called Vanessa at the big house. She answered, sounding rumpled and satisfied. "Marjory, is that you? Is it time?"

"I think you'd better call over to Billy Jack's ranch and dust Reverend Bruce off, wherever they've got him stashed. They're about to pop."

"Oh, we'll get right on it. Over there, or over here?"

"Your place. We've got everything planned." Marjory set about actuating the scheme.

Matthew caressed Cait's hair and the side of her face, marveling. "You're as soft as I thought you were. Like a baby chick…" They kissed again, sitting on the couch. "I never thought…"

"Why don't we stop thinking?" Cait said, straddling him and kissing him for real.

She hopped off like he was radioactive. "I can't do this. This isn't right. It's not just me feeling bad about Thad. There's something wrong."

"I know. It's wrong." Matthew felt like he was being fed lines by a cosmic prompter. "Cait, I love you. Even when you threatened to kill me, I loved you. You're beautiful and brave. Fearless. You handle the worst disasters and come out whole. I love you, and I love *you*…"

He caressed her, running his hands from the back of her head down her back. "I really love you. You're like…an Afghan woman. That's who you remind me of. Beat to hell, nothing left, but still standing and proud. I saw so many of them. You're like that.

"I love you, Cait. I want to marry you. I don't want to do anything to cheapen what we have. I want it straight up, on the level, legal in the sight of man and God.

He dropped to his knees by the couch. "I love you, Caitlyn Cummins. Will you marry me?"

"Yes. I've loved you since the first time I saw you. You're so beautiful. You're noble. You're heroic. But every time I'd look at you, I'd feel guilty. I loved Thad, but he wasn't like you. He was a kid in a lot of ways. I'd realized that, and then felt guilty for dissing Thad. And then I'd miss him…" She was talking too much, as usual.

"I love you. There. I said it. Thad is gone. This is a new time and it's okay to love another man. Thad would be happy for me." Cait burst into tears, and Matthew held her tighter. "Any time anything important happens, I bawl." She pulled herself up.

"Yes, Matthew. I'll marry you. Now let's do the deed so we can get back to what we were doing legally."

Mrs. Naughton entered the room wearing a purple suit with a long skirt and wide-brimmed hat with a veil and fluffy plume. "Come along, darlings. Everyone's waiting over at Will's. Matthew, George Yeoman is outside with the helicopter. He will take you to Will's where you can dress. Cait and I will get ready here. Go! People are waiting!"

"Oh, Marjory, it's beautiful!" Cait held up a Victorian confection of a wedding dress in peau de soi, trimmed with lace and pearls, and an overskirt of more handmade lace that flowed into a long train. "It's the most beautiful dress I've ever seen."

"'Tis, isn't it? It was my grandmother's. People were smaller then. I've not found a bride tiny enough to fit into it until now. You'll be a vision."

She was a vision, making her way down the central aisle in Will's big ballroom. Will walked next to her, holding her arm. Amazingly, the room had been set up for a wedding, with rows of chairs and flowers. Ribbon festoons. An altar. At the head of the room was undeniably an official minister in black robes and a white collar.

Cait gasped at the crowd. Who were these people? She didn't know them, but they knew her. All smiled and waved triumphantly. Could they be fans of her show?

Will gave her arm a little pinch, time to let go and face her groom.

Her eyes opened wide, and she clutched Will again, just briefly. No more fainting! But he was so beautiful.

Matthew wore his dress uniform, navy blue and white with his ribbons and medals on the chest. He stood so tall, his chest magnificent. Everything about him was beautiful. He dazzled her. He was a masculine god, the lord of her heart. He always had been, she just didn't know it until then. Cait stepped forward to join her husband.

"Do you take this woman?" the minister said. "Do you take this man?" He said a lot of other stuff, but she couldn't process it. They were married. An hour or two ago, they were making out on her sofa. Now, they were married.

It was righter than right, better than the best. The only thing that made sense in the world, that could make sense. She and Matthew were wed, for ever and ever.

People cheered. "We live here on the mountain, just wanted to pay our respects." "We work over on the other side. Couldn't stay away." There was a cake and food. They met Reverend Bruce, who was as awkward and gangly as they could imagine a man being.

"Bruce is an old friend," Will explained. "He was the minister of the community church in Oregon where Elizabeth's family lived. He's a special friend. We have a lot of impromptu weddings up here. He likes to officiate."

Music and dancing and someone took photos. A perfect night. Mathew bent to put his arms around her for a waltz of the ages.

The music stopped, but he kept holding her, looking into her eyes. Starlight flew off them, illuminating the room, opening hearts and minds.

They stood on the dance floor with light undulating around them. When the rapture of their marriage allowed people to move, Mrs. Naughton approached and said, "It's time to whisk your bride off to your honeymoon palace. The helicopter is outside. I brought the baby here. Ye c'n have a wee bit of alone time the next few days."

What happened was sacred. He joined with her, and she joined with him in a way both spiritual and physical, emotional and righteous. And then they joined again. And again.

41

HOME

OPAL LAY ON her bed in the screened porch, her sleeping babies scattered around. She listened to the sweet, soft sounds of her humans mating. Her heart expanded. This was what she wanted, had wanted, would always want. The warmth of home with her people and whatever pups they might have. With her pups and theirs and theirs, forever forward from that day.

Her heart opened and sent out a call to her mate, wherever he was. She couldn't love him as she once had, but she could keep him safe. He and his pack could live here, and her humans would guard them. They would live forever on this magic mountain, where the soul's deepest yearnings became real.

Come here and be with me in the heartland, my love. Stay with me in our true home.

Opal relaxed and lay back in her bed. Her eyes closed slowly and she drifted into oblivion. Stars and soft lights danced in her mind, whispering stories of easy hunts and breezes filled with the scent of the forest. Whether her lover heard her or not, Opal was home.

Opal, Always

WHAT'S COMING
NEXT IN THE
BLOODSONG SERIES?

Do you believe in time travel? If you're reading the Bloodsong Series, you'll know it's possible. We're going to do some right now. The Bloodsong Series started with *Numenon* and *Mogollon*, both set in 1997. From there, the books show up all over the temporal map. *Opal: A Poodle's Journey Home*, this book, takes place in 2018 and 2019. It's a canine-assisted jump into contemporary events.

With *Willy Fish & the Mighty Fine Mule*, we go back in time to 1997 and the Native American spiritual retreat that started it all and the great Medicine man Grandfather and his people. You'll find out some things that are key to earlier...uh, later, Bloodsong books. For instance, Willy Fish is an established figure in *MINDSPEAK/HEARTSPEAK*, my thriller about alternate universes set in 2016. Here you find out about his beginnings. It's quite a trip.

So, welcome again to the Bloodsong Series! I expect to bring our more shorter books such as this one in 2020 and beyond.

Sandy Nathan

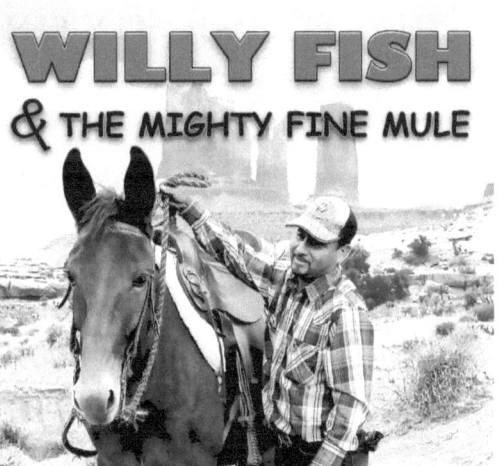

WILLY FISH
& THE MIGHTY FINE MULE

SANDY NATHAN

WILLY FISH & THE MIGHTY FINE MULE

Willy Fish almost lived at Mike the Mechanic's in Tulsa, Oklahoma, where he worked. He could fix anything with a motor or an electronic pulse. That was a blessing in that he could support his wife and kids. And a curse because he couldn't support them very well, and no one could understand what was in those notebooks he made, full of drawings of inventions and equations. He muttered to himself about how to make the drawings real. But everyone—especially his wife Rocky—knew they would never be real.

Most people thought Willy was nuts. Short and stocky, he wore Day-Glo cowboy shirts, his hair in long Native braids, and a high-crowned hat. He was a disappointment to everyone, mostly himself. He couldn't help it; his ideas for inventions were realer to him than his own needs or those of his family. They crowded everything out. He had to write them down.

At the first Meeting——a powerful spiritual retreat—the great Native American holy man, Grandfather told Willy he would be a great Medicine man. "You will change the world, my son. You will be a great warrior."

That was eleven years earlier. Willy and Rocky were getting ready to leave for New Mexico and the last Meeting. Nothing had happened to him. He still wore wacky shirts and muttered, filling more and more notebooks with ideas. This was it—his last chance to make something of himself.

When Willy saw the TV coverage of that poor mule stranded on the barn roof during the Great Flood of 1997, something broke inside him. He *had* to save the mule, and he drove north across four states from his home in Tulsa to do it. Not knowing what else to do with the creature, he took it to Grandfather's final retreat. It was in New Mexico: a *long* drive.

That was the beginning of an adventure that would change Willy forever—along with the whole world. Grandfather's final retreat was the biggest ever. More than four thousand Native American souls would attend. So would someone who *could* see what Willy was and knew what to do with those notebooks.

Could they find each other in that huge crowd? Would they recognize what the other had to give?

Maybe they needed a mule to push things along.

WILLY FISH & THE MIGHTY FINE MULE,
A Bloodsong Novella, is coming in 2020.

ABOUT SANDY NATHAN

Sandy Nathan is a mule-riding, poodle-loving word slinger from the San Francisco Bay Area, which is what Silicon Valley was called *before* it was Silicon Valley. Her life has been one of exaltation, transformation, loss, and redemption.

"I used to be a princess. My parents created the 9th largest residential construction company in the United States in the early 1960s. They did this from *nothing*, being dirt poor during the Great Depression. I didn't know anything about the poverty part of my family's past. I knew the royal status conferred by great success in our culture. I was a princess and expected that I always would be.

"In 1964, when my father was killed by a wrong-way driver on a freeway offramp, I learned otherwise. My life of horse shows and power boats, luxurious Atherton houses, and limitless shopping sprees went *poof*, disappearing like my father's ghost.

"I lived at close to the poverty level for a while, something I'm sure no one who knew me back then would believe. Attempting to regain my lost status, I went on an achievement binge, getting two master's degrees and working on a PhD. I worked as an economic analyst and tried to predict things like where employment growth would happen in Santa Clara County. My team failed miserably: no one in the early 70s could imagine the computer revolution and rise of Silicon Valley.

"All that time, I was haunted by what I'd lost. Haunted, generally.

Fortunately, the Human Potential Movement was in full swing then, promising enlightenment in a couple of weekends for a few hundred bucks. I went for it—and I got something: the sense that what was didn't have to be. That I could create a life that I wanted. So I did."

From there, Sandy went on to true success: a wonderful family life, more horses, a mule, a poodle, and lots of time at a computer, writing quirky, but meaningful books. They've won thirty-one national awards so far and have been Amazon bestsellers. This is one of Sandy's books. Hope you enjoy it.

To join Sandy's Mailing List and Readers' Club, go to her website at SandyNathan.com

OPAL: A POODLE'S JOURNEY HOME

Thad Cummins and his wife Cait fled the high prices and craziness of San Francisco to breed designer dogs. They found their dream in an idyllic town called Paradise, in the California foothills. Thad bought dogs while Cait transformed their rundown mini-mansion into a farm-style masterpiece. They were in it together and couldn't pass up the beautiful Grand Champion poodle, Opal, or leave their enchanting Victorian farm in the woods.

Unfortunately, Opal carried baggage. The manager of the fancy kennel where Thad got her warned that she had bitten people and was a legal liability to her owners. "She could be put down as a vicious dog." Thad and Cait knew they could overcome Opal's aggressiveness, with time. Couldn't they?

The Camp Fire of 2018 turned Paradise into an inferno. Thad and Cait's heaven became a blazing firestorm. The survivors had to fight their way back from a horrific natural disaster, braving loss and pain. Through it all, Opal struggled to find her destiny and be the dog she was born to be. Would she ever find her true home?

Resources

Mon Amie Standard Poodles
http://monamiestandardpoodles.com

Animal Compassion Team of California
https://www.animalcompassionteam.org/

Tracy Bellion
https://traceysfancy.com/

Confessions of a Serial Do-It-Yourselfer
https://www.confessionsofaserialdiyer.com/

Thrifty Décor Chick
https://www.thriftydecorchick.com/

Do Dodson Designs
https://www.dododsondesigns.com/

Artsy Chicks Rule
https://www.artsychicksrule.com/

Serena Appiah
https://thriftdiving.com

William Renn, Illustrator
http://www.williamrenn.com/

Damonza.com
http://damonza.com

www.ingramcontent.com/pod-product-compliance
Lightning Source LLC
Chambersburg PA
CBHW022025240626
47154CB00007B/2270